ROYAL REPLICAS

MICHAEL PIERCE

To little baby Dari.
My other new adventure.

*B*eatrice Ramsey stood against the wall by the bookshelf while the doctors were working on her daughter; the girl was still lying unconscious from the procedure and looked so peaceful in her bed. Beatrice gazed upon the wooden crucifix above the bed that—once upon a time—had been her own. She felt the full weight of guilt for everything the poor girl had been subjected to.

Doctors Sosin and Crane had been taking care of Victoria since before she was born. They had good reason for their investment and concern with her wellbeing. Her current state was a definite cause for worry.

A lot of equipment had been loaded into the small, dark room, so much so that the portable dress rack and dresser needed wheeling outside. The machines blinked and beeped, connected to her daughter in a multitude of ways; some were more invasive than others.

"When will she wake?" Beatrice asked.

"In a few hours. Maybe a little longer," Dr. Sosin said.

"You don't sound so sure."

"There's always some degree of guesswork in science. For all the many things you believe you control, equal numbers of variables and unseen factors challenge that certainty. You're a woman of faith; you must understand there are things beyond our control?"

"And things we should not even be attempting to control," Beatrice said.

"I'm not here to have a theological discussion with you, but to help keep you in good standing with the Queen," Dr. Sosin said.

"After this, I don't see how we can continue to be in good standing," Beatrice answered.

"To the Queen's knowledge, this is another routine checkup. Nothing more."

"I don't know whether I should be worried or relieved." Beatrice stepped forward, approaching the bed. She reached out to touch the still girl lying beneath the covers but pulled back. "What will she remember?"

"We've reset her to last summer—that should be far enough—before their first meeting. We didn't want to take too much from her." Dr. Sosin checked the screen of one of the chirping instruments. "Just so you know, this isn't the first one we've had to reset. Teenagers can be... well, unpredictable."

"Tell me about it," Beatrice said with a pained chuckle. "I practically have three."

"I fear you're getting too close," Dr. Sosin said. "You do realize she'll have to be returned soon?"

"I know. I've been preparing for it—though it doesn't make it any easier."

"You should really distance yourself more."

"Are you telling me you always do the right thing?"

"Of course not. We all have our... vices and regrets."

"I don't regret this." Beatrice gently laid a hand on her sleeping daughter and waited for her to wake.

"Neither do I," Dr. Sosin said, removing a roll of gauze from his bag and beginning to wrap Victoria's head. "She's my daughter too."

I was only ever allowed to wear shoes when sent on errands into town. This was mandated by Master Ramsey and had been so ever since I was a little girl. I wasn't a Ramsey though; I was a Sandalwood and was reminded of that every single day of my life.

The Ramsey estate was large and sprawling, a testament to their position as Duke and Duchess of the 24th Ward. We were in the ring of the outermost wards in the Kingdom, considered the Borderlands. The electric fence protected us from whatever stirred in the Outlands, but from my limited experience, protections from things inside our very own Kingdom were most needed.

From one of many hallway entrances, I padded outside on calloused, bare feet and followed a path through the East garden, making my way to the gaping mouth of the hedge maze. On one side of the maze entrance grew a cascading willow tree, and on the other, a copse of young birches, hazels, and hickories.

I approached one of the hazels with its low-lying branches, gripping the handle of my paring knife in one hand. There were fewer and fewer branches every time I came out here, but I found two that were sturdy yet flexible and cut them down. I'd become something of an expert in choosing and smoothing them, always returning with two just in case one snapped before my time was up. If only one was supplied and it broke before the determined time, then I'd only have to fetch another, and the whole act would begin again.

I returned with haste to the Master's den—the one where he loved to sit by the fire, read from one of his hardbound books from his library, and occasionally watch television. I found him waiting there, and presented him with the switches.

"These look adequate enough," he said, taking them from me and proceeding to bend and flex them. "They shall do nicely."

Master Ramsey pulled the leather-bound bench away from the wood-paneled wall. Above where the bench was stationed, sat a shelf displaying a stuffed mountain lion; the Master had shot it himself in his younger years before the shades of gray hair had completely overtaken his beard.

I got into position, lying down on my stomach across the hard leather and placing my hands behind my back. I gazed at the open doorway as he secured my upper body and lower legs to the bench and bound my hands.

Mina passed by, stopping in her tracks when she saw what was happening—my preparation for punishment. She was only twelve, but already a stunning copy of her nineteen-year-old sister, Johanna. And the boys were taking notice of her—even Johanna's regular gentleman callers.

"Mina, darling, please fetch your sister for me," Master Ramsey said in an even, but commanding voice. "And you come back with her as well."

"Yes, Father," she said as she scampered off.

The only thing worse than the switching itself was having an audience. Mina and Johanna sat in quite often, so they could learn their life lessons vicariously through me—through my pain and shame. I felt my pain rising like the tide from the last session. I was supposed to be learning. I was supposed to be more disciplined and obedient. I seemed to be none of those things.

Master Ramsey pulled on the ropes securing me to the leather bench; he said they were for my own safety. My skirt was pulled up to just past my knees, and he leaned the second switch against the wall where it would wait for its chance to kiss my imperfect skin. He stood silent and stoic, awaiting the girls' arrival.

Waiting was also excruciating when all I wanted to do was get this over with and go back to my room. And this was not the only time I'd be forced to wait in terrible anticipation of the coming waves of pain.

When the girls entered the room, I knew it was time and my whole body tightened.

"Good, now we can begin," Master Ramsey said.

The girls knew exactly where to stand.

"What are you being punished for?" Master Ramsey asked, stepping to the side of the bench where he could see my face and I could see his.

If I did not answer, then it would only be worse. "For going into town unescorted," I said.

"Yes. You know the rules."

"It is a new rule," I pleaded. This rule hadn't been implemented until after my recent accident.

"A new rule or an old rule, it makes no difference. Disobedience does not have varying degrees," Master Ramsey said. "What interested you in town? Was it to meet *him*?"

"I don't know to whom you're referring. I was simply asked to retrieve a few supplies for the kitchen."

"Be that as it may. I cannot allow this insubordination to go unpunished."

"Yes," I said and closed my eyes, anticipating the first strike. A single tear escaped at the mere thought of what was to come.

The switch came down with full force across the vaults of my feet, followed immediately by searing pain. I cried out, as I did every time on receiving the first blow. Only so much tolerance could be built up, not enough to keep me from screaming; the girls standing before me melted away in the blur of tears.

I tried to catch my breath, but there was no time during the initial onslaught of strikes. One after another, they rained down on me. I could feel the welts forming on the bottoms of my feet already; Master Ramsey didn't hold back. He hit me again and again, as fast and as hard as he could. And as I screamed, I strained against my restraints, but there was no escape, no reprieve; I couldn't shield my sensitive flesh from his powerful blows.

Johanna and Mina watched on with blank, almost black expressions. Mina cried too, sometimes, but I could never hear her over my own sobs. Johanna had become hardened over the years and no longer empathized with my pain.

"I'm sorry, Father," I cried, unable to form any clearer thoughts. And I hadn't even realized what I'd just said until I heard his reply.

"I've told you never to call me that!" he yelled,

finding some extra strength in the yell to make me sorry for those words too.

The bottoms of my feet burned like they were being poked by a red-hot iron. I tried to go somewhere else in my head, but the pain kept me present. After a few minutes—though it felt like an eternity—the blows slowed as Master Ramsey grew tired. The strikes became more infrequent, bringing back the horrible anticipation of when the next one would land.

"Johanna, come here," Master Ramsey commanded. From the watery blur of my vision, I saw her join her father's side.

"Aim for the weals in the center of the feet and strike fast. What do we do to stubborn mares that insist on remaining wild?"

"We break them, Father."

"Good girl."

I took a few labored, deep breaths while the switch changed hands. Then I felt the familiar sting of being struck again. The first one seemed almost hesitant. A pause. The next one was less so. A shorter pause came.

"Yes," Master Ramsey said. "She needs to know you mean it."

Then the full force and volley returned and I found myself screaming again. Johanna grew tired faster and her blows weakened but I knew it wasn't over.

"Mina, come take your sister's place."

But Mina didn't budge; she stood glued to her spot and shook her head. Her face matched mine as a ruin of tears, partially concealed by the pink and red locks accessorizing her naturally blonde hair.

"If you do not, you will only be making it worse for her." Master Ramsey's voice was deep and sinister. He did not shout.

Mina dragged her feet as she reluctantly complied. When she took the switch, it was almost a mercy; she missed the primary target half the time, and the blows she landed correctly had a greatly reduced severity. But even the touch of a feather hurt at this point.

She didn't last long and then the real punishment continued, causing me to wail once again like a dying animal. I knew I wasn't even bleeding—Master Ramsey was too practiced—but the pain inflicted by each calculated blow felt like my feet would split open at any moment, like overripe fruit.

Just when I thought I couldn't take another licking, it was over. The girls were sent on their way with warnings of disobedience, while I was untied from the bench. My arms fell limply to the floor. I lay across the leather unable and unwilling to move.

"You may go about your chores, Victoria," Master Ramsey said, snapping the sticks into smaller ones before throwing them into the lit hearth. Next time would require new ones I'd also have to supply. It was all part of the ritual.

He gave my butt a pat and left the room, allowing me the slight dignity of hobbling out of the den in solitude, but not before returning the leather bench to its original location under the trophy.

CHAPTER 2

I carefully made my way to my room in the cellar, another reminder of my place in the family and within the community. The wooden stairs killed my feet, but the cold concrete at the bottom slightly dulled the pain.

The lights down there were dim and the air cool and musty. This was where much of the extra furniture for parties was stored, tables and chairs that would fill the main ballroom. It was all kept under white linens to maintain the items relatively clean between uses; I felt I was living amongst the dead.

My room was far from the stairs, far from access to anyone, and I treasured my moments of seclusion. There was one overhead lightbulb I could turn on using a string; it didn't provide much illumination for the whole room, even though it wasn't much more than an oversized closet. Two small windows close to the ceiling let in a little more light, though I usually kept my curtains drawn. The furnace and water heater were on the other side of the wall and I listened to them crackle and cough, on and off, throughout the nights.

Besides an intercom by the door and the crucifix over my bed, the walls of my room were bare. The Ramseys were a God-fearing family, and the crucifix they'd given me as a little girl was the reminder that He sees everything and I was being watched and judged wherever I went.

I had a nightstand with a digital clock and a few candles, a metal clothes rack for my dresses, a portable plastic dresser for the rest of my clothes, one pair of casual dress shoes for when I was permitted to wear them, and a small bookcase containing hardbound copies from Master Ramsey's library. I made sure each book received no more than an extra crease in my care; they were so sacred to me. They were my escape.

I lit a candle on my nightstand and lay on the bed. Curling up on one side, I kept anything from touching my damaged feet. I was missing memories since the accident a week or so earlier; according to Dr. Crane, acute head trauma could cause temporary or even selectively permanent amnesia. But all the memories of my switchings throughout the years remained intact. Why couldn't some of those have been erased? I closed my eyes to see what else I could forget, but the memories of being beaten flooded back with gruesome, terrifying clarity.

Who was the boy?

It hadn't been a lie. I honestly couldn't remember. There was no one I could meet in town, no one I knew outside of the Ramsey estate. Johanna and Mina went to school with the other children, though they arrived in more style than their peers, but my studies were confined to the estate with the Governess. I was taught to be proper and polite, like any other noble young lady. But I *was* no noble young lady; I was just a Sandalwood.

I could hear footsteps echoing in the hallway outside my room, so was not surprised when there was a soft knock at the door.

"May I come in?" It was the melodic voice of Lady Ramsey.

"Yes," I said, and the door creaked open.

She entered the room holding a couple of embroidered hand towels and a porcelain basin filled with water. She was an indisputably beautiful woman, making it clear how her daughters came by their good looks. Her blonde hair was up in a tight and perfectly held bun. Her face matched her daughters' soft and subtle features, and she only bore a few more lines of age.

Lady Ramsey glided over to my bed, wearing a flowery apron skirt over her dress. I scooted to the far side so she could sit. She set the basin beside her and maneuvered my hurt feet onto her covered lap. Looking over at me, she tucked a lock of my dark hair behind my ear and wiped my tear-stricken cheek.

"You're a strong girl," she said. "I wish I had your strength."

"I'm not strong," I said. "I don't know how much more I can endure."

"We're never asked to endure more than we're capable of."

I used to call her Mother, but there'd come a time when it just didn't seem appropriate anymore. I was without a family and it was no use pretending I was a part of this one. I often wondered why the Ramseys accepted to care for me at all.

Lady Ramsey dipped one of the hand towels in the basin and wrung it out before gently applying it to my right foot. I cringed despite how careful she was being. My feet were always dirty; no matter how hard I scrubbed, I could never get them totally clean. She wiped around the wounds and gently patted the injured portion of my foot, reminding me of the real mother I was missing so much.

"I know you didn't mean to go against our wishes by venturing into town alone," she said as she continued her work.

"I forgot to bring someone with me," I said. "There's so much I'm forgetting right now. My head is in a fog."

"Dr. Sosin said you'd feel like that for a while. But you'll be back to your old self soon."

"The past few months are a blur. Master Ramsey mentioned a boy."

"A boy…" Lady Ramsey moved to my left foot, gently dabbing at the fiery welts. "Yes. He had been harassing you. It culminated in a confrontation while you were riding, causing you to be thrown off Misty. It was a miracle you weren't more hurt."

"I so love riding," I said, having no recollection of the fall.

"I know you do, sweetie. And you'll be able to again once you're well enough. I'm sure Dr. Crane will clear you for riding in a few weeks' time." She dropped the wet towel into the basin, the water now cloudy and brown. Then she took the dry one and patted my feet dry. "It's for your own safety," she said, laying a comforting hand on my ankle.

"What is?" I asked.

"For you to take someone with you on your trips into town. The boy has escaped reprimand thus far and we are concerned for your safety. I don't know what else he's capable of. You know you must follow the rules."

"Who is he? What's his name?"

"You never mentioned his name, and by the time the accident occurred, it was too late to ask. But I'm grateful you don't remember him. It helps for you and the rest of us to move on."

"I'm not grateful for it," I said. "I want to remember. There's enough in my life that's lost to me. Like my parents."

"You're my little girl."

"I'm not a—"

"No matter what happens, you'll always be my little girl." Lady Ramsey moved my legs aside and rose from the bed. She wiped her hands on her apron skirt before picking up the soiled basin and turning to me. "You're excused from any unfinished chores for the rest of the day. If anyone questions you, tell them to come talk to me."

"Yes, Ma'am. Thank you for your kindness." My feet ached, but they felt slightly better knowing they'd get some time to rest.

Lady Ramsey left the room without another word and I closed my eyes, trying to remember the face of the boy who'd supposedly tormented me.

CHAPTER 3

The most severe pain from a switching lasted for a few days, but the following day was always the worst. Each step felt like a fresh strike from my time on the bench.

I limped to the kitchen and helped prepare breakfast with the hired help, and was allowed to sit down and eat once the family had finished. I crossed my legs under the table to keep the soles of my feet temporarily off the floor. I had a compulsion to keep checking them, examining each red ribbon stretching out across the arches.

I ate my porridge and cut fruit while the rest of the kitchen staff cleared the table from the family's breakfast.

"Are you finished, Miss Victoria?" Berta asked when there was nothing more to take away. Only the tablecloth was left to be changed. "I'll take your dishes for you."

"You know you don't have to do that. I'll get out of your way," I said, removing my almost empty bowl. Many of the estate workers were extra nice to me the day after I'd received a switching. I glanced down at Berta's shoes and envied her.

"I'm not trying to rush you," she said.

"I know you need to finish up," I replied. "I need to get my day started as well before meeting with the Governess." I finished the fruit while hobbling into the kitchen to wash my own dishes; I wasn't about to have the others waiting on me.

Once I was finished in the kitchen, I headed to the stables. The Ramseys had a total of twelve horses. Misty was an Appaloosa and I thought of her as my own, even though she wasn't specifically given to me. She was the mare I mostly rode and the closest thing I had to a real friend. I tended to all the horses but gave Misty the most attention.

"I'm sorry I haven't been able to ride you lately," I said as I brushed her. "I should be allowed to, soon. I'm told Dr. Crane will return in a few days and he'll hopefully give me a clean bill of health."

Misty whinnied and nodded, and I knew she understood.

"One day, we'll ride and you'll jump the fence and we'll just keep going… going far away from here. I wouldn't be able to do it without you."

I adjusted my stance, but everywhere I stood had more pieces of straw digging into the soles of my feet. It was uncomfortable even on regular days; on this day, though, it was nothing less than excruciating.

I couldn't linger too long, I kissed her on the cheek before continuing to the next stall to tend and clean.

It was mid-morning by the time I had worked through each of the occupied stalls. There wasn't much time before my lessons would begin with the Governess, but I had a few minutes to rest.

I ventured into the meadow. Part of it was fenced in, where the family did much of their riding, as did I whenever I was allowed. I leaned on the wooden fence and watched Mina practicing with her trainer. It was Sunday, so the school was closed, yet I wasn't excused from lessons.

Her thoroughbred, Pumpernickel, trotted in circles around the trainer who barked commands to the horse and his rider. Mina sat tall on the saddle, keeping the reins tight; her riding skills were already almost surpassing mine.

"I know you miss it."

I turned to see the Governess striding up behind me.

"I can't wait to get back out there," I said.

"It shouldn't be long now." Now, the Governess stood beside me at the fence, resting her forearms on the top slat. "Dr. Crane will be back on Tuesday, correct?"

"Sometime this week, I was told."

"How are you feeling?" she asked.

"Okay, I guess," I said.

"And your head?"

"It's still a little fuzzy, but not hurting as much," I said, mainly because the pain in my feet had overshadowed it.

"Good, then you're fully prepared for today's lesson?"

"As ready as I'm going to be. Can't I have a little more time off?"

"You've missed quite enough already," she said. "Today is the day we resume."

"Okay," I said, hanging my head low. I knew she wouldn't go easy on me and had to make sure she wouldn't have a less than satisfactory progress report to deliver to the Ramseys.

When she was silent for longer than usual, I glanced up. Her expression was dark as she focused on the far side of the field. She was no longer looking in the direction of Mina and her trainer.

Then I saw him too. There was a boy who looked about my own age standing at the far fence. His hair was short and light and he wore a tan leather coat. It was hard to make out many of his facial features from this distance, but he seemed tall and trim, gauging his height from how far his upper body extended above the fence-top. I'd never seen him before, but the Governess seemed to know exactly who he was; it was clear she was not the least bit happy about his presence.

The boy was staring directly at me with haunting eyes, the color of which I couldn't distinguish but I felt them reaching for me, pulling me to him.

"What is it?" I asked. "Who is he?"

"He is the boy who caused the accident," she replied. "I should alert the Master immediately, but I know as soon as I turn to leave, he'll be gone again like a ghost."

"That's him?" I now had a face to paste into my missing memories. Now all I needed was a story. "He doesn't look—"

"Well, he's dangerous and should not be on the Ramseys' property, especially after what he's done."

The boy never tore his gaze away from me and I couldn't manage to look away either; his unyielding attention was mesmerizing.

"Now he knows you're up and about, he may be here to finish the job." The Governess snapped two fingers to grab my attention. "You're sure you don't remember anything?"

"No. What should I remember?" I asked, finally turning to her. "What do you mean by *finish the job*?"

"To kill you," she said ominously.

CHAPTER 4

I couldn't shake the boy's face from my mind, becoming so engrossed in my thoughts that I forgot about the pain in my feet for a short time. But the Governess didn't allow my distractions for long.

Who was he? What was his name? And why would he want to kill me? I thought seeing his face would have triggered one of my lost memories, but it didn't. It just created more questions.

The locations of my lessons depended on the subject matter of the hour. Oftentimes, they started and finished in the library of wall-to-wall bookcases complete with rolling ladders and an assortment of study tables in the center of the room. Master Ramsey's desk was in the corner by the stained-glass window.

The Governess—attired in her black dress with

long billowy sleeves—methodically circled the table at which I was seated. She held a long wooden pointer that she tapped against the palm of her free hand as she paced.

"That's as far as I can go," I said and could sense her displeasure from behind me. "I'm trying."

"Reciting three generations of Queen Dorothea's lineage is not *trying* hard enough; Mina can do that in her sleep. You were previously able to go back seven generations."

"I was previously able to do a lot of things."

She rapped me on the shoulder with the pointer. "Save your smart mouth. Sit up straight. I will not have you slouching in my presence. A proper young lady will sit up straight with her feet crossed at the ankles until she is ready to rise."

I crossed my feet at the ankles to appease her, causing me to remember the pain in them, and then said, "Why is this so important anyway?"

"Why is the Queen of Westeria so important?" she asked, her tone dripping with disapproval. "The question is downright offensive and I hope it is never heard uttered beyond these walls. The Queen of Westeria should be important to everyone within the Kingdom. She's been the sole ruler throughout your lifetime and her family has ruled for thirteen generations. Open the book and read to me—direct lineage only. We won't branch off too far."

I opened the heavy leather-bound text *The Great*

History of Westeria and flipped to the genealogy charts in the back. I began reciting the names, starting with Queen Dorothea Hart III and her only child, the reclusive Princess Amelia, who hadn't been seen in public for nearly a decade and a half. She was only a few years older than I was, and I could see myself in the few pictures of her as a child.

Every girl wanted to picture herself as a princess, but I *really* could. Oh, to be young and naive again!

She looked happy in pictures, but she was sickly, with some debilitating illness that seemed to be worsening as she aged. As rumors spread of her declining health, the Princess was locked away within the palace, which certainly didn't stop the spread of rumors.

I knew many people thought the Princess had passed, though the Queen assured everyone her daughter was alive. In fact, during a live teleconference, she'd recently stated that—due to new experimental treatments—the Princess was doing better than ever; her condition was not just improving, but actually reversing, and we'd all be reintroduced to her very soon. You would be right to assume that many in the twenty-four wards remained skeptical.

IN MY LESSONS with the Governess, other mundane facts I'd previously had to memorize and regurgitate included details about our Kingdom of Westeria.

It had survived 579 years, three wars, five natural disasters, and numerous instances of civil unrest. The aftermath of the last war fifty-seven years ago led to the building of the electrified fence, separating us from the lawless Outlands on three sides. The Great Ocean made up our fourth border. Over the generations, we'd been reduced from thirty-five wards to twenty-four—several lost to the Outlands and the rest to restructuring.

Four faction kingdoms were born out of the ruins of a seemingly untouchable empire: Westeria, Easteria, Northeria, and Southeria. This land we now inhabited had once belonged to a cooperation of small kingdoms called the United States of America. In their timeline, 2064 marked The Rift and the collapse of their great cooperative. This collapse was followed by a decade of anarchy before the new kingdoms emerged, becoming our Year Zero.

"Now, close the book and recite them again," the Governess commanded. "Have both hands flat on the cover like you're summoning the names from within the pages."

But that wasn't why she wanted my hands outstretched. I made it to the fifth generation before faltering, the Governess then slapping me across the knuckles with the pointer, producing a welt almost rivaling those on my feet. Luckily, my hands were tougher.

"This isn't a joke," the Governess said, waving the

pointer at me.

"I'm not laughing," I said. My hands burned, but I didn't remove them from the book cover.

"This is important. Everything I stress to you is important."

"If my studies are so important, then why am I not in school with everyone else?"

"Because we're not focusing on general education. We're focusing on the specific knowledge you require." The Governess looked like she wanted to hit me again, but I remained seated tall and straight.

"And I'm required to know the Queen's entire lineage by heart?" I said, exasperated.

"Yes."

We went through the ridiculous drill again. I read the names from the genealogy chart, then recited what I could remember with the book closed; the Governess struck me with the pointer as soon as I reached my memory's end.

Not getting hit was supposed to be the motivation, but I'd become so accustomed to the response that it just became part of the exercise. By the time we took a break—after I reached the twelfth generation—my knuckles were bloody and swollen, less inconspicuous than the weals on my feet.

"Let's move to the dining room," the Governess said. "You may have a minute to grab yourself a glass of water. Then we'll continue with a review of formal dining decorum."

$\mathcal{I}$ was tidying up the front formal sitting room when the doorbell rang. It wasn't an unusual occurrence; deliveries were made regularly and guests of the Ramseys were always coming and going. The estate workers were also in constant rotation to a point where I couldn't keep up with learning all their names.

One of the housekeepers scrubbing the floor in the foyer answered the door. A small messenger drone flew in, which stopped and hovered once inside, its twin propellers whirling.

"Who may I ask for?" the housekeeper asked.

"Duchess Beatrice Ramsey and Victoria Sandalwood," the machine answered in its electronic, monotone voice.

I was speechless. The housekeeper glanced over at me nervously.

It must be some mistake, I thought. I was included in the same message as Lady Ramsey? I'd never received or been included in a message from a drone in my life, only a few items I had ordered being delivered by small package drones; I had no outstanding packages I was aware of.

"I carry a private message for Duchess Beatrice Ramsey and Victoria Sandalwood. Are both present this morning?" the drone asked. A red eye pulsed when it spoke.

The reiteration brought gooseflesh as I considered my response. It didn't seem to be a mistake. Maybe just a misunderstanding?

"I am Victoria Sandalwood," I said as I exited the sitting room and stepped up to the foyer. "What is this regarding?"

"I need both recipients present and authenticated before I can deliver the message, Miss Sandalwood."

"I will find the Duchess," the housekeeper said, hurrying down the hallway and turning a corner.

"I will wait on standby," the machine said, continuing to hover.

"I'll do the same," I said, not sure what else to say or do. I stood idly for a few minutes, then asked, "Can you tell me who it's from?"

The messenger drone did not answer. It either couldn't hear me in standby mode or was flat out ignoring me.

"I'm one of the supposed recipients. There must be something you can tell me."

Still no response.

After a few more minutes of no interaction and no one returning, the hovering drone began to move about the space.

"Please open the door. I shall return when both recipients are present," the drone said.

"No!" I exclaimed. "She's home. Please wait a short while longer."

"I have other deliveries and must continue on my route. Please allow me to exit." The drone moved toward the door, hovering inches away from it like a waiting dog—well if a waiting dog could hover!

"Do you have a message I can relay to Lady Ramsey?" I asked, approaching the door slowly and trying to bide as much time as possible.

"I shall return when it is more convenient."

I apprehensively opened the door and the messenger drone flew out, returning to the open air. Before I'd fully closed it and finished scolding myself for not persuading the drone to wait longer, the housekeeper came running down the hall with Lady Ramsey in tow.

"The Duchess is here! The Duchess is here!" she yelled, waving her arms like a maniac.

I threw open the door and sprinted onto the front landing and down the steps. "She's here! Lady Ramsey is here!" I yelled after the departing drone. I ignored the screaming in my feet and continued down the asphalt roundabout, determined to make sure that damn machine heard me.

After a few more attempts to grab its attention, the drone returned and lowered.

"Beatrice Ramsey and Victoria Sandalwood are both present?" the drone asked, its red eye fixated on me. By this time, Lady Ramsey had emerged onto the front landing.

"I am Beatrice Ramsey," she said.

"I must authenticate each message recipient," the drone said as it flew back into the foyer.

My adrenaline was dropping and my feet felt like they would burst into flames at any moment. I carefully limped back up the steps and through the front door, to stand beside Lady Ramsey.

"Please be still while I authenticate your identity," the drone said in its mechanical voice. A fan of red laser light shot from its cyclops eye and scanned the Duchess's face.

"Identification confirmed."

The drone floated over to me and repeated the process, confirming my own identity.

"The message is marked *confidential*, so only verified recipients may be present during the replay."

"We can go into Mr. Ramsey's office," Lady Ramsey said.

"If the room can be closed off, then it will be adequate," the drone said.

"It can," she said and led the way down the hallway.

Once the three of us were in the office—a room I was never allowed to set foot in alone—Lady Ramsey closed the French doors.

The messenger drone hovered about the room and scanned the walls with the same, fanned-out laser light. "Privacy confirmed. Please stand by while I retrieve the message." The red eye dimmed.

I glanced over at Lady Ramsey, who was fidgeting with the cuffs of her sleeves.

"Do you know what this is all about?" I asked, but before she could answer, the red light from the drone shone brightly again and projected a hologram into the center of the room. We both stepped back to a comfortable viewing distance while simultaneously realizing who was being depicted.

"Good day, Beatrice and Victoria," said the Queen of Westeria.

CHAPTER 6

*T*he hologram of the Queen was colored in shades of red. She had a long flowing gown, her neck and wrists dripped with jewelry, and tendrils of dark curly hair cascaded over her bare shoulders. Atop her head was set the crown she never seemed to be without.

And in the hologram, she was not alone. Beside her stood a young man who couldn't have been much older than I was, dressed as regally as the Queen. His facial features were defined, yet soft, and there was a kindness in his eyes and radiance in his smile.

"In case you don't know, I would like to introduce you to Prince Byron of Easteria. He has taken temporary residence at my palace in the 1st Ward and is eager to meet you, Victoria."

My jaw almost came unhinged and dropped off

my face entirely. Lady Ramsey immediately noticed my state of shock and put a comforting arm around me.

"I am working hard to advance our relationship with Easteria, and a royal marriage between our two mighty kingdoms is a perfect way to do that. I'm sure you're asking yourself what this has to do with you? There is much that needs to be said, most of which should be done in person. But first I must get you to the palace. So, this is your official royal invitation.

"Victoria, this concerns you because—and I hope you're hearing this from me first—you are my younger daughter and the second heir to the throne. I have arranged for you and Prince Byron to meet and build a connection, with the hope that we can make this union between our two kingdoms come to fruition.

"Beatrice, I want to thank you for raising Victoria and grooming her for her proper place at my side. I'm sorry I could not provide you with more warning, but arrangements have been made for Victoria to leave three days hence.

"Victoria, I'm sure this is a lot to absorb, but I'm excited to officially meet you and also for the future of our Kingdom. All your questions will be answered upon your arrival at the palace."

The Queen turned her attention to the Prince.

"Prince Byron, is there anything you would like to add?"

"Victoria, the pleasure is all mine," he said, cheerfully. "I've heard such wonderful things about you from the Ramseys." And there was that radiant smile again. "I'm confident we'll hit it off and excited to discover where this can lead. We shall explore the 1st Ward in style. I wish you safe travels to Capital City."

"We both do," the Queen added. "I don't want to say too much in this message, but I assure you, things will be much clearer once you're here. I very much look forward to meeting you. We shall see you soon."

Abruptly, the holograph dissolved and the light went out.

"That concludes your private message," the drone said. "Thank you for inviting me into your home. Good day to you both."

Lady Ramsey showed the drone out. When she turned to face me after closing the front door, there were tears in her eyes.

"What's wrong?" I asked. If she had been expecting this message from the Queen, it didn't show.

"My little girl's finally all grown up and leaving us," she said, producing a pained smile.

"It seems I'm not your little girl," I replied.

"You always knew that."

"I still don't believe what I just heard. It can't be

possible. I can't be the Queen's daughter—a Princess of Westeria."

"How does Victoria Hart sound?" Lady Ramsey started walking down the hallway.

"Wrong," I said, instinctively following her.

After a few turns, I found myself back in the office with Lady Ramsey. She once again closed the French doors.

"Yes, I knew this day was coming—not when, but that it would be upon us before too long. It may seem impossible or a cruel joke, but you are the Queen's daughter and we were instructed to raise you until you were called back. I'm happy for you, but can't say I'm happy about you leaving." Lady Ramsey paused and took a deep breath. "I know you'll do the Kingdom proud. But don't forget about us way out in the 24th Ward."

"What does this mean?"

"It means you are going to return to your mother, marry a handsome prince, extend the Royal Family, and one day rule the Kingdom. You'll have more shoes than you can count. Does that about sum it up?"

"I don't understand," I said.

Lady Ramsey took a few steps toward me and pulled me in for a hug. She cried then, on my shoulder, in turn bringing tears to sting my eyes.

CHAPTER 7

I couldn't get the hologram and message delivered earlier in the day out of my head. I'd been a second-rate family member and servant for so long, I couldn't picture myself as anything else. No one jumped this many caste levels in a lifetime, let alone in a moment.

The 1st Ward was by the coast; I'd never been there before. In fact, I'd never been out of the 24th Ward. The Ramseys regularly traveled to other wards for business, and occasionally were invited to the Queen's palace for special events. And soon, I'd be living there; that thought was so surreal.

It was late, but I wasn't expecting to do much sleeping that night. I lay on the bed with an open novel, but couldn't concentrate on the story either. Each time I turned a page, I realized I'd completely forgotten what I'd just read and had to go back and reread many pages. I finally gave up and simply gazed around my sparse room, thinking of Johanna's and Mina's rooms and imagining my new one dwarfing theirs. My rolling rack of dresses would soon be replaced by a closet larger than my present bedroom; there'd be a four-poster canopy bed I could stretch out on without reaching a single edge, and I'd have racks of shoes of all different colors and styles. My attention fell to my single pair of scuffed flats on the floor.

I looked up at the sound of a knock at my door. Instead of waiting for my reply, someone opened it; Mina apprehensively entered. Of the two Ramsey daughters, she came down to my room more often—which was still far from regular.

"Good evening, Miss Mina," I said, sitting up. "What are you doing up so late?"

"I overheard my parents talking about you."

"I'm sure they were."

"And they said you were leaving," she said. She remained standing by the door.

"It seems I am."

"And you're a princess."

"I—I don't really know what's going on yet."

"You don't look like a princess."

"I suppose a princess without her elegant ball-gowns and tiaras doesn't much look like herself."

"I can't picture you like that."

"If I'm being honest, neither can I," I said, laughing. "I'm pretty much a wreck most of the time."

Mina smiled, but it was short-lived. "I don't want you to go."

"I'll miss you," I said. "And once I'm settled in, you'll have to come and visit me."

"If my parents let me."

"I'm sure they won't deny a request from the Queen," I said with a wink.

Mina approached, dragging her feet, and sat beside me on the bed. Her expression was haunting as she peered over at me. "I'm afraid of what will happen once you're gone."

I turned on the bed to better face her. "What are you afraid of?"

She didn't want to face me. Her head was down, her attention all given to her fidgety hands in her lap. "I'm not as strong as you are."

"What are you talking about? You're plenty strong."

"I can't take the punishments like you do. I just can't," she cried.

"I didn't think you got the same types of punishment as me."

"Me and Johanna have gotten switchings ourselves. You get most of them. But we've been hit by the switch too."

"Oh... I didn't realize..."

"Ours are behind closed doors."

"Does Lady Ramsey—your mother know?"

"I think so," she said weakly. "I never brought it up to her."

I wanted to tell her everything would be all right, but I couldn't. I thought that since I was the outcast, I was the only one receiving the agonizing, humiliating treatment. I didn't want to believe he was subjecting his own daughters to the same tortures. But I guessed like everything else I'd discovered that day, I'd been wrong about that too. Johanna was almost a grown woman and could potentially be out of the house soon, leaving little Mina all alone. Now I *was* afraid for her.

"We won't lose touch. We'll talk on the phone and write letters and you'll tell me everything that's happening. If things do get worse like you fear, I'll do whatever I can to get you out of here."

"Do you promise?" she asked, finally gazing up at me.

"I promise," I said and hoped I didn't come to regret those words.

"Pinky promise," she insisted, holding up a hand and extending a delicate pinky finger.

I did, which made me more afraid for her but stoked the fire within to uphold the promise.

"I'll write to you every day," she said, and I laughed.

"That seems a little excessive, but I appreciate the sentiment."

"I didn't want to hit you," she said.

"I know."

"Johanna wouldn't admit it, but she didn't either."

"I know that too. She's not one to give away her hand."

"What do you mean?"

"Never mind." We sat there silently for a minute and then she lay down and put her head in my lap. I stroked her blonde hair with its locks of red and pink. It felt just like silk.

"You should probably go before someone realizes you're not in your room and comes looking for you."

"Can't I stay the night?" she asked, looking up at me with sorrowful eyes. Those eyes would be absolutely irresistible to the boys in a few short years.

"No. You should get back. I don't want to get either of us into trouble."

Mina sat up and hopped down from the bed. "Are you really going to be a princess?"

"I wish I knew," I said. "But it seems I'll find out soon."

"I hope so," she said as she made for the door.

In truth, I didn't know how I felt about it; the information was all too new and still seemed too unbelievable. So, I simply smiled, but she didn't turn back to see it.

After she was gone, I went back to my thoughts, which were becoming more overwhelming by the second. Now, I had to add Mina's physical and emotional wellbeing to my growing list of concerns. If I really was to become the next Princess of Westeria, there was no doubt I'd be able to keep my promise to Mina. But what if I wasn't? I had no idea what to expect in three days' time. What if I was simply exchanging one house of chores for another? What if this was some cruel joke or some other situation or circumstance I wasn't even considering?

I didn't know who to trust. As nice as Lady Ramsey had been to me over the years, I'd never felt she was telling me the whole truth. I would never in a million years consider trusting Master Ramsey. I didn't personally know the Queen, but, historically, royal figures were not known for being forthcoming and trustworthy. And as handsome and kind as Prince Byron seemed from the hologram, I didn't know him either. The only person I truly trusted was a brokenhearted, twelve-year-old girl, whom I well knew could be taken advantage of or manipulated to betray me against her better judgment. I suddenly felt the full weight of my loneliness.

I was startled by the sound of a few quick taps. My attention returned to the door, but when I heard a few more raps, it was obvious they weren't coming from there.

Three more resounded, louder this time.

I recognized the sound as something rapping against glass—against one of my small windows. I looked in their direction, but my curtains were drawn.

Already on edge from all the stress of the day, this was not helping; my stomach tightened and my pulse increased. I waited, hoping whatever was causing the sound had left or blown away.

But the rapping returned in a quick burst.

I finally gathered the nerve to get off my bed and approach the window where the sound was coming from. I didn't know why I was suddenly so fearful of a faint noise from a window too small for anyone to fit through, but my rationale was overtaken by my sensational over-imagination.

I slowly reached a hand up and pulled the curtain to one side as the next burst sounded.

I was hit with the beam of a flashlight, as its head knocked against the window. A figure was lying in the grass outside—a figure looking vaguely familiar. The flashlight then turned onto his face so I could better make out who was calling on me—or who was here to *finish the job*. It was the boy I'd seen from across the field, the one the Governess had warned me about.

My heart pounded against my chest as he stared at me through the window. He'd obviously known exactly where to find me.

CHAPTER 8

J closed the curtain in a flash, stepping back.

"Victoria, please talk to me," I heard the boy say from outside, soft enough as to not call too much attention to himself. "I need to talk to you. I need to make sure you're all right."

His words took me aback. He didn't sound like the Governess had described but I wasn't about to drop my guard for a few sweet words of concern.

"Then talk," I said, standing in place, my attention on the closed curtain. "How about starting with who you are and how you know me."

"I don't know what they did to you," he said. "You know me. I'm Kale. Please come outside. I need to see you."

"Are you mad?" I scoffed. "I'm not going outside with you out there."

"I'm sorry. Will you at least come to the window? What could I possibly do through this tiny thing?"

I sighed, but stepped forward and reopened the curtain. "There. Now you can see me. Happy? Why are you here? What did you do to me?"

"Me? I didn't do anything." He sounded offended. "Are you hurt?"

"What would you know about that?"

"I know what the Duke does to you. You've shown me the wounds. You've cried in my arms. I swore to take you away from here." Kale's eyes were pleading. He put a hand to the glass. "I don't know what happened after they took you and I've had to lie low and be careful since it happened."

"Who took me?"

"The guards of the Ramseys. They hauled you back... home. So, are you hurt?"

"I'm fine," I said, even though I felt anything but.

"No, you're not," he said as if reading my mind. "You're forgetting how well I know you. I can read it all over your face. You're far from fine."

"You can't. You don't know anything about me."

"I know you like to eat peanut butter straight out of the jar. You love the smell of the honeysuckles growing out past the stables. Your favorite book is *Pride and Prejudice* and you've read it nine times. You want to see all twenty-four wards. You want to ride Misty on the beach and splash in the ocean. You feel like a real big sister to Mina and wanted to take her with us. You—"

"Take Mina with us?" I asked, cutting him off.

"Yes." Kale brought his face closer to the window. "Take her away from here because you were afraid she was receiving the same type of treatment as you. It was deplorable just to think about."

"I was… I thought that?" I thought how surprised I was when Mina had brought up the subject earlier. I had no recollection of such thoughts. Then I grew more upset with what else I wasn't remembering. Like Kale… He was telling me specific details about myself that I thought no one else knew. How much else of what he was saying was true? There was a lot I was having a hard time remembering, but it was so strange I had no memory of him at all.

"I can see the gears turning," Kale said. "What are you thinking?"

"I don't know what to think," I said. "I wish I could remember at least one thing about you. It would help make all this seem real and give some validation to what you're telling me."

"That would make things a whole lot easier."

"How long have we known each other?"

"About four months."

"That's all?"

"It may not have been a long time, but I've felt like I've known you for years. We just clicked, you know? We still can."

I stared at him through the glass and wished I felt the same way. He seemed sincere with everything he was saying, and God knew I needed a friend right now—someone I could trust. But trustworthy people were very hard to come by.

"Can I persuade you to come outside yet?" Kale asked.

I shook my head. "I don't think that's such a good idea," I said. My room still felt safer than being out there with him. Maybe not much, but enough.

"Can I at least call on you again? If we must start over, then so be it. I'm not letting you go."

"There isn't time to start over," I said, sadly.

"What do you mean. Of course, there is. You're not going anywhere. *I'm* not going anywhere—"

"That's just it," I said, my voice catching in my throat. "I'm leaving in three days."

"Where to? When will you return?"

"I don't know when I'll be back... if I *ever* come back." I didn't know how much I should tell him, so tried to keep my answer vague and hoped he wouldn't pry too much. "New accommodations have been made for me in the 1st Ward."

"Wow..." He seemed lost for words, which helped me. "Stepping up in the world, Lady Victoria."

"Don't call me that."

"Maybe you'll even get to meet the Queen." His tone was sarcastic.

I shrugged. "Your guess is as good as mine."

"I don't know what to say," Kale said. "At least it gets you out of here, which is what you wanted. I really want you to be happy, so I should be happy for you."

"But you're not."

"We had a plan."

"So you say."

"I know… I'm asking too much, putting too much pressure—"

There was a booming knock at the door.

"Who are you talking to?" It was the voice of Master Ramsey. The door opened and he stumbled into the room.

Perhaps it hadn't been a knock at the door, but him crashing into it as he fumbled for the doorknob. He wasn't typically one to knock in his own house.

I closed the curtain before he could take an inventory of the room, and I spun around to face him.

He still held onto the doorknob for support. In his other hand, he held a whole bushel of freshly cut switches. Six, seven, maybe eight—I couldn't count them all, nor did I want to as I considered their implication.

"You think you can just leave?" All his words ran together. The stench of whiskey and cigar smoke poured into the room like a tidal wave. "You will not leave until I say you can leave… and especially not without a proper send-off." He sneered at me, gathered his balance, and closed the door behind him. "Come. Bend over. And place your palms flat on the bed."

CHAPTER 9

I backed up against the far wall. I knew Kale was only a few feet away, but there was nothing he could do to help me from outside. I knew if I screamed, I'd only make things worse for myself.

"Please don't do this," I pleaded. I was as far away from the drunken Master as I could get, but it was a dead end. I had nowhere left to go.

"I gave you a direct order, *Princess*." Each slurred word was laced with venom, but he didn't raise his voice. He rarely found the need to do so; he was a big and powerful man, used to the world bending to his will. And I was a small girl who could easily be bent.

"Do as you're told, or so help me God, I will make it so you never sit comfortably again."

The thought sent chills throughout my entire

body. I inched forward, making my way to the bed while giving him a wide berth.

"That's it, darling," he said and placed all but one of the switches on the nightstand. He flexed it, slicing the air with a heavy swing. "Everything will go much smoother if you follow directions."

I reached the bed and placed my hands on the mattress, bending forward as directed. I shut my eyes tight, trying not to think of what was to come. In his drunken state, there'd be no holding back. And I would have to remain standing.

Then there was a crash and the sound of glass shards raining onto the concrete floor. A metal flashlight bounced off the side of my bed, hitting the ground.

Master Ramsey stumbled back into my dress rack and pulled a few dresses off their hangers, trying to regain his footing.

"What the hell was that?" he roared.

No other sound came from the broken window. My eyes shot open and I was upright in a flash, ready to run.

Master Ramsey shuffled past me, toward the broken window. He grabbed the curtain; I think he meant to just slide it to the side, but instead ended up ripping the curtain rod right out of the wall. He gazed out into the cold night, but on this side of the house, there weren't many lights so there wasn't much to see. There seemed to be no trace of Kale.

Master Ramsey shifted from one side to the other, disoriented and confused. He finally picked up the flashlight and examined it, turning it on, then off again.

"Who were you talking to?" he asked, waving the flashlight at me.

"No one," I said. "I was talking to myself. It gets lonely down here, especially at night."

He kept the flashlight pointed at me and looked like he was about to say more, but then ran out of the room without uttering further reprimands. From the force of him throwing open the door, the doorknob had slammed into the wall, leaving a hole in the drywall.

I hurried over, closed the door, and fell back against it with a heavy sigh. But after a moment to regain my breath, I ventured toward the broken window.

"Kale?" I called into the night. "Kale, are you still there?"

There was no reply.

Then I heard the crunch of multiple sets of booted feet trekking through the grass and gravel. Master Ramsey had already gathered a posse of guards and was checking the perimeter of the house. I heard a few sets of the same booted feet just outside my broken window, and after a few seconds, they stomped away.

My heart went out to Kale and I hoped his head start had been enough for him to get away.

I lit a candle on the nightstand. With the flickering light in hand, I ventured out into the cellar, first looking around to ensure I was alone, then burrowing into the cave of stored furniture, all the while being careful not to set fire to any materials. The wood smelled of varnish and mothballs. I pulled at the sheet covering a stack of chairs, then crawled under another until I found a large enough space to rest. The sheet I'd taken provided something other than the concrete to sleep on, and once I was settled in, I blew out the candle and drifted to slumber amongst the ghosts.

WHEN I AWOKE, there was light outside my indoor tent. Two servants were talking to each other, probably down here to get extra supplies for breakfast.

"No, I didn't hear if they caught the intruder," one said.

"No place is safe anymore," the other said. "I heard them patrolling half the night. I hope I can get some sleep tonight."

"Me too. I've already had three cups of coffee. It's barely keeping me awake and now it's giving me heartburn."

They continued their conversation as they made

their way up the stairs. Then the lights to the cellar were extinguished, and all was quiet once again.

I had to feel my way around to get back to my room, which wasn't overly difficult. Last night hadn't been my first time sleeping in the stored furniture grotto; I'd hidden from a drunken Master Ramsey before. He didn't seem to hold those times against me like any other type of open defiance. Perhaps he just didn't remember them.

My room should've had light coming from the broken window, but was just as dark as the rest of the cellar. I pulled the string for my overhead light and found the broken window had been boarded up from the outside, glass shards still littering the floor.

I pulled the curtain for the second window and discovered it boarded up as well. There, the glass was still intact but it was still covered with plywood on the outside.

My room had never felt so much like a prison. I started to consider I may not be leaving after all. At least Mina would be happy if that were the case.

I defiantly wore my one pair of shoes as I cleaned up the glass. The last thing I needed was glass embedded in my slowly healing feet.

Before I could finish, the intercom on the wall crackled and a tiny voice came through. "Are you coming up for breakfast?" The voice was Mina's.

I glanced over at the clock and hadn't realized how late it was—how much I'd slept in. I ran over to the intercom and pressed the button. "I'll be right there."

It wasn't like the rest of the kitchen staff couldn't help them, but I was expected to be there every morning to help out. I didn't want any more trouble. I didn't worry about wearing the same dress as the day before, and went out of my room, across the cellar and up the stairs.

CHAPTER 10

I passed through the formal dining room and greeted the family on my way to the kitchen. Master Ramsey wasn't present at the table.

"Victoria, wait," Lady Ramsey said. "Come join us."

I stopped and turned. "Are you sure?"

"Quite sure," she said. "Come. Sit."

I didn't know what to think, but certainly wasn't going to argue. I pulled out a chair next to Mina, and as I sat down, I noticed the shoes I was still wearing. I glanced nervously around, but no one else seemed to have seen them. Johanna was talking about a new boy she'd met and Mina kept chiming in with the latest things she'd learned in her riding lessons. Lady Ramsey had to split her attention between the two chattering girls.

I sat down and smiled, making sure to adjust my

posture like the Governess constantly reiterated. I crossed my legs at the ankles and tucked my feet under the chair.

There were already assortments of breads, pastries, meats, and cheeses in the middle of the table along with pitchers of juice and water.

Bertha came over and asked if I wanted tea or coffee? I always made coffee for myself, but her asking suddenly made the decision a whole lot harder.

"I'll take an Earl Grey tea," I said because it sounded fancier than coffee and it was a day for a change. I needed to try something new.

"Victoria, before I forget," Lady Ramsey began. "Dr. Crane will be here at ten for your check up."

"Okay," I said. "I'll see what chores I can get done before then."

"No chores," she said with a smile. "I want you to relax today—for your final few days here. You'll still have your lessons with the Governess. It's important to stay on top of your studies. But all your chores will be delegated to the rest of the staff. They are no longer your responsibility."

I couldn't suppress a smile. The next two days without chores would be as good as any vacation I could imagine. I didn't know what awaited me when I arrived at the palace but didn't want to think about that now; I just wanted to enjoy the fact I had two full, chore-free days!

"Think you can come riding with me?" Mina asked.

"Wait at least until Dr. Crane has had a chance to examine you," Lady Ramsey said.

"This afternoon," I told Mina.

"Wait, you didn't even hear the best part..." Johanna said and went right back to talking about her new gentleman caller.

While Johanna was talking her mother's ear off, Bertha brought my tea. A few minutes later, the main dishes were served. We each had a tower of waffles, assorted fruit slices, and whipped cream that I knew would taste divine. Lady Ramsey and Johanna ate slowly and elegantly like they were sitting with the Queen herself. Mina mostly picked at her food, stabbing at the fruit slices and placing them into small piles, then taking a forkful of nothing but whipped cream. I didn't even want to eat my food, didn't want to ruin its presentation. But I was enjoying watching everyone else eat.

"Aren't you hungry?" Lady Ramsey asked in between bites.

I nodded, but it wasn't until everyone was almost done with their meals that I finally began eating. I'd had our kitchen's waffles many times before, but they'd never tasted as good as they did on that morning while sitting with the family.

The Governess retrieved me after breakfast to fit in our session before Dr. Crane arrived.

"Did Lady Ramsey inform you I'd be accompanying you to the palace?" she asked.

"No. She didn't," I answered.

"Well, I will be. I'll travel and stay with you. I haven't been told how long as yet, but I'm sure it will be for at least a few days to help ease the difficult transition."

"That'll be nice," I said. I meant it too. The Governess was a strict woman, one I didn't want to cross, but I didn't hate her. She didn't seem to enjoy punishment the way Master Ramsey did.

The Governess was quizzing me on general information about the Kingdom of Easteria and the ruling DuFours—of whom Prince Byron was the youngest son—when Lady Ramsey entered the library to inform us Dr. Crane had arrived.

She led me to one of the upstairs guest bedrooms, where he was waiting.

"Good morning, Victoria," he said with a warm smile, shaking my hand. "I've been told the good news."

"You knew I was the Queen's daughter?"

He seemed happy for me, but not terribly surprised. "I wasn't able to disclose such information by order of the Queen," he said. "I'm sure you can understand."

"I'm sure it's a sensitive subject."

"Extremely."

I was asked to sit on the bed while he checked all

the regular things: my blood pressure, breathing, pulse, and blood sample, and he ended the examination by giving me a visual examination and a small cup for a urine sample. Dr. Crane recorded all the results on a small tablet computer.

Lady Ramsey, meanwhile, stayed seated on a leather loveseat in the corner of the room while the doctor worked.

The bedroom had an en-suite, so I used the bathroom and returned with the cup filled. Dr. Crane labeled it, along with the blood sample, and placed both containers in a portable cooler.

"How do you feel, Victoria?" Dr. Crane asked.

"Good," I said.

"How about your memory?"

"It's about the same. Most of what I lost is from the last few months and it hasn't come back. Though it doesn't seem to be getting worse."

"That's not uncommon. There's a good chance what you lost will come back in time, but there's no guarantee." He ran his fingers along my neck, pressing just below my ears and then pushing gently on numerous spots on the back of my head. "Tell me if you feel any pain or discomfort?"

None of the areas hurt.

"Have you had any dizzy spells? Lightheadedness? Nausea?"

I shook my head for all the listed symptoms. "Can I start horseback riding again?" I asked.

"I don't see any reason why you shouldn't be able to. As long as you feel up to it, then I have no objections."

I was excited to run out and tell Mina; I couldn't wait to be back in the saddle, my hands on the reins, the wind in my hair. The sun was out and the temperature was fair; I couldn't have asked for better riding conditions.

"Well, I think this is it," Dr. Crane said as he started to gather up his supplies.

Lady Ramsey rose from her seat. "Thank you as always, Doctor."

"My pleasure," he said and glanced over at me. "And the next time I check on you, it will be in the Queen's palace."

"It'll be nice to have a familiar face there," I said.

"I'm sure it will feel like home in no time. Enjoy the rest of your day, and safe travels," he said, picking up his black leather bag of personal equipment.

Dr. Crane shook both our hands and then Lady Ramsey escorted him out.

CHAPTER 11

I had one of the best afternoons I could remember, riding through the meadow with Mina. Misty and Pumpernickel seemed to be having a grand ol' time too.

I kept glancing at the far fence where I'd first seen Kale—or, at least, the first time I could remember seeing him. He'd said we were planning to run away together and that I'd wanted to take Mina with us—away from this place, this façade of glorious, luxurious living. I wanted to ride up to him and talk face-to-face in the daylight, to see him clearly and be able to make out all of his features previously veiled by distance or shadows.

Mina kicked Pumpernickel into a full gallop and I chased after her. Her trainer, Samuel, stood by and let her go, confident in her ability to remain in control. She was on track to compete in a few years;

I hoped I'd be able to see it. When she reached the edge of the property, she pulled Pumpernickel to a halt and waited for me to catch up.

"You're a slow poke," she laughed.

"You had a head start. Not fair!" I protested.

"I guess you'll have to practice more," she said.

"I hope I'll be able to."

That dissolved her smile. The seasons were changing. The carefree afternoon in the sun had temporarily pushed it from her mind.

"We have tomorrow," I reminded her.

Her spark returned. "Maybe I'll let you win tomorrow."

"Maybe you won't have to," I said.

We trotted back to the stables together. I untacked Misty while one of the stable hands took care of Pumpernickel. I wasn't ready to delegate this chore because it didn't feel like one. Mina stood by and watched as I finished with Misty.

On returning to the main house, we went our separate ways to clean up and I retreated to my room in the cellar. As I approached, I saw my light was on, so entered cautiously.

"Oh, sorry. I was just dropping this off," Johanna said, pointing to a suitcase and matching shoulder bag on the floor. "Mom wanted me to bring them down for you. They were mine, but I'm going to get a new set. These are getting worn."

"Thank you," I said. "They look nice to me."

"They were top of the line when I bought them a few years ago. I didn't bring the rest of the set because you don't have much stuff."

"Yeah; these will be more than enough," I said. "I wouldn't be able to carry more than this anyway."

She gave me a confused look. "We have people for that," she finally said.

"Of course."

Johanna made her way to the door, noticeably keeping her distance from me. Then she stopped and turned back.

"Why?" she asked open-endedly. "Why are you like this secret princess? It's not fair. I should be the one getting out of here first."

"It's not like I asked for this," I said.

"Yeah, but it's happening. You'll be living it up at the palace while I'm stuck here in the outskirts of the Kingdom—in the wretched Borderlands."

"You can come and visit if you want."

"So you can rub all your good fortune in my face and have me serve you? No, thank you."

"I wouldn't do that."

"Everyone starts off saying that, but..." Johanna stood silently in the doorway for a moment, then turned and left.

I went after her as far as the doorway, then decided to let her go, watching her go up the stairs and back into the primary living quarters of the main house where she belonged. I simply reminded myself there was no love lost between us.

I returned to my room and gazed upon the bags she'd brought, one more reminder that this was really happening. Two days. My nerves were shot already, my excitement giving me heartburn. I felt sick and overrun by emotion.

I perused the dresses hanging on the rack to determine which one was suitable enough for arriving at the palace and presenting myself to the Queen—and Prince Byron. I couldn't find a single one, not that there were many to choose from; I started throwing down the ones I thought were trash and ultimately found myself with three left hanging from the rack. None of them seemed suitable for royalty, but they were the best I had and would have to do.

I looked upon the fallen heap of unbefitting dresses and started to cry. They seemed to be all different parts of myself, none of them good enough. This was all too much. I sat among them, scooping them all up into my lap, unable to control the tears. If I wasn't good enough for the Ramseys, how would I ever be good enough for the Queen? Why would the Prince even want to meet me? I was nothing.

One by one, I took a dress from the pile and folded it, then placed each one into the larger suitcase. They may not be worthy, but they were all I had.

When I was folding one of the final dresses—one with pockets in the skirt—I felt something. I reached into the pockets and pulled out a crumpled piece of paper. Once I'd flattened it out, I discovered it was a note:

Meet me at the devil's tree tomorrow at twilight. –Yours always.

I checked the back of the paper to see if there was more, but there wasn't. I couldn't remember finding this letter before but assumed I'd known about it at one time—before the accident. I thought of Kale and his tale of us running away together; maybe this was from that night? I did know the tree to which he was referring and took the note as another sign he wasn't the bad guy the Ramseys made him out to be.

I placed the note inside my nightstand drawer, beneath *Pride & Prejudice*, and continued packing my few belongings.

CHAPTER 12

The next day, Master Ramsey found me under the willow tree at the mouth of the hedge maze, reading from his hardbound copy of *Pride & Prejudice*. Kale had been right, and this would be my tenth time through the book.

"You've read this one before," he said, bending down to get a closer look at the cover.

"I have—multiple times actually," I replied.

I then noticed him glance at my shoes and waited for a disciplinary comment or to have him grab me by the arm, drag me into the hedge maze, and punish me out there. But he didn't.

Instead, he said, "You may keep it." He rose and was quiet for a time, standing beneath the willow's thick canopy, gazing out at the East garden. "I guess this is it," he finally said. "You're finally going back to where you belong."

From his tone, I couldn't tell whether he was happy or sad to be ridding himself of me.

"I know you're looking forward to moving on, but don't be fooled into thinking this is some dream-come-true or happily-ever-after. Everyone in the 1st Ward is treacherous and narcissistic, especially the Queen and all her bottom feeders."

"Don't worry. I don't trust anyone now. That won't change when I leave. I'm not expecting the world to be handed to me."

"I feel partially responsible," he said, finishing with a grin. He obviously had no regret for anything he'd done to me. "How are your feet?"

They tingled merely from his words. "Still sore, but I'll live," I said sharply.

"I'm sure you will," he said. Master Ramsey said nothing further before heading back to the house, leaving me to my reading.

I didn't want to think too much about his warnings of what lay ahead; I knew I couldn't just go in as a naive teenager, but needed to have my guard up, at least until I fully understood what was going on. This conversation was a good reminder of that.

My reading was interrupted about an hour later, this time by Mina coming from the direction of the house, tramping through the East garden.

"Mom would like to see you inside," she shouted while still a little way off. It didn't seem serious; she sounded excited. I bookmarked my page and rose from my place in the grass.

"What's going on?" I asked.

"You'll have to come in and find out for yourself," she answered with a smile.

She skipped ahead of me as we both went inside the main estate. I followed her through several hallways and rooms, stopping at the doorway to the front formal sitting room.

Lady Ramsey was speaking with a few members of staff about rearranging furniture to better suit the room.

"Oh, Victoria, there you are," she said, excusing herself from the servants. She walked over to us and stepped up, into the foyer. "I have an errand for you to run." She reached into a pocket hidden within the folds of her dress and produced a stack of bills. "I want you to go into town and buy a dress and shoes for your travels tomorrow. Go to Adriana's and tell her I sent you."

Adriana was the best seamstress in town and had handcrafted some of Lady Ramsey's and the girls' finest dresses.

"I get to go with you!" Mina exclaimed, practically bouncing in place.

"Yes. Mina has developed a wonderful eye for style. She'll help you choose. Get the best one that suits you and if this isn't enough, ask for some credit and I'll handle getting her paid."

I took the money; it felt so very heavy in my hands. I'd carried this much before but never was the purchase intended for me.

"Yes, Ma'am," I said. "We'll leave right away."

Lady Ramsey laid a hand on my shoulder and smiled. "I want you looking your best."

I hurried down to my room to put away the book, but before I left, I removed the bookmark—the note I'd found from Kale the previous night—and stuffed it into the pocket of my dress with the money.

The walk into town was calming. Mina asked all about the 1st Ward and I told her everything I could remember from my lessons with the Governess.

A bell above the door chimed when we entered Adriana's. She was a lively little ball of a woman with poufy, almost white hair, colorful makeup, long fake fingernails, and a pair of black-rimmed glasses hanging around her neck.

"Mina, my dear, how are you this fine after-noon?" she said in a loud, manly voice. "And this isn't Johanna. Who have you brought with you today?"

"This is Victoria, my other sister," Mina said.

"The mysterious *other sister*. I have seen you around town, have I not?"

"Yes, Ma'am," I said. "I've been on errands around town many times. I just never had the pleasure to come in here."

"The pleasure's all mine," she said boisterously. "How may I be of service?"

Mina did most of the talking. She could describe the dresses while I simply tried on what was given to me. I ambled around the room as they discussed fabrics and style. I looked at all the dresses dangling from hangers and draped on mannequins; there were a great many to choose from, and I didn't see a single one unfit for a princess.

"Is this for a special occasion or event? For everyday elegance?" Ms. Adriana asked.

"Victoria will be meeting the Queen tomorrow," Mina said.

Ms. Adriana's eyes lit up and she clapped her fleshy hands together. "Oh, then I have just the thing!" she said as she disappeared through a curtain into a back room. In a flash, she returned with a flowing emerald green ballgown with beaded lace appliqués and a plunging V-back.

"It's the Queen's favorite color. I made it two years ago for the Queen's last scheduled visit, as a gift for Princess Amelia. I'd requested her measurements and got everything a few weeks before the arrival. But the Queen's itinerary changed only a few days before she was due and she didn't end up coming to the 24th Ward. I knew Princess Amelia wouldn't be traveling with her but thought the Queen would appreciate the gift. I've been holding onto it ever since, waiting for her to schedule another visit. It didn't seem right selling it to someone else, but maybe you're the girl this dress has truly been waiting for."

"It's gorgeous," I admitted.

"Try it on!" Mina insisted.

Near the back of the shop, a series of partitions created a semi-private changing area.

Ms. Adriana helped me climb into the emerald gown; its fabric lining was so incredibly soft as it perfectly hugged every curve. I gazed down at the beadwork and embellishments and couldn't remember ever seeing something so beautiful before. Then she led me by the hand over to the small pedestal, where I stood before a full-length, trifold mirror and was able to gaze upon the full impact of such a striking dress.

"This dress is amazing," I said, doing a half-turn so I could view the gown's back.

"It sure is," Ms. Adriana said. "I don't think I have to do any alterations. It fits you perfectly and I can't think of a time that's ever happened before. It's like I'd made this dress specifically for you without even knowing it. Truly amazing!"

"Now, you look like a princess," Mina said.

I lifted the skirt and twirled in my scuffed flats. My hair was unkempt and I had no makeup on, but the dress elevated everything about me. I now felt a tiny bit of confidence to meet the Queen—my mother.

"So?" Mina asked.

"Is there really a question?" I said. "This is *the* dress. How much do I owe you?"

Ms. Adriana had taken a few steps back and put on her glasses. She was examining me intently with the eye of an artist, with me her willing muse. "This dress was made as a gift, and a gift it shall remain."

"No," I said. "I need to pay you for it. Too much work went into this adorable piece of art for the artist not to be compensated. I can't leave without—"

"I won't hear any more about it," Ms. Adriana said, shaking her head. "The dress is yours."

"I don't know what to say."

"How about a *thank you* for starters."

"Well of course! Thank you! A million times *thank you!*" I threw my arms around her and nearly cried.

Ms. Adriana hugged me back. "Some things were just meant to be. Go and make an entrance."

CHAPTER 13

J still had plenty of money left over, even after Mina helped me decide on a pair of black leather boots to do justice to my new dress. The pair I bought didn't have a heel too extreme since I'd had zero experience walking at such an angle. And I was too intimidated by all the high-heeled shoes Mina recommended.

I had both outfit pieces wrapped and boxed, not wanting to dirty them before the following day; I carried the dress and Mina the boots. With some of my extra money, I also bought Mina the same pair of boots in a smaller size; she insisted she wanted us to match.

Evening was approaching as we made our way back. I told Mina I wanted to make one more stop before going home and she was thrilled to prolong our afternoon adventure.

I led us in the opposite direction of the Ramsey estate, toward the edge of town. We walked along the paved road, all the way until it ended. At that point, a forked set of dirt paths led into the forest, and between the two paths grew a small tree with two trunks twisted together. At one time, it may have at been two trees, but now it had joined and grown into one. Further up the entwined trunks, branches were also entangled in a thick web and their trunks were engraved with hundreds of names and initials, some now barely legible. This was the devil's tree.

"Why are we here?" Mina asked.

"I wanted to see something," I said. "Have you been here before?"

She shook her head.

I walked up to the tree and circled the tangle of trunks, reading the engravings. On the back of the tree trunk, I found the initials VS + KC. I didn't know Kale's last name to be sure they were ours, but three out of four—along with the note—made me feel confident enough.

"Is that you?" Mina asked, pointing at the carved VS.

"I don't remember doing it, but I have a feeling it is," I said.

"And are those the initials of the boy my parents are after?"

"Again, this is part of the hole in my memory, but I believe so."

I removed Kale's note from my dress pocket and read it again. Mina peered over my arm to see the note as well.

"Is this the devil's tree?"

"Yup."

"You were supposed to meet him the night of the accident, weren't you?"

"Do you have any light you'd like to shed on that night?" I asked, putting the note away.

"I—I heard you yelling and screaming when you were brought back. I hid in the pantry when they brought you in, so I didn't see anything. I didn't know if you were hurt or angry."

"So, I was awake when I was brought home and then lost months of my memory. It doesn't add up."

"I didn't want to ask questions," Mina said.

"I know," I said, bringing a hand to her cheek, rosy pink from the blush she wore. "I don't want to get you in any trouble."

We left the devil's tree and headed home. The street lamps were lit when we passed through town again.

LADY RAMSEY MADE me show her the dress and boots as soon as we entered the foyer. Mina was excited to show off her own fine boots too.

I tried to give back what money I had left over, but Lady Ramsey wouldn't take it. She insisted it be my traveling money.

The emerald gown wouldn't fit in my hand-me-down suitcase, so I'd have no choice but to wear it all the next day. I hung it on the empty metal rack and stared at it for a long time, unable to believe it was mine. It was the only item I had that actually *was* my own.

That evening, I ate dinner with the Ramsey family, an occasion at which everyone was present; I wore my new boots to start getting used to them before I'd be in them most of the next day. Mina showed me she was wearing hers too; she could walk in them better than I could.

"Are you all set for tomorrow?" Lady Ramsey asked as we were served our main course of roast duck, scalloped potatoes, and an assortment of steamed, seasoned vegetables.

"I think so," I said.

"Johanna can give you another bag if needed."

"She doesn't need one," Johanna said.

"I'm fine. Really," I said.

"Did you see the dress Victoria got?" Mina asked Johanna.

"If you were there to help her, then I'm sure it's beautiful," she responded and grabbed at a dinner roll in the center of the table.

"It's *so* beautiful. Ms. Adriana had made it especially for Princess Amelia. And she gave it to Victoria," Mina explained.

"You must have really made an impression," Master Ramsey said, sitting back and leering at me.

I didn't respond, not wanting to provoke any further comments. I wanted the attention off me.

"Eat your dinner, dear," Lady Ramsey said to Mina, who hadn't yet touched a single item on her plate.

I quickly retreated to my room after we'd eaten, as there wasn't much else to do. I mainly wanted to lie low for my last night and headed for the employee bathroom in the cellar, a place I often used for showering and freshening up.

I took a long, hot shower and kept reminding myself that the next day was an exciting one. There were so many unknowns it was difficult to cultivate that excitement, but the knowledge of leaving should have been enough.

I changed into my nightgown, halfway dried my hair, and brushed my teeth before returning to my room with my towel and a small bag of toiletries. I hung the wet towel on the dress rack, next to my new gown, then tucked the toiletry bag into the suitcase. My room didn't look any more bare than usual, but there was an added feeling of emptiness.

I was reading in bed when the door to my room opened and Master Ramsey barged in. The familiar stench of whiskey followed him, but he was not stumbling drunk like a few nights prior. He seemed quite alert and aware, which frightened me even more. One of his guards entered behind him and closed the door.

"No one gets in or out," Master Ramsey said to his guard, before turning to me with a rapacious grin. Once again, he held a new bundle of switches in one hand. "We shall not be interrupted this time."

I pulled the bedsheets as high as they'd go, not that they would provide any protection. The guard stood in front of the closed door, barricading it, with his muscular arms crossed.

"I want to make your final night here memorable," Master Ramsey said, slowly approaching the bed.

"Please don't," I pleaded. "I've tried to be good. I didn't do anything wrong."

"How about the shoes you've been wearing? Don't think I didn't notice."

"I thought—"

"That the rules no longer applied just because you're leaving? Let me be clear. You're still in my house. They still apply."

"I'm sorry."

"Not yet, you're not," he said and ripped the covers away from me.

The hardbound copy of *Pride & Prejudice* was on my lap. I grabbed it and threw it at his head. It missed and the book bounced off his shoulder and onto the ground.

Master Ramsey let go of the bundle of switches, allowing them to rain down onto the floor. He grabbed me by the nightgown, tugged me toward him and slapped me hard across the face. The rings he wore cut into my cheek, which now felt like it was about to explode. I tumbled backward from the blow and collapsed onto the concrete floor.

"That one's going to cost you. I hope it was worth it." Master Ramsey walked up to the rack and examined the gown with clear contempt. "So, this is the dress everyone's been raving about? You'll be able to waltz into the Queen's palace looking a million bucks." He ran a hand down the V-line hem of the back.

I knelt on the floor, peering over the side of the bed, watching him grope my new dress. Just when I was about to tell him to stop touching it, he gripped each hem of the V and tore it apart.

"No!" I screamed, scrambled to my feet and raced around the bed. He tugged and tore until the back of the gown was nearly ripped in two.

I reached him and tried to pull him away, but he easily tossed me aside, and I landed back on the bed.

Master Ramsey went back to the ruined dress and continued ripping it until the two halves were completely severed. "There. Now it's a dress befitting a Sandalwood," he said, just as it slipped off the hanger and pooled onto the floor.

My tears could no longer be contained. I covered my face with my hands and wept, but was only given a moment to grieve. Master Ramsey grabbed a fistful of my hair and forced me off the bed.

"Now, where were we before being so rudely interrupted last time? Oh, yes... Bend over. Palms on the bed." He let go of my hair, allowing me an instant to breathe. I glanced at the guard by the door, then did as I was told.

I didn't know what could possibly interrupt the switching session this time, but I wished for anything to get me out of this.

It was bad enough when the girls were brought in to witness my humiliation and shame, but it seemed like a whole new violation with another adult man in the room.

Master Ramsey pulled the nightgown up to my waist to expose the full lengths of my legs. My feet were still healing. He wasn't going to focus on them. The backs of my legs—and perhaps the fronts— would be the focal points of tonight's visit.

"Stay on your feet, *Princess*," he commanded. "You know what happens if you don't."

"Yes," I sobbed. I didn't move—couldn't move. The muscles in my legs were already knotted tight— awaiting the first of many, many strikes.

I heard the familiar swish of a switch cutting the

air. Now, my whole body tensed so tightly I thought I might crumble. Tears cascading uncontrollably now, I looked up—in clear view of the two boarded-up windows. No matter what wishes I made, there truly was no one coming to save me. In Master Ramsey's own words, I'd get my proper send-off.

CHAPTER 14

"Oh, dear God," I heard Lady Ramsey say.

It had to be the next morning. I felt the chill of the cellar when she removed the bedsheets from me. The bloody nightgown clung to my marred skin.

I squinted from the severe overhead lightbulb; I lay on my side because I couldn't bear to be on my back. That wasn't to say I was comfortable on my side either; every position hurt. My left cheek throbbed and felt twice its normal size from the incredible slap across the face, but it was nothing compared to the horror of my butt and the backs of my legs. They were covered in crisscrosses of bright red welts, some specific areas attacked so ferociously the skin had split. My sheets were a mess of dried blood.

"I can't believe he'd do this to you," Lady Ramsey

sobbed. She was already dressed, made up, and perfect—even through the sobs.

I could certainly believe he'd do it, and it was only a matter of time before he inflicted this kind of damage on his own girls, but I couldn't say that aloud; it was too horrible to verbalize.

I didn't know how long Master Ramsey had been assaulting me because when it was over I was ready to lose consciousness and couldn't see the time on the clock through my tears. And the guard who'd stood there and done nothing to help me got to witness quite the show.

I had been punished many times over the years, but never like last night; I'd finally seen Master Ramsey without restraint.

Lady Ramsey's red eyes shifted nervously about the room. "The Queen can't see you like this."

Everything packed in the suitcase had been strewn around. He'd torn more of my clothes, spat on some, and completely desecrated others.

Lady Ramsey picked up the emerald gown and gasped. "Why?" was all she could manage to say.

After she got over her initial shock of finding me and my room in the condition in which we'd been left, Lady Ramsey started to help me clean up. Actually, she did most of the cleaning while I did my best to get dressed in something still relatively wearable. The dress I chose was enough to make me decent, but nowhere near suitable for public viewing, let alone meeting the Queen and Prince Byron.

Ripped out pages from *Pride & Prejudice* were also scattered about the floor. I even saw the wad of crumpled pages he'd used at one point to gag me and slightly suppress my screaming.

The only truly salvageable things in this room were my boots.

Lady Ramsey led me upstairs and I followed her to Johanna's room. She disappeared into the large walk-in closet, emerging with three or four dresses draped over her forearm. Johanna was a few inches shorter and bustier, but most of my old dresses had been hand-me-downs of her own, more casual ones. I had never been given one of her fancy gowns to wear.

"Which one of these do you like the best?" Lady Ramsey asked, displaying all four gowns on Johanna's four-poster canopy bed.

Nothing compared to the destroyed emerald gown, but they were all still stylish and lovely. One of the dresses on the bed was a similar emerald color, and I probably would've liked it the best, but it reminded me too much of the one I'd lost so I took it out of the running. I ended up choosing a baby blue one.

"Very well," she said. "You'll wear this one today, but you'll take the rest with you." Lady Ramsey went into Johanna's dresser and picked out a small assortment of undergarments and a replacement night-gown. Once she had a neatly-stacked pile of clothes, she retrieved a new suitcase from the closet and packed everything that had been piled onto the bed.

"Now, you're going to take a bath in my wash-room, and then I'll fix you up and get you ready for your departure."

"No, I can't do that," I cried.

"You'll be okay," she said, resting a soft hand either side of my face and kissing me on the fore-head. "You'll be okay, dear."

Her luxurious bathroom was four times the size of my bedroom. Two female servants came in, got the bath ready, and helped me in. I was given an extra pillow from the bed to sit on. Lady Ramsey sat at her powder table as the servants tended to me. One soaped me up with a soft washcloth while the second massaged my scalp, washing my hair. Both were sensitive to my injuries and washed delicately around them.

Once the bath was finished, I was given a plush, white robe, which hugged me like a life-sized teddy bear. I stood while the servant women combed and dried my chestnut-colored locks. Then Lady Ramsey took over to apply my makeup, doing what she could to conceal my bruised cheek. When she was done, I took a peek in the mirror and hardly recog-nized myself. I actually looked healthy and beautiful. I touched my cheek just to check if the bruise was still there or if the magic concealer did more than hide the blemish. Unfortunately, it was still there.

"There, the Queen won't even know," she said. "Now your first impression will be memorable because you'll make it so, and not because you'll walk in looking like a poor, battered, broken girl."

It hurt to smile, but I did it anyway. "I don't know what to say."

"Say you'll miss this place just a little bit?"

I gestured *very little* with my thumb and forefinger, which made her laugh.

"Fair enough," Lady Ramsey said.

"I'll miss *you*," I said. "And Mina and Misty."

"And Johanna?"

I repeated the *very little* gesture.

"Mina adores you. She's heartbroken you're leaving."

"I wish I could take her with me," I said.

"It's bad enough losing one of you."

"I'm leaving, but you're not losing me."

"You're going home to your true family. I can't see how this isn't losing you. But I knew this day was coming and just didn't know how hard it was going to be until it was upon me." Lady Ramsey shrugged and glided into the adjoining master bedroom. "I'm not very good at goodbyes."

She was facing away from me when she said it. I could hear her sniffling.

The blue dress I'd chosen was laid out on the bed.

Lady Ramsey helped me get dressed like she'd done when I was younger, and I welcomed her assistance. She gave me toiletries from her washroom and finished packing my suitcase.

"All done and not a moment to spare," Lady Ramsey said. She pulled me in for a hug. "You'll do great, *Princess*."

I cringed at the word and let her go.

She extended the handle of the suitcase and passed it to me. "The Governess will be waiting for you in the town car. It's time if you're going to make your train."

I left Lady Ramsey—the Duchess of the 24th Ward—in the bedroom as I rolled my suitcase out of the house and up to the waiting town car.

The driver tipped his hat before taking my luggage and tossing it in the trunk. He then opened the side door and helped me climb into the extended back seat. The Governess was already inside. She wore a black A-line dress and a black, wide-brimmed dress hat that shadowed her face.

"Good morning, Victoria," she said. "Big day. How are you doing?"

"Never better," I said as I carefully sat on the leather bench seat.

She seemed to notice my pained movements but didn't comment on them. There was no way to sit comfortably, so I just had to deal with it and appear as normal as possible. I crossed my right leg over my left, which ended up being worse. So, I went back to sitting with both feet on the floor.

"Anything you want to talk about?" the Governess asked. She looked concerned.

"Not particularly," I answered. Then after a minute, I changed my mind, and asked, "Why is everyone lying about the boy we saw in the field?"

"No one's lying," she said. "What gives you that impression?"

"I don't believe he was harassing me. I spoke with him—"

"Is that so?"

"His name's Kale and I don't believe he wished me any ill will. There has to be something I'm not being told. It's hard putting these recent things together with a several-month memory gap."

"Is anything more coming back?" the Governess asked. "Or are you taking what he tells you at face value?"

"It's not just what he told me."

"Then what else is there?"

I didn't know how much I could trust her with, so I ended the conversation. She wasn't willingly giving up any additional information.

It didn't take long to reach the train station. Our train was already there and passengers were boarding.

The driver had our luggage ready on the platform before the Governess and I stepped down from the town car. He wished us safe travels and left as we made our way to the closest boarding train car.

Luggage attendants took our bags and the Governess handed the porter our tickets. The small white-haired man in a striped jacket welcomed us to the Inter-Ward Express, offering a hand to the Governess as she climbed aboard.

I glanced back at the station, and beyond it, at the rest of the town. As the porter called for my attention, I noticed a familiar face in the crowd. Kale leaned against a wood pillar by the ticket booth and waved.

"Miss?" the porter asked.

I gave a small wave back and took the porter's hand, allowing him to guide me into the Inter-Ward Express and take me away.

CHAPTER 15

The Governess and I had our own private train car with sofas, chairs and a dining room set, complete with a chandelier. It could easily accommodate twenty people.

I ran to one of the windows facing the station and scanned the area looking for Kale, but he was gone. I found the pillar he'd been leaning against, which now had a family of four standing in front of it.

"Do you want to order anything?" the Governess asked. I turned my attention back inside. The Governess was standing with a dining attendant.

"I'm having some tea," she said.

"Sure. I'll have some too," I answered.

"I would like some tea as well. Thank you." Her tone was sharp. Luckily, she didn't have her pointer.

"I would like some tea as well," I recited. "*Thank you.*"

The horn blew at the top of the hour, signaling the train's departure. I gazed out of the window as we started to move, seeing families and loved ones of others waving from the platform. I searched for Kale again but still didn't see him. There was no one out there seeing me off, but I'd had my send-off the night before.

The dining attendant returned a few minutes later with our tea and a platter of assorted fruits, meats, and cheeses. I perused the provided teabags and this time chose *Lemon Chamomile*. The name sounded fancy.

"So, I suppose my last name is Hart now?" I said.

The Governess added sugar and cream to her tea, so I did the same.

"I suppose you're right," she said. "But let's not go making any drastic changes until the Queen approves them."

"I'm not changing anything. I'm just saying. I wish I could fast-forward a few months, to a time when I knew what was going on, knew what to expect, and had my new life in order."

"If only life worked that way," she said. She stirred her tea and clinked the spoon on the saucer before taking a sip. "Didn't you come home with a new dress yesterday? I thought I overheard Mina going on about one."

"I did, but it ended up not being very comfortable so Lady Ramsey gave me this one instead," I said. It even sounded like a poor excuse.

"That's also a very beautiful dress. I'm not suggesting otherwise," the Governess said. "I thought I overheard the new dress was originally crafted for Princess Amelia. I was curious, that's all."

"Ms. Adriana had said that. I don't know if it's true. It was—is quite a dress."

"You'll have to show it to me sometime."

I nodded while I sipped my tea.

"This will be a first for both of us," she said after a short pause.

"What will?"

"I've never been to the palace either. It will be quite a privilege."

"Good. I won't be the only dummy gawking at everything."

"I have no intention of gawking," the Governess said with a smile.

"How long will it take to get there?"

"About five hours. So, there's plenty of time to relax. Try not to get too anxious."

"No last-minute lessons?" I asked.

"I won't subject you to that—not today. This will be the perfect opportunity to sit back with a good book."

"If only I had one."

"Oh… I assumed… I'll ask the attendant for one when she returns."

The train didn't have a supply of books. They had a few used newspapers, but I decided to pass on those. The attendant suggested I go into town at the next stop—the 21st Ward—which had a bookshop not too far from the station.

To pass the time, I lay down on one of the luxurious sofas. I could lie on my side, which was much more comfortable than sitting. My legs and backside ached terribly, and I closed my eyes and tried to get some sleep; in the dark, though, I saw Master Ramsey coming for me again and again—switching me over and over. The more I cried, the more excited he seemed to get. It was a vicious cycle of pain and humiliation. Staring across the train car became much safer.

The train pulled into the 21st Ward station about a half hour later. I decided it was in my best interest to venture out and find a book to help get me through the rest of the ride in relative peace.

"I'm going into town to find the bookshop," I told the Governess.

"You don't know where it is."

"I'll ask the porter on my way out."

She glanced down at her watch. "You have less than twenty minutes before the train leaves."

"I'll hurry," I said, confident I'd make it back in time. I had to; I didn't want to continue the ride stuck with only my thoughts, and needed something else to distract me.

The porter gave me directions to the bookshop when I disembarked. He warned me the train would not wait for me, so I needed to be back in time. I assured him I would.

A mass of people stood waiting to disembark and even more waiting to board. I pushed through the crowd, trying not to let the waiting people slow me down. In my haste, I bumped into another teenage girl.

"I'm sorry. I'm just trying to get through," I said.

"That's okay," she answered as she turned to look at me straight on.

She was about my size, and when I fully saw her face, I almost stumbled back in shock. She wasn't someone I knew or had ever seen before—except in a mirror. Her hair was cut shorter and styled differently, and she wore darker makeup accentuating her look. But her natural features were exactly like mine. She looked as much an identical twin as I could ever have imagined.

The girl gave me a strange look, as much so as the shocked expression I was probably giving her, but she didn't say any more and continued on. She moved through the crowd with a shoulder bag slung over her arm, approaching the train. I waited and watched as she handed her bag to one of the porters and climbed aboard.

I stood there, dumbfounded for at least another minute until I realized I was wasting my precious and dwindling time to purchase a book for the rest of the trip. And, with that, I took off running toward the town, trying to remember all the directions the porter had provided.

CHAPTER 16

"*Y*ou should have seen her," I said to the Governess as the Inter-Ward Express left the 21st Ward. "She looked *exactly* like me."

"That's so strange," she said.

"Does the Queen have more children she'd put into foster homes—like me?"

"You'll be able to ask her yourself in a few short hours."

I always had a hard time reading the Governess. She didn't seem surprised by my discovery, but then again, she never looked surprised at anything at all.

I'd gone through all the trouble of finding a book to read, scanned the *used* section and decided on a tattered, old paperback with a pretty cover. But now I couldn't concentrate on reading. My mind kept going back to the strange girl and our brief interaction. She wouldn't have been Princess Amelia, her health fully restored, and out and about like one of us commoners so she had to be another sibling.

The Governess was on the matching sofa, reading The *First Ward Tribune* provided by the dining attendant. She periodically glanced up at me to see if I was reading, which I was not.

"Are you all right?" she asked.

"I wonder if she's coming too," I said. "What if I'm not the only long-lost daughter going to meet the Queen?"

"You weren't lost. The Queen knew where you were all that time."

"You know what I mean. Fine, then *abandoned* daughters all coming home at the same time. What does this mean? Who will be the true successor?"

"As is customary, succession goes to the eldest full-blooded royal child."

"So, would I be considered full-blooded? The King's been dead for years. Was he my father?"

"I don't know," the Governess said with an exasperated sigh. "These are all questions for the Queen."

"I know. I just have a lot going through my head. It's hard to wait, hard to read. This train has too many stops. This is like the longest day of my life."

I stood up and paced around the train car, partially due to my impatience, but also partially due to my aching backside. Master Ramsey had threatened to make it so sore that I could never sit comfortably again. I sure hoped that wasn't the case. Hopefully, these wounds would heal like all the others.

"Pacing doesn't make the time pass by any faster," the Governess said, folding the newspaper in her lap.

"But it makes me feel better. I'll stop burdening you with my anxiety," I said, continuing my rounds.

"That's not what I'm saying. You may talk about your concerns. But there are only so many answers I can provide regarding your current situation. I have not been privileged with many details either."

"Yet you're the one sent to accompany me."

"Yes. That's not uncommon."

"You can go back to your paper. I'll pace quietly," I said and went to one of the windows to watch the landscape speed by.

The next few hours were broken up with snacks, more tea, and an early dinner. The dining attendants checked on us constantly. Even though most of the time I didn't require anything else, I didn't mind the interruptions; any distraction was a good thing at that point.

By the time the train pulled into the station for the 1st Ward, I had lost count and wasn't expecting it to be the final stop. A pleasant voice over the loudspeaker welcomed us to Capital City in the 1st Ward.

My heart skipped a beat when those words finally sank in.

"We're here? We're actually here?"

"You've managed to pace the whole rest of the trip," the Governess said, finishing the tea she'd been sipping on for the past twenty minutes.

"Not the *whole* time," I said. "I did stop to eat dinner."

"Yes, and you seem to have forgotten everything I showed you about dining decorum."

"It was just us. There was no need to be overly formal."

"But it was a good opportunity to practice like I said. There are no more dress rehearsals. We're finally here. This is the real thing."

Her final comment hit me harder than I wanted to admit. This was it; my life was about to change forever. A short ride away, I'd be meeting my mother —the Queen of Westeria—and my older sister, Amelia, the Princess of Westeria. And after my run-in from earlier in the day, there'd potentially be more estranged siblings. Then I was hit by the strange realization I was also a Princess of Westeria.

All the dining attendants who'd served us throughout the trip came in and thanked us for our patronage, beginning to ready the car for the next guests. It was also our cue to leave.

The porter helped us down the steps to the landing, where our luggage was already waiting for us. This station was much larger than the others; the main terminal was an artistic building of colored glass, and there were so many train lines loading and unloading never-ending streams of people.

"If you're looking for rentals, you can follow the signs going that way," the porter said, pointing off to the right.

"Thank you," the Governess said.

We took our rolling bags and ventured into the dense crowd. After a few steps, I noticed a man in a black suit and cap holding a sign with my name on it.

Victoria Sandalwood. Was that still my name? Really? I didn't even know anymore.

The man holding the sign saw me and seemed to recognize me.

"This way," I told the Governess, then she saw the sign as well.

As we approached, the man addressed me. "Good evening, Miss Victoria. My name is Edward. May I take your bag?"

I nodded. Edward took the Governess's bag after mine.

"The car's just over here," he said, leading the way through the busy station. "I trust you had a pleasant journey from the 24th?"

"Very much," I said.

"The accommodations were exemplary," the

Governess said. "The Queen did not have to go to so much trouble to—"

"The Queen does not go to any trouble," Edward said, flatly. "What she requests is done." He strolled quickly like he was on a schedule that had to be kept, which may have been true.

Once we reached the road, Edward led us to a black limousine with another man waiting. When the man saw us coming, he lifted the trunk and opened the rear door against the sidewalk, holding it wide.

"Good evening, ladies," he said, gesturing for us to enter. "Please. Help yourselves to any refreshments."

I climbed in first and lightly scooted across the bench seat. The leather was softer than that of the town car, which cushioned the pain. Inside, there was a flat screen TV, refrigerator, and an ice bucket with a chilled glass bottle. Two glasses were set on their sides and wrapped in cloth napkins on the same silver platter as the bucket. The Governess got in and the door was closed behind her.

The second man's face appeared on the other side of the lowered partition. "With current traffic, we should reach the palace in about forty-five minutes. Is there anything you need before we leave?"

"Nothing. We're anxious to get there," the Governess said.

"Very well. We'll give you your privacy. There's a button directly under the glass if you need anything," he said. His face disappeared behind the rising partition.

Neither of us indulged in any of the provided refreshments. I peered out of one of the tinted windows as we drove through Capital City, gazing upon the monstrous skyscrapers I'd previously only seen in textbooks and on the television, on the rare occasions I was allowed to watch it.

The flat screen in the back of our limousine turned on and began showing sweeping sky views of the city. A narrator cited city facts and history as the camera panned from the downtown area and over the sprawling, densely populated communities surrounding it. In the distance, I could see the sparkling water of The Great Ocean that seemed to extend forever.

The skyscrapers disappeared from the screen. The buildings below got smaller until they were more the sizes I was used to; they were only one- or two-story mixed-use buildings, but instead of being confined to a small town, they were everywhere. Soon, the storefronts were replaced by houses, as the camera continued onward. The upcoming foothills were peppered with houses the same as any flatland neighborhood I'd ever seen. Mansions with no yards to speak of hung precariously over cliff edges while other grand homes had been torn apart, lying with their innards exposed at the clifftops and the rest in ruins at the bottom of canyons.

The camera passed over the mountains, leading to more towns and neighborhoods—all seeming to merge into one sublime metropolis. The aerial camera steadily dropped in altitude as it entered another neighborhood zone; the estates here were more spacious, with lush, green properties everywhere. A parade of palm trees lined the street the camera now followed, and our view dropped to the vantage point of a car driving down it. The vehicle came to an abrupt end at an iron gate with a large heart in its center; the heart parted as the gate opened and we drove up a neatly paved drive with perfectly manicured grass either side.

An immense white estate with a semi-circle of pillars accenting its front façade sat visible in the distance. I recognized the estate from books and television; it was the Queen's palace—Château le Hart. The narrator spoke of the palace's history as the camera drew closer to the front door, which soon magically opened, thus marking the beginning of a grand interior tour.

I was captivated by the images on-screen and had lost all interest in the world passing by outside the windows. For a few minutes, I didn't even feel my injuries, but as soon as I made the realization, the aching returned.

"Impressive, isn't it?" the Governess said, her

attention also on the screen and the current tour of the Queen's palace, with the narrator describing every room the camera entered.

"It's unbelievable," I said. "All of this is."

"Believe it," she said.

CHAPTER 17

I soon recognized the street leading to the palace from earlier in the video; the long lines of palm trees were still there. Every few minutes, we passed another gated driveway to a private estate. There was no shortage of money there and each one of these estates rivaled the Ramseys' back home.

Back home. What was home now? I didn't want to think of the Ramseys' estate as my home but had no other to associate with.

We couldn't see straight ahead, so I didn't set eyes on the broken heart of the Queen's gate until we passed it. There was a uniformed guard stationed just inside, who nodded as we entered with a rifle held low across his body, the barrel pointing downward. I looked out of the opposite window and saw another guard stationed on that side as well.

At the roundabout, the limousine stopped, and after a few seconds, our door opened. Edward stepped back so we could exit. The other man who'd been in the front seat gathered our luggage and walked toward the front door.

"We can..." the Governess started.

"Your bags will be brought to your rooms," Edward said.

Two female servants in bright and beautiful dresses waited by the front door. One was blonde, and the other brunette, both maybe mid-twenties with exquisite postures and graceful mannerisms.

"Welcome to Château le Hart," the brunette said as a greeting to both of us, then turned her attention specifically to me. "My name is Indira. I will escort you to your room."

The other woman introduced herself as Gertrude and guided the Governess inside.

The foyer was an exquisite two-story room with wood flooring and walls decorated with royal portraits and mirrors. In the center of the room was an elegantly crafted wooden table, upon which sat a marble head of King Samwell Hart I. He was the first of the royal Harts line, lineage I'd memorized for my lessons with the Governess. But I wouldn't have recognized the statue without it being mentioned in the video during our ride to the palace.

Indira did not start me off with a tour of the palace, though I supposed that was what the video was for. We ascended one of the two curved staircases to the second level, leading to a long hallway of closed doors. The Governess had been led through the foyer and into another room on the first level.

When we reached an open bedroom door on the left, Indira invited me to enter first. This was a major improvement from my meager accommodations in the cellar. This room was about the size of Johanna's and Mina's rooms combined, with a large four-poster canopy bed, a flat-screen, wall-mounted television, several sofas and chairs, a bench window seat, a cozy office nook, a walk-in closet probably the size of my old room, and a private washroom of my very own. Multiple large windows made the room light and airy, and this was accentuated by the yellow color scheme. Indira even presented it as such.

"The Yellow Room is yours," she said.

"It's really something," I said. I noticed my luggage positioned by the closet door.

"If there's anything you desire, dial zero on the phone on the nightstand. Are you hungry?"

"We had an early dinner on the train, but it's been a few hours now."

"Then I will have some food brought up to you. Do you have any special requests? Any specific dietary requirements?"

I'd never been asked that before. "I don't think so," I said meekly.

"Then I will bring up a portion of what the chef has been preparing this evening," Indira said. She circled the room, peering into the closet and washroom before making her way back to the door. "Have a good evening, Miss Victoria." She curtsied and closed the door when she left.

I had been about to ask her what I should do now, but was tired from the long day of traveling and didn't feel like chasing after her. There'd be plenty of time to explore, and since the Queen hadn't greeted us on our arrival, she was probably attending to some business and unavailable at the moment anyway.

I paced around the room and took it all in. It was mine. This was *all* mine now. I peeked into the washroom and saw a long sink, vanity unit, shower, and large tub similar to Lady Ramsey's. I ventured into the walk-in closet, so long it was practically a hallway, and literally turned a corner. And the most amazing thing was that it wasn't empty, but filled with dresses, coats, shoes and accessories. And I bet every one of them would fit me perfectly. I ran a hand along the luxurious clothing as I passed, confirming they were real.

I peered out of one of the windows at a view of the front yard, with the driveway and gate included. The property was enclosed by a tall brick wall extending past what I could see from my window. If the Ramseys' estate was any indication, the Queen's land stretched a long way.

I removed my boots and dropped them haphazardly on the floor before climbing up on the bed, then lying down on what could've been a cloud. My backside almost didn't hurt at all as I lay sprawled out in the middle of the heavenly softness. I closed my eyes, but the pain from the night before still returned in crushing detail. When I reopened my eyelids, I almost expected to be back in the cellar again with *him*. But I wasn't. I was still lying in my new room—the Yellow Room—surrounded by more luxury than I'd ever thought possible for myself.

I rolled over at the sound of the phone ringing, reached for the nightstand and picked up the receiver.

"Hello, Miss Victoria. Your dinner order has been placed and will be brought to you in the next twenty to thirty minutes," said the female voice on the line.

"Thank you," I said, surprised to be receiving an update at all.

"My pleasure," the voice responded and then the line promptly disconnected.

I was growing even more impressed and awed by the accommodations and treatment I was receiving; this was like nothing I'd ever experienced, but everything I'd dreamed of.

Since I knew approximately when the food

would arrive, it gave me some downtime, which I thought would be a great opportunity to explore.

I strolled into the closet, found a pair of comfortable-looking flats and headed for the door. But when I went to turn the knob, I quickly realized it was locked. Upon closer examination, I discovered there was no lock on the inside—no keyhole, no thumbturn, no pushbutton. Nothing. Which could only mean the lock was on the outside; I couldn't believe my luck. This surely couldn't be happening; I'd simply traded one prison for another.

CHAPTER 18

I knew this was all too good to be true!

I couldn't breathe. I tried the door knob again, stepping away, then trying one more time to see if I was making some silly mistake. Still locked. I didn't know what kind of game was being played with me, but it was definitely starting to freak me out.

I ran to the phone and dialed zero.

It was just a mistake. A misunderstanding. There's a very good reason... the locks are on the outside of the bedrooms.

A woman on the other end of the line picked up on the third ring. "Good evening, Miss Victoria. How may I be of service?"

I was all ready to say, "My name is Victoria and I'm in the Yellow Room," but she obviously already knew that, and her greeting threw me off.

"Hello? Are you still there?"

"I'm here," I finally said. "I seem to be locked in my room."

There was a pause.

"Yes," the woman said. "Queen Hart has directed our new guests to be confined to their rooms until everyone has arrived."

"When will that be?"

"The final guest is scheduled to arrive tomorrow afternoon."

"So, I'm stuck in here until then?"

"You are free to enjoy the accommodations of your palace suite, and if there is anything you require, we'll promptly bring it to you. Your dinner order is in. Would you like anything else?"

"I'd like to know why you guys are holding me prisoner?" I commanded. "My mother is the Queen! I am a princess here! I demand you unlock my door immediately!"

"I understand your concern and frustration, but we are under strict orders from the Queen. You will be freed as soon as she gives the word."

"And my orders mean nothing?"

"At this time, your orders have no clout. Would you like anything else this evening, Miss Victoria?"

"I'd like to see my governess."

"I'm sorry, but that is also not permitted at this time."

I hung up the phone before my voice cracked. I

dropped my face in my hands and wept. I thought I'd arrived, but I'd just been placed into a new limbo and still had no idea what was happening. This was becoming increasingly terrifying. My life with the Ramseys provided for some terrible times, but at least they were familiar and I always knew what was coming. My punishments were typically expected, whereas this unknown was becoming a worse torment than any switching.

I went to one of the windows and looked out at the brick wall holding us all in. Placing my hand on the glass, I saw that the window didn't open. To get out, I'd have to break the glass and jump two stories into the shrubbery below. With my luck, the glass wouldn't even break and whatever I used to hit the window would probably bounce off.

I resigned myself to my comfortable prison and began unpacking the few belongings brought from the 24th Ward. It didn't take long before I was fully settled in. I took an extra pillow from the bed to place under my butt as I took a seat on a sofa facing the wall-mounted television.

There were three remotes on the coffee table and it took me all three tries before I could turn the unit on. I expected to find a bunch of channels to sift through but instead was greeted with a screen of unfamiliar icons. Clicking on the first, lists upon lists of movies and shows appeared; there were so many I'd never seen before or even heard of.

I had watched the first few minutes of a handful of television shows when I was interrupted by a knock at the door.

I stood up from the sofa and the door opened before I even had a chance to cross the room. A young woman in a black dress and apron entered with a silver tray of food.

A uniformed soldier remained in the doorway, blocking any attempt at escape. In his hand, he held some type of electrified baton; he pressed a small button on the handle and a blue current sizzled around the ball on the end. It was obvious he was showing me the power of the device to deter me from attempting any dramatic acts. He was a big, intimidating man I had no intention of rushing.

"Here you are, Miss Victoria," the young woman said as she laid the tray on the coffee table near where I'd been sitting. "Lamb shank with buttered potato shallots and pickled greens. I also brought you an ice water with lemon. The Queen is quite fond of this dish. I hope you enjoy it as well."

"Are you going to lock me back in when you leave?" I asked, already knowing the answer. I wanted to see her expression when she told me what no one had yet been able to do in person.

"I'm afraid so," she said, stepping away from the tray—and from me.

"Why did no one warn me ahead of time? It's a little disconcerting."

"Which is why no one did warn you ahead of time. We're under very strict orders from Queen Hart. Your arrival with the others is a very sensitive matter."

The soldier at the door cleared his throat—exaggeratingly so.

"Enjoy your dinner, Miss Victoria," the woman said.

"Wait," I insisted. "Why is my arrival a sensitive matter? Who are the others? Where is my governess?"

"I'm sorry," was her only reply as she exited the room.

The soldier glared at me as he closed the door. I ran to try the knob, but already knew it would be locked again.

I returned to the sofa and stared at the elegantly presented plate of food. It looked delicious, but I was no longer hungry.

I didn't sleep in the bed that night but repositioned the pillow I'd been sitting on and lay on the sofa. I also never turned off the television. I wasn't really watching the titles I chose; it served more as background noise than anything else.

My breakfast the next morning arrived with the sight of the rising sun over the brick perimeter wall. The dining servant wasn't the same as the night before, though the soldier accompanying her was certainly the same, staring at me with the same cold eyes. The woman commented that I hadn't touched my dinner; I only grunted a response.

At 11:58 a.m., my lunch arrived, and my breakfast tray was removed from the room. This time, the dining servant and the accompanying soldier were both new.

At exactly 3:30 p.m., came another knock at the door. The young woman who had served me dinner the night before entered the room. The soldier from lunchtime was still on shift, and instead of guarding the doorway, he followed her in, closing the door behind them both.

This is new, I thought.

The soldier strolled over to the desk, pulled out the chair, and sat down.

"It's almost time," the woman said. "You need to be presentable for meeting the Queen this evening."

CHAPTER 19

I sat up on the couch. "You mean I'm finally going to be allowed outside this room?"

"Very soon," she said. "First you must bathe and change. I'm here to help you with both."

"And he's here to make sure I cooperate?" I said, gesturing to the soldier in the corner.

"There's no need for any problems," she said. "I'm here to help. But we haven't much time. We must get moving so you're not late. The Queen does not like tardiness."

"I'm sure she doesn't," I said, rolling my eyes.

She proceeded to the washroom and turned on the water to what I assumed was the bathtub, and returned to the bedroom wiping her wet hands on her apron. "Come, Miss Victoria."

I pushed up off the couch and staggered to the

washroom. I wanted to close the door, but she insisted it remained ajar. I told her I could do this on my own, but she wouldn't hear of it and began unlacing my dress and pulling it down. When my slip was also removed, she gasped at the sight of the puffy red welts and cuts emblazoned across my lower cheeks and down the backs of my legs.

"Who did this to you?" she asked.

"A monster," I responded.

"I will be as gentle as I can." She took me by the hand as I stepped into the warm bath.

I let her do her job and bathe me without putting up a fight. All I had to do was move when she told me, and once all the makeup from my face was washed away, she noticed my bruised cheek as well.

"What's your name?" I asked the young woman as she wet my hair.

"Kimera," she said after a pause as if she hadn't been asked the question in a very long time.

"Have you worked here long?"

"As soon as I was allowed to work. My mother's been on the Queen's staff for many years. My father is a part of her Royal Guard. It was only natural I remained in the palace too."

"Do you like it here?"

Oh, yes. It's such a lovely place to live and work," she said and sounded as excited as the words suggested.

"Why am I not allowed to see my mother? Why am I being locked in here?"

This caused her to clam up. Her excited tone evaporated. "I'm not at liberty to discuss anything regarding your stay in the palace."

I lowered my voice. "It's okay," I said. "I won't tell anyone. This can remain just between us. We're alone in here. There's nothing to worry about."

"You're never truly alone in the Château," she whispered, her words coming across like a warning.

Once out of the bath, Kimera applied ointment to my wounds, which seemed to have an icing effect, giving me chills. Then she helped me into a white cotton robe that had been hanging from the back of the washroom door and proceeded to do my hair, makeup, and nails. It felt amazing being pampered, even as a prisoner; when she was done, I looked at myself in the mirror and was amazed by the transformation. She was even more skilled than Lady Ramsey! My face looked flawless, though it certainly didn't feel it.

We then moved from the washroom to the closet, where Kimera closed the door once we were inside to escape the gaze of the waiting soldier, and began putting an outfit together. I would simply have chosen the first dress I saw, but Kimera carefully and deliberately picked out each piece of the ensemble. Nude undergarments that were elegant, yet comfortable and understated. A yellow cocktail dress that matched my room's decor. Lavender pumps echoing the color of my nails and eyeshadow... And a golden tiara with amethyst accents.

The closet had a full body mirror. Kimera positioned me in front of it to view the finished product.

"Fit for a princess," she said.

"If I didn't know any better, I'd swear I was looking at one," I said.

"Perhaps you are."

"I wish you would talk to me."

"You're very beautiful, my lady," Kimera said and exited the closet.

"Thank you," I said under my breath, following her back into the bedroom.

The soldier had barely moved. He sat so still I couldn't be sure at first that he was still breathing.

Kimera removed a watch from her apron pocket and latched it to her wrist. "We have ten minutes," she said, adjusting the timepiece. "Right on schedule."

"What do we do in the meantime?" I asked.

"We wait," the soldier said from the corner of the room. I glanced over and it still looked like he hadn't shifted from the spot.

"Yes. We wait," Kimera repeated.

I'd already done more waiting than I could handle. And I'd done more pacing in the past two days than any time I could remember, but after all this time, what was another ten minutes? It was ten minutes of pure emotional torture—that's what.

"Take a deep breath," Kimera said.

I was pacing again, and doing it in heels, without thinking. Once I realized it, I stumbled, twisting my ankle and falling to my knees.

"Are you okay?" Kimera rushed over to my aid. She was the only one displaying any concern.

"I'm fine," I said, back on my feet before she could help me out. I took the deep breath she'd suggested, feeling how it slightly calmed my nerves.

She brought me a half-full glass of water from my lunch tray. "Drink. It will help."

"What's going to happen when you lead me out of this room?" I asked, after emptying the glass.

"I'm not at liberty—"

"Okay. Forget I asked." This still all felt like a dream—sometimes a dream come true and other times (like right at that moment) a nightmare. I pictured the hologram of the Queen and Prince Byron and the message that changed everything—everything I thought I knew about myself, my life, and my past. I vividly remembered trying on the emerald dress for the first time in Ms. Adriana's shop. I relived the gut-wrenching pain of Master Ramsey tearing that dress in half and leaving it and me for ruin. And now, I was here in the palace, fixed up as beautifully as I'd ever been in my life, waiting to be granted an audience with the Queen of Westeria. I feared some other part of my life soon being torn apart.

The clock seemed to tick slower than a minute at a time, but time didn't truly stop and the ten minutes finally passed. The soldier was the first to acknowledge it by rising from the desk chair and heading for the door. He stopped at the nightstand, to pick up the phone.

"It's Williams. Unlock on Yellow," he said, and my door seemed to magically open. "After you."

Kimera led the way out of the room and back down to the first floor. I periodically glanced back to see if the soldier, Williams, was still behind me. He was, and moving as quietly as a cat.

We followed the open foyer under the stairs, passing a formal sitting room, a dining room, a games room, and a long lounge that could have also been a hallway, all the way to a closed set of ornately-carved wooden double doors.

Kimera waited for Williams to open the door, allowing us to enter what looked a large, two-story ballroom. The room was empty of furniture except for a rectangular dining room table with place settings for eight.

"What's this?" I asked.

Kimera didn't reply, instead proceeding into the cavernous room, the clicking of her high heels on the wood flooring echoing and ominous, like the ticking of a doomsday clock. The sound of my own heels as I crossed the room was just as unsettling. Williams remained close behind.

Kimera pulled out the exquisitely-crafted wooden chair at the head of the table closest to where we'd entered. She directed me to sit, took hold of my napkin and placed it across my lap. I scooted my chair in with assistance. Kimera remained standing directly behind. Williams joined other soldiers standing to attention against three of the four walls.

Six other places at the table were taken, leaving only the head of the table on the opposite side empty. From the length and style of her hair and the instantly reciprocated recognition, I was sure the middle girl on the left was the one I'd bumped into at the 21st Ward train station. And I still considered that chance encounter very strange. But stranger still was the fact that the other five girls seated around the table also looked exactly like me.

CHAPTER 20

e seven carbon copy girls sized each other up. But—with each girl having a servant stationed directly behind her and the soldiers along the perimeter of the room—the table remained quiet.

There were variations in hairstyle and color, some probably dyed, as well as in piercings, skin tone, and muscle definition, but the general build, natural features, and approximate age of each girl seemed incredibly similar. There were also no two dresses of the same color, and I figured each color identified the room to which each girl was assigned.

I was confident from the expressions of agitation, impatience, uncertainty, and fear that none of the girls had any more information than I did. The realization made me feel slightly better about my current predicament.

I sat tall like the Governess had always instructed and crossed my ankles beneath my chair. The biggest issue for me would be sitting there for any extended period with the injuries to my backside screaming out in protest at the chair's naked wooden seat. I tried not to let the growing pain show on my face while I waited like everyone else for the last seat at the table to be filled.

Then, the far doors burst open; two lines of servants entered, parted, and provided a pathway for the Queen who followed on. I'd never thought of myself as sharing her features, but I could see it now. She wore a sparkling emerald dress with extensive needlework in the corset, and a voluminous train stretching out behind her like a shadow. Her arms and neck dripped with diamonds and her shimmering crown looked like it could have been carved from a single jewel. Her smile was as radiant as her jewelry and only seemed to shine brighter as she crossed the expansive room.

"You should rise," Kimera whispered in my ear and I noticed the other servants also providing instructions to their respective girls.

I was delighted to stand and give my injuries a moment to calm. The other girls did the same as the Queen approached.

Before the Queen could reach her chair, however, one of the servants rushed over and pulled it out for her.

"And then there were seven. Welcome, ladies, to your new home—the Château le Hart," the Queen said as she took a seat. "I hope your accommodations have been to your likings thus far. I do apologize for all the secrecy, but the reason why will become clear very soon."

The seven of us were seated in relative unison.

"Princess Amelia is dead," the Queen said bluntly. "I know this comes as a shock to you, but it is the reason you are all here. You obviously know she has been out of the public eye for quite a few years. You see, she was born with a degenerative disorder that was detected soon after birth. She began to exhibit mild symptoms soon after. With her condition worsening over the next few years, I decided to take her out of the public eye after her eighth birthday; I didn't want the entire Kingdom to see the primary heir to the throne deteriorating before their eyes. I'd tried for many years to have a baby without any success, so when baby Amelia came along, she was my miracle. Then the doctors discovered her condition and I saw how cruel fate could be. As soon as she was given to me, she was taken away—a small piece at a time. And now, my little miracle is gone.

"I worked with the best doctors in the Kingdom and brought in the best medics from around the world too, but they all were unable to reverse or even halt the worsening of her condition. That was when I received another option and the lovely young ladies seated at this table were born. My daughter was two when this new option was presented to me and I knew at my age, and following my difficulty to conceive the first time, the chances of me having another child were extremely unlikely.

"There had been success in other kingdoms with human cloning trials, and I was presented with an opportunity to have Amelia cloned. With much deliberation, I chose to proceed. Her cloned genes were wiped of the degenerative disorder, so the new baby could have a fresh start. And from the advice and recommendations of the geneticists, we ultimately implanted eight cloned embryos into surrogates. The true nature of the pregnancies was kept secret and confidential, of course, which is why you are hearing about it only now. Only your surrogate parents were told the true nature of the pregnancies and you were all closely monitored for any complications or abnormalities. All of you have remained perfectly healthy—as healthy as any naturally-born child."

The Queen paused to take a sip of water, then let out a long breath. "I've been waiting eighteen long years for this day. I've imagined this initial meeting countless times and recited this speech like a daily prayer since you were all born. Seeing you all sitting here now, I still feel unprepared. Like I said, there were eight embryos and eight girls born, but only seven remain surviving today—the seven beautiful young ladies seated here. Please don't worry; the death of the eighth girl was unrelated to the cloning process and Amelia's disorder.

"So… this is the big secret and will remain so to everyone outside of the palace walls. The seven of you are clones of my daughter, Princess Amelia, and one of you will replace her."

CHAPTER 21

*L*ooking around the table, I knew I wasn't the only one floored by this revelation; I'd heard rumors this technology existed—or at least, it did at one time—but I figured someone who was a clone would know it. A clone would surely have to feel something wasn't right, that she was less than human? But I'd never had that suspicion, not for one moment.

I am human. I am human. I am human. I am—not—*human.*

So, the Ramseys had known this too. Lady Ramsey carried me like her own daughter—but I was something else entirely. Master Ramsey knew what I was. Was this why he…? I couldn't bring myself to think about what he really thought of me.

"What does that mean?" asked the middle girl on

the left, in an orange dress—the one I'd bumped into at the train station.

"Perhaps we should do introductions, but first I'll answer your question," the Queen said. "If you recall in recent press conferences, I addressed the Kingdom with the exciting news of Princess Amelia's improving health and that she would soon be reintroduced to the people of Westeria."

"And now you've said the Princess is dead," said the girl closest to me on the right, in a royal blue dress.

"Which is where one of you will come in. Princess Amelia's re-emergence will be one of you, as a symbol of hope and health for the Kingdom. We will then announce your upcoming union to Prince Byron, tying the DuFours of Easteria to the Harts. Then you will focus on producing an heir for the Hart family to live on and remain in power, in control of Westeria for generations to come."

"Which one of us?" The question was asked in rapid succession by at least three girls at the table. I may have been one of them. The conversation had quickly become overwhelming.

"Ladies, we will get into all that. Please stay calm. Be patient. I understand this is a lot," the Queen said.

I noticed some of the soldiers inching away from the walls, taking subtle steps toward the table.

The Queen raised her hands for them to hold back. "We're okay. No one here is going to cause a disturbance. Isn't that right, ladies? Before we go any further, let us do introductions." She nodded to the girl on her left.

"My name is Constance Redwood from the 23rd Ward. I've been raised by the Mackenzie family." Constance wore a bright red dress.

"My name is Danielle Cherrywood from the 19th Ward. I was living with the Thortons." Danielle wore a lilac purple dress.

"I'm Piper Rosewood from the 20$^{th.}$ I lived with the Boyes family." Piper wore the royal blue dress.

I was next. "Victoria Sandalwood," I said. "From the 24th Ward. I was employed by the Ramsey family."

The Queen frowned at my choice of words but didn't comment, allowing the introductions to continue.

"My name is Jane Ironwood and I'm from the 17th Ward. I am part of the Kincaid family." Jane wore a champagne-colored dress.

"Thank you, my Queen, for inviting us into your home. My name is Bethany Marblewood, coming from the 21st Ward. I've been raised by the Nobel family." Bethany wore the fiery orange dress.

The Queen nodded with a smile at Bethany's remarks.

"It's a pleasure to be here and officially meet you. I am Eleanor Muskwood from the 18th Ward. I've been raised and taught by the LaBelle family." Eleanor wore a shimmering silver dress.

"Very good," the Queen said and her smile faded as she considered her next words. "Lastly, the one of you who could not be here, who departed nearly three years ago, was Tabatha Dogwood. She lived in the 22nd Ward with the Hendrix family. She was a very bright and kind girl, and it is heartbreaking she was also taken from us at such a young age."

"When did Princess Amelia pass?" Bethany asked.

"Six years ago," the Queen said. She didn't have to think about it.

"Which one of us will be replacing her?" Constance asked, repeating the earlier question.

Before the Queen offered an answer, the doors on either side of the room burst open and two parades of servers rushed in holding silver trays.

"I took the liberty to order for all of us," the Queen said as a plate of meticulously presented food was set before her.

A server handed Kimera a tray, who then set it in front of me. There were thin slices of some type of roast on top of a layer of couscous and a rainbow-colored assortment of vegetables paired into flowery designs.

"Enjoy," the Queen said, taking her first bite.

I knew it was customary for the highest caste at the table to take the first bite or sip before the rest of the table followed.

"Which one of you—an excellent question." The Queen dabbed at the corners of her mouth with her cloth napkin. "With seven very fine candidates, it's difficult to simply choose one of you to replace my dearly departed Amelia. Each of you grew up in different wards with different ruling families. I don't truly know what your experiences have been like and how they have shaped your current personalities. I don't know who's truly up for the task. So, I've devised a small competition."

"A competition?" I found myself asking.

"Yes, Victoria. Each of you will be competing to become Amelia. Genetically, all of you are Amelia, but socially, I'm sure each of you is quite different. One of you will be a best fit, and it will be between Prince Byron and me to determine who."

"Prince Byron will be a part of this process?" Bethany asked.

"An integral part," the Queen said. "He will be deciding which one of you will be the best fit for him—the one to take back to Easteria and introduce to the King and Queen—since you'll be destined to wed. You'll be competing for his heart, while I will be looking for the best princess to represent my family name as ruler of Westeria. Royal refinement and decisive action are key. At the end of this process, we will jointly decide."

"And how long will the competition last?" Jane asked quietly.

"I believe one month will be enough time to confidently make a decision. And with that time-frame, I thought it only fitting to have the new Princess Amelia introduced to the Kingdom on its birthday—at the Foundation Day celebration."

"When do we get to see Prince Byron?" Bethany asked.

"He will be arriving tomorrow. I know you're all anxious to meet him. You'll only have to wait a short while longer."

"I'm stealing him first!" Constance announced. She received a few scowls from the table but seemed to be above them.

The Queen chuckled. "I admire your initiative. I'm sure the competition will get fierce." She was watching everyone at the table.

I readjusted my posture to look attentive. The backs of my legs burned from the extended pressure of sitting. I focused on eating the delicious food we'd been served, trying to push the pain from the fore-front of my attention.

The competition between the seven of us for the hand of the Prince and all the Kingdom's glory did not start the next day; it had already begun.

And the winner would not just become the new Princess Amelia—but essentially become human, like we'd all previously taken for granted.

Who am I? I no longer knew the answer to that.

CHAPTER 22

*T*he Queen said we now had free range of the palace grounds, minus a few rooms that were specifically hers and that she wanted to remain private. We were not permitted to attempt to leave the property for any reason, though there'd be special occasions where we'd be escorted off-site individually—described as exclusive one-on-one dates with Prince Byron.

"Are you excited to meet the Prince today?" Kimera asked. It turned out she would be my personal assistant throughout the competition, always on call for whatever I required. And, right now, I required help with my makeup to conceal my bruised cheek.

The creams she used on my face to help my skin seemed to be helping heal the bruise as well. Soon, I would just need general makeup assistance.

"I don't know. Should I be excited to meet him?" I asked. "He's handsome from what I've seen and seems nice enough, but it's not like I have butterflies in my stomach at the thought of meeting him."

"I'd be excited if I were you. Actually, I'm excited *for* you," she said as she finished powdering my face to even out the color and dull the shine. "I've seen him around the palace several times and his smile melts my heart."

"Maybe you should replace me in the competition, then," I said.

"You're funny." Kimera stepped back to give me a moment to assess her work in the mirror.

"You're a professional," I said. "I'd be a mess without you."

"You're beautiful all by yourself... I simply enhance."

I didn't know what Kimera knew about me—about any of us *clones*. It seemed like a dirty word, so I decided it was better to not bring it up; it was enough for the realization to be consuming my every thought.

I strolled into the bedroom wearing my robe as Kimera ventured into the closet to put together the day's prince-meeting ensemble. It was much more relaxing not having a soldier watching from the corner of the room, wielding an electrified baton. Kimera now trusted I had no intentions of harming her.

When she emerged from the closet with the chosen dress, I asked, "Am I going to be wearing yellow for the next month?"

She glanced down at the dress, then back at me. "It's *canary*."

"I don't care what shade of yellow it is. Is it the color I will be confined to throughout the competition?"

"Only for formal events with the entire group."

This dress was shorter but still reached my knees, covering the weals on the backs of my legs, though I'd probably have to be strategic in how I sat.

Once dressed, I left the room, enjoying my new-found freedom. The bedroom doors had some type of electronic locks controlled from a central location and they'd all been turned off. It was a little unnerving not being able to lock the door while I slept, but I guessed it wasn't much different from my time in the cellar. The ability to keep others out did not outweigh being forcefully locked in.

The house was beautiful and inspiring, but I'd much rather be outside, walking the grounds. I meandered through the gardens at the rear of the estate; there were stables beyond, and I leisurely headed in that direction.

From a distance, I could already see several unsaddled horses grazing in the field. I held onto my shoes as I walked through the grass and up to the wood plank fence. I'd always resented not being allowed to wear shoes, but the feeling of the cool grass on my healing feet felt familiar and calming. Walking shoeless in the fresh grass was the one thing I could control.

Among the unsaddled horses was a tan and white thoroughbred with a male rider. The horse galloped along the fence line, its rider slim and fit in white and red riding attire, helmet, and dark sunglasses. I watched him enviously, knowing there was no way I could join him in my current condition. My butt hurt just thinking about bouncing along on the saddle or straining my leg muscles to hover above it.

When the horse rounded the perimeter of the fence, approaching me, the rider pulled on the reins to slow his horse to a trot.

"Hey there," the man said as his thoroughbred stopped before me.

I reached over the fence and stroked the magnificent creature's muzzle. "Hey there, yourself."

The rider removed his sunglasses and riding helmet. "You must be Victoria."

"Good guess," I said, suddenly recognizing the rider from the hologram message received at the Ramsey estate. "And I presume you're Prince Byron?"

He didn't quite look like the clean-cut Prince Byron from the hologram, but it was definitely him.

His dark hair fell in all directions creating the perfect mess. Thick stubble covered his face, his eyebrows bold, and his gray eyes smoldering, making him look at home with the brawny riders of the Outlands, not royalty.

"Guilty," he said. His gaze on me was intense. "I'm not supposed to be here yet. I arrived early and thought I'd get in a little riding before cleaning up. It clears my head."

"I know what you mean."

"Do you ride?"

I nodded. "I do, but not today."

"Oh, but you must join me. I insist."

I knew I wouldn't survive if I went out there. "It wouldn't be proper. I'm dressed for our official introduction later this afternoon." I held up my shoes dangling from one hand to reinforce my point.

"I can see that. And a very lovely shade of yellow, I might add."

"*Canary*," I said with a smirk, gaining a bit of confidence.

The intensity of his eyes on me only seemed to strengthen. I found myself leaning into the fence like my body was being pulled forward. His boot in the stirrup was only inches away.

"Okay... I do appreciate learning new things. Since I can't convince you to ride with me, what else interests you, Miss Sandalwood?" Prince Byron asked.

"Do you know what ward I'm from too?"

"The 24th."

"Did you memorize the basic information on all of us?" I asked.

"I've done my homework," he said with a smile that deepened the dimples in his cheeks, giving him a boyish charm beneath the hard stubble. "We'll soon see if it was enough."

"Well isn't this a pleasant surprise," said a voice from behind me.

The expression on the Prince's face had made no indication anyone was approaching until that moment; his gaze left me for the first time since the start of our conversation. I turned and saw Constance ten yards away, approaching fast.

"It seems we have a frontrunner already stealing the Prince away for a little one-on-one time before he's even scheduled to arrive," she said, stopping beside me and linking an elbow with mine. "Isn't my sister super cute in yellow? She's like a perfect little doll I could set on a shelf and stare upon for hours."

"Canary," Prince Byron said, giving me a knowing grin.

"I beg your pardon?" Constance lay her head on my shoulder, staring longingly up at her possible prize.

"The shade of yellow is canary," he clarified.

"And I see you're more than an Adonis—knowledgeable, worldly and wise."

"Not as much as your sister here."

Constance lifted her head and gave me a sidelong glance, seemingly deciding how to take the comment. She turned her attention back to him. "I also love to ride. Would you like company out there?"

"I wouldn't want to mess up your dress or your hair or anything else when you're so perfectly put together," the Prince said.

"Don't be silly. I have plenty more dresses in my closet and an assistant to fix any errant strand of hair before our official meet-and-greet. I want to take advantage of all the time we have together. It will go by in the blink of an eye. Would you like a riding partner?"

"I'd love one," he said.

She offered him her hand and he shook it.

"I'll meet you at the stables and help you get set up."

"I'm so excited!" she squealed.

I forcefully took my arm back from the snake beside me.

"It was a pleasure meeting you, Miss Victoria Sandalwood. I'll see you inside later," Prince Byron said, strapping on his helmet, sliding on his sunglasses, and riding off toward the stables.

"Yes, you will," I said, more to myself than him. I should have pushed through the pain and joined him in the field when I had the chance since it literally hurt to watch him ride away.

Constance grabbed my upper arm and gripped it tightly. "Nice try, sweetie. You won't get him. Why don't you go back to the house and wait with the rest of the runners-up? The Prince is *mine*."

$\mathcal{T}$he palace was buzzing with excitement and activity. The time to meet the Prince was swiftly approaching and most of the other girls could barely contain themselves. On the other hand, Constance—who had changed into a new red dress since riding with Prince Byron—was huddled with Danielle and Jane, both shooting dagger-looks in my direction. I could only imagine what she was telling them about me, and I'm sure her words were painting a gigantic bullseye on my back.

Beyond the girls' eager anticipation of the arrival of their regal suitor, the palace staff seemed to be working on some important project with a quickly-approaching deadline, judging by their hastening urgency. It was difficult to navigate through the palace without either being redirected or running into rushing staff members. Was this all for the Prince?

I tried to innocently maneuver past a palace worker carrying a ladder, when he made a sudden turn, causing me to jump out of the way. Just when I thought I had succeeded in escaping unscathed, a messenger drone weaving past the same ladder came at me head on. It pulled up at the last second, but still clipped the top of my head with its small plastic legs.

I was already off balance, and the surprising force of the impact sent me toppling backward.

"Excuse me," a mechanical voice called out as the whining propellers merged with the din of commotion.

I knew there was no way to recover. I was going down and was about to brace myself for impact when two wiry arms caught me before I could hit the ground.

"That could have been bad," a female voice said.

The weals on my butt tingled just from the thought of hitting the floor. "That's for sure," I said, looking up and over my shoulder to find one of the cl—girls, Bethany, gazing down at me.

I quickly regained my balance and placed a hand to my stinging head.

That's going to bruise.

"I think I saw the Prince in the crowd," Bethany

said, giving me some space. "I thought maybe he'd caught your attention too."

"Nope," I said. "I simply wasn't paying attention." Then I pulled over to what seemed like a safe island in the shifting sea of task-focused personnel. "What's going on?"

Bethany inched closer to me, to avoid being hit by two men carrying a long table.

"I overheard someone say something about tonight," she said.

"You do realize that tells me nothing, don't you?"

She shrugged, people-watching now. "They like their secrets. You try asking someone and see if you can get more information."

If I went back to my room, I could call on Kimera; I thought our relationship had grown enough for her to tell me what all the commotion was about. But we'd soon be meeting the Prince in the Garden Room, anyway, so I decided to let them have their secret.

"We should probably get going," Bethany said. "Do you know where the Garden Room is? This place is so big, it's too easy to get lost. Was your family's estate in your home ward anything like this?"

"They thought it was," I said. "But no. This is a whole other level."

"Comes with the title, I guess."

"Did you not get a map of the palace and

grounds?" I asked. Kimera had given me one while getting me ready in the morning.

"I did, but I've never been much good at translating from paper to the real world," Bethany said. "I heard you met the Prince earlier. Is that true?"

"Word sure does travel fast. And you're still talking to me?"

"Why should it get me upset?"

"It seems to be ruffling the feathers of other girls," I said. "And it wasn't just me."

"No?"

"Of course, that hasn't been part of the story going around. Constance showed up too."

"That's not what she's saying," Bethany said, but it didn't sound accusatory.

Not surprising. "I think the Garden Room is this way," I said, leading Bethany into the chaos.

We maneuvered through the bustling palace staff, Bethany almost running right into a woman carrying vases of flowers in each hand; she nearly caused a disaster. I remained on the lookout for passing drones.

My decent sense of direction got us to our desired destination. We weren't the first to arrive, but also not the last. Constance and her newly-formed coven with Danielle and Jane entered behind us.

The Garden Room was an offshoot of the main house, with three walls and a slanted ceiling made almost entirely of green-tinted glass. There was an assortment of seating areas, throw rugs and scattered tables with flower vases, drinks, and hors d'oeuvres. A lit hearth was cut into the one true wall. Sunlight poured into the room, which was muted by the tinted glass but still remained bright and airy.

I received more icy glares and whispers among the girls once we were all in the room, waiting together. Bethany, though, stayed by my side, seemingly unfazed by the other girls' responses toward me.

"Hello, ladies," came a bold voice from the entrance of the Garden Room.

Squeals of excitement erupted when everyone finally noticed Prince Byron standing there, with the Queen standing at his side and numerous staff members waiting directly behind. I may have squealed a little on the inside.

The Prince wore a gray suit to match his eyes, with a white shirt and a skinny black tie. His dark hair was combed back away from his face and he was now clean-shaven. His ruggedness was gone, replaced by striking noble refinement.

He held a champagne flute in one hand and adjusted his crisp shirt cuff with the other.

The Queen also held a glass of champagne and clinked it with a butter knife, requesting us to quiet down. "I would like to officially introduce you to Prince Byron DuFour the Second, of Easteria."

The staff members scooted around our royal host and hostess. One table bore filled glasses of champagne, and the staff distributed one to each of us.

"Let us raise our glasses," started the Queen. "To the next Princess of Westeria and to finding love with this fine young man. May this experience change your life forever."

"I thought we were all princesses now," I whispered to Bethany.

"I have no idea what we are," she whispered back.

The Queen took a sip of champagne, followed by the Prince, allowing the rest of us to then drink.

"Thank you to Queen Dorothea for this amazing opportunity," Prince Byron said. "All of you look so incredible. I'm excited to begin this journey with all of you and confident my future wife is in this room right now. And I'm determined to find her—to find *you*.

"This process will be difficult for all of us, not just you. If at any point it becomes too overwhelming, please come and talk to me. Be honest with me and I promise to always be honest with you. Do your best to make this feel as normal as possible in this very abnormal situation."

Our eyes met from across the room and I felt he was looking straight at me while he spoke. Maybe we did have an actual connection?

"Go forth and mingle with these lovely young ladies of mine," the Queen said, putting a hand on the Prince's shoulder and nudging him into the room. "I'll be back to check how things are progressing in an hour or so, at which time, there'll be another announcement."

"Is that a good or bad thing?" Piper was standing near Bethany and leaned in to us.

"I would think bad news would just be sprung on us," Bethany said.

Prince Byron entered the room as the Queen departed and he was instantly mobbed by Eleanor, Jane, and Danielle. He started out by looking past them, but then gave the raving girls his attention, breaking our connection.

Constance came up beside me with her champagne flute nearly empty. "I had such an exhilarating time riding with him. I don't know about you, but Byron and I had instant chemistry."

Bethany was now talking to Piper, neither one of them listening in on the conversation in which I now found myself. Constance leaned into me and kept her voice down; I could smell sour champagne on her breath.

"When he helped me down from my horse after our ride, he kissed me." She pulled back and smiled, a smile looking anything but sweet.

"I don't care," I said, but inside knew that wasn't entirely true.

"It was *soooo* good." She licked her lips as if she could still taste him.

I felt queasy.

Piper left to join the mob of girls around the Prince, and Bethany turned her attention to us.

"What are we talking about?" she asked.

"Victoria says we should all just give up and go home. She's already got the Prince's heart in her back pocket," Constance said.

"Seriously?" I scoffed. "I said no such thing. If anything... never mind."

"Exactly. No sense in getting yourself in more trouble. I can't listen to any more of this." Constance downed the rest of her champagne, set down the flute on the nearest table, and stormed off.

"She's absolutely evil," I said.

"It'll come out to the right people eventually," Bethany said.

Then Prince Byron was before us with the female throng in tow.

"Hello. You must be Bethany," he said.

She giggled shyly. "How did you know?" She offered him a hand.

He kissed her knuckles. "Process of elimination."

"I hope you're not eliminating me."

"Certainly not," he said and shifted his gaze to me. "Hi, there."

"Hi, yourself," I said. "You clean up nice."

"You look exactly the same."

"Which is hopefully a—"

"I'm not complaining," Prince Byron said, offering me a hand as well.

Some other girls tried to chime in on our brief exchange.

"Yes, I'm the baby of the family. Two older brothers and one sister."

I tried to stifle a laugh. *They should already know that.*

"May I steal you away?" Prince Byron asked, his hand still in mine.

"You may," I answered.

"Excuse us, ladies," he said and guided me by the hand to a loveseat by the hearth.

CHAPTER 24

There was moaning and grumbling behind us, but the rest of the group allowed us to leave privately, though the corner of the room could hardly be considered private.

We parted hands. I smoothed out the skirt of my dress and placed both hands in my lap. He sat back, his body turned toward me, laying an arm across the back cushions and crossing his legs.

He started out by saying, "I missed you out in the field earlier."

"I heard you enjoyed yourself quite a bit," I countered.

"Is that so? Would this be from the biased opinion of the girl who stole me away from you?"

"Perhaps," I said, melting under the heat of his smile—not counting the fire in the hearth. "Did you kiss her?"

"Proper ladies wouldn't be kissing and telling."

And Constance was no *proper* lady. "So, you don't deny it."

"We did kiss," he simply said, and I noticed his careful choice of words. "Is that a problem? You do realize I must get to know each of you. Connections will be made and kisses shared; it's all a part of building relationships."

"I know," I said.

"So, let's not spend our short time together talking about someone else. Let's talk about you. Who is Victoria Sandalwood? I know you love horses and riding. I know you can identify *canary* as a certain shade of yellow. What else should I know about you?"

"You'll have to come closer because it's a secret and I don't want the others to hear."

Prince Byron leaned in. "Do tell, m'lady."

"This has to stay just between us," I started, then brought my lips to his ear. "I'm a clone of the late Princess Amelia." I pulled back and judged his reaction. I'd tried to make a joke of the revelation currently destroying my entire world. It was easier to make light of the situation than attempting a serious discussion.

He took a moment to reply, but his expression didn't reveal much. "Your secret's safe with me. We should be sure not to tell the other girls."

"Ha ha, very funny. Does this seriously not bother you?" *Because it sure as hell bothers me.*

"Are you any less *you*?"

"I don't know. I thought I was me, but that was before discovering I was a genetic copy of seven other girls," I said. I didn't know who I was anymore —*what* I was. I no longer knew the correct pronoun.

"You're unique to me," he said as he took back my hand, stroking my fingers with his thumb. "Your thoughts are *you*. Your reactions are *you*. Your likes and dislikes. Your style." Prince Byron brought his free hand to my neck and pulled me toward him, my face leaning in to his.

His lips were nearly on mine when I pulled away. I pictured him kissing Constance and was saddened by the thought we were so interchangeable.

The hurt and confusion on his face was immediate. Prince Byron sat back, creating a huge chasm between us.

I froze, waiting for a reprimand. Disobedience would only result in further punishment—or so I had grown accustom to back in the Ramsey estate.

"I'm sorry," he said. "I thought…" But the Prince couldn't seem to finish his thought.

My mind was reeling from self-consciousness and embarrassment, even though I didn't have anything to really be embarrassed about. He had made the first move and I had shot him down. I didn't know if I'd get another opportunity. Maybe this one act just destroyed any chance of us having a future.

I lowered my head and took a deep breath. "No. I'm sorry, Your Highness. I'm not used to all this—to this kind of attention. It's a little overwhelming."

Prince Byron's confident smile returned. "You've turned me down twice now." But his words weren't accusatory.

I hadn't thought of that.

"I'm not here to pressure you," he continued. "I'm just looking for my perfect match. I respect your apprehension. And we can move more slowly—but our time is limited, you realize."

And as if on cue, a forceful voice broke our connection. "Prince Byron, may I steal you away?"

We both looked up. Danielle was fixated on the Prince, her made-up eyes sparkling. Her teeth were so white, they practically sparkled too.

He glanced at me, then at Danielle. He slapped both hands on his knees before pushing off the loveseat. "Of course, Danielle. Victoria, until next time," he said before being led away by another beautiful version of me.

I remained on the loveseat by myself for a while. I heard the other girls talking behind me and didn't want to turn and face the conflict.

"She's playing games with him." The voice was recognizably Constance's.

"She's luring him with playing hard to get. It was *so* obvious."

"Totally obvious."

"Watch out for her."

"She's not a threat."

A few minutes later, Bethany plopped down beside me. "How are you?"

"Okay, I guess." I sank into the loveseat until my head hit the back cushions. The Prince was preoccupied. I wasn't presently concerned with being proper.

"Don't listen to them," she said and waited for me to react. When I didn't, she continued talking. "They're just jealous."

"This is crazy."

"The world is full of crazy things. Like us for instance."

"I know. You do realize you're ostracizing yourself from all the other girls in the house by sitting and talking with me, don't you?"

"I'm not here for them," she said. "I'm here for him. I don't want to get tangled up in the negativity. If you end up winning his heart over me, I'll be sad, of course, for myself, but happy for you."

"Wow," I said. "I haven't come across many genuinely nice people in my life. My little sister back home, Mina, is one of the few. A real gentle soul. You remind me of her."

"Well, we are sisters too."

"I like that much better than the C-word," I said, feeling confident about my place in this competition. If she won, I'd be happy for her as well.

"Clone," she said. "It isn't so bad. You say it."

"I prefer not to." I couldn't bring myself to say it aloud. I didn't know how she could.

It wasn't long before the Queen returned to the Garden Room. Five of us had spent semi-private time with the Prince; Constance had stolen a second kiss, Jane had received a peck on the cheek, and Bethany earned a full hug. And Eleanor had had her hands all over him begging for more than he reciprocated for her desperate efforts.

"Well, ladies, how are you enjoying Prince Byron's company?" the Queen asked.

The reaction was unanimously positive. Though I wasn't a raving fan, I had to admit I'd enjoyed his company and was curious to spend more time with him.

"Happy to hear it. I trust connections are already forming. What do you think of my girls?"

Prince Byron made his way to the Queen by the doorway. "Each one of them is absolutely extraordinary," he said. "I'm excited for the process to continue. My wife is in this room. Of that, I have no doubt."

"Of course, she is." The Queen smiled. "There will be more formal and informal mixers, group dates, and personal dates over the coming weeks.

Don't hold back. Time will not be on your side. You will need to take advantage of every moment—which is also a good lesson in life.

"I am stealing your Prince away right now. But you'll see him again later tonight, that is if you can recognize him. To formally commence this process, I am throwing a masquerade ball this evening. It will be a truly elegant affair. High society from all over the 1st Ward will be in attendance. Which now also means you. Carry yourselves as such."

CHAPTER 25

The ballgown Kimera chose for me was a jasmine shade of yellow, definitely more muted than the dress I'd worn earlier in the day. Naming the shades was still beyond me; luckily, I had Kimera to teach me.

The gown was strapless, cut straight across the top, with crystals tucked into the skirt pickups. The flaring skirt brushed the carpet even in my purple open-toed pumps. I'd have to be extremely careful if I didn't want to break an ankle that night.

I tried on the mask lying on the dresser, tying a bow at the back of my head with the black lace. The mask covered the top half of my face down to the tip of my nose and was finished with violet scales and feather plumes adorning the top.

"Aren't you a sight. A real princess if I ever saw one."

I turned and saw the Governess standing in the doorway, also dressed for the occasion; she was holding a black mask by her side, matching her dress.

I would have run over to her—if I could in those heels. Instead, I walked slowly and carefully in her direction. "You're still here," I exclaimed as I threw my arms around her.

"It was the Queen's orders to give you girls time adjusting to your new living situations," she said.

"It's good to see you," I said. "Kimera, this is my Governess."

"We've met," Kimera answered, but she curtsied nevertheless. "I was introduced to her on your first night here."

"Oh, okay."

"Shall we go?" the Governess asked, shading her face with her mask. "The ball has already begun."

Kimera stood behind me and adjusted my mask. She turned me around to square my shoulders. "Shoulders back. Chest out. Chin down. There, perfect."

"Too many things to remember," I complained. "I need to concentrate on walking."

Kimera held the door open for us as we exited the room and headed for the masquerade ball downstairs. I could already hear the classical music drifting through the hallway. The Governess linked arms with me as we descended the curved staircase to the first floor.

We joined the influx of anonymous guests pouring in through the front door. The Event Room was on the opposite rear side of the palace from the Garden Room, and multiple sets of doors stood propped open for easy access.

The main floor of the Event Room was down another wide flight of stairs. Private balconies were stationed around the room's perimeter one floor up, while massive crystal chandeliers hung overhead. Seating areas bordered the lower room while the entire center of it was reserved for dancing, the floor filling up fast with graceful, mysterious couples.

The sophisticated, intricate music filling the room came from a small orchestra on one of the middle balconies. We passed several speakers on our way down the stairs.

"What do we do?" I asked as we reached the edge of the dance floor.

"Mingle. Dance. Have fun," the Governess said.

"I'm not very good at any of those things."

"Now's a good time to learn because a princess *is* good at those things. Everyone's hiding behind a mask tonight, which should make conversations less intimidating. How about starting off with some familiar faces?"

The Governess led me through the crowd around the edge of the room and interrupted a group engaged in conversation. As soon as I could hear the voices, I knew exactly who she was bringing me to.

"Victoria!" Mina squealed and crushed me in a hug.

Master and Lady Ramsey, as well as Johanna, were gathered in a small group talking with a few others I didn't recognize by their voices.

"Mina, it's so good to see you," I said. When I let her go, Lady Ramsey was the next, and last, to embrace me.

Both Master Ramsey and Johanna provided short, stiff greetings.

"So, this is your new home," Johanna said.

"For now," I answered.

"When do we get to meet the Queen?"

"That would be up to her," I said. "I have no idea where she is. I've only just arrived myself."

"We haven't been invited to a party here in over three years," Lady Ramsey said.

"And you didn't take me," Johanna grumbled.

"You weren't invited," Master Ramsey said.

"Have you been to the Queen's stables yet?" Mina asked.

"I've been out to the field and seen some of the Queen's horses," I said. "But I haven't been in the stables yet."

"Misty misses you, you know." Mina stopped and looked over at her mother, then back at me. "She missed you so much we had to bring her with us."

"You brought her?" I asked, directing the question more to Lady Ramsey. "She's here?"

"In the stables!" Mina exclaimed.

"She's yours now," Lady Ramsey said. "She didn't want to ride with anyone else. She belongs here with you."

"I—I don't know what to say," I said, feeling my eyes well up.

Master Ramsey passed me a handkerchief. "Don't get all mushy on us. You could start with a simple *thank you*. I thought we at least taught you that much."

I thought of the last time he'd said something nice to me and shivered. But here, I wouldn't be left alone with him and there was no way I'd allow him to separate me from the party. There would always be people around, and the guards here were not his own.

"Thank you," I said, keeping my attention on anyone other than Master Ramsey. "You don't know how much this means to me."

"You can take me riding here," Mina said. "It will be just like it was."

"How about tomorrow?" I asked.

"We're leaving tonight," Master Ramsey said.

Even though I wanted to spend time with Mina, Master Ramsey's answer brought a sense of relief.

"Next time, then," I said.

A young man in a tuxedo emerged from the

crowd and asked Johanna to dance. She was willingly dragged away and onto the dance floor.

"We'd love to meet Prince Byron," Lady Ramsey said.

"I'm sure he's around here somewhere," I said. "There wouldn't be a party without him."

More and more mysterious guests poured into the ballroom. The dance floor was full and the chatter now a small roar above the volume of the orchestra.

"Hi, Victoria. Is this your family?"

The voice was familiar, but it took me a moment to recognize it. Then I appreciated the mandated dress colors we wore to match our rooms, saw the orange dress and realized the voice belonged to Bethany.

I introduced everyone to each other. I didn't know how to describe Bethany to the Ramseys because I didn't know what they knew already, especially with Mina standing there too.

This is too complicated.

"Come, I want to introduce you to my family," Bethany said excitedly as she pulled me away.

On the way, we snagged glasses of champagne from a server making her rounds in the crowd. Earlier that day was the first time I'd had the bubbly refreshment, and I'd immediately developed a taste for it. The alcohol also seemed to reduce my anxiety, which was certainly welcomed.

"They're just the other side of the dance floor," she said, just as a hand grabbed my wrist.

"Excuse me, m'lady. But may I have this dance?"

I instinctively snatched my hand away, then gazed up into the blue eyes of a guy with short, light brown hair. He was also in a tuxedo like so many others there, and the upper half of his face was concealed by a black mask with silver embroidery.

"She'll have to take a rain—" Bethany started to say, but I cut her off.

"Yes," I answered, fixated on the man before me. "I'm sorry, Bethany. I'll find you in a little bit."

"But…"

"I don't want to be rude," I insisted. "It would be my honor, sir." I performed my best curtsy, which felt forced and fake, and I wobbled on my heels a little.

Bethany didn't put up any more of a fight and left me with the fine-looking stranger.

"I feel I know you," I said.

He moved me onto the dance floor and placed a hand on the small of my back before leading me to the music.

"You don't recognize my voice?" he asked.

"I feel like I should, but…"

"Well, you said you didn't know if you were coming back, so I came to you."

"Kale," I said, sensing it had been him all along.

"At your service," he said with a smile, taking back my hand and spinning me around.

Miraculously, I remained on my feet. "You shouldn't be here."

"I'm not leaving without you," Kale said.

CHAPTER 26

J remembered seeing him at the train station, but I never thought he'd follow me to the Queen's palace. It had been a relief seeing him there because at least I knew he hadn't been captured by Master Ramsey. But I was more than just concerned for his wellbeing; there was definitely a part of me that was happy to see him.

"How did you get an invitation?" I asked Kale.

"Who said I received one?"

"Then how did you get in?"

"I'm crafty like that," he said with an *I'm-so-proud-of-myself* grin.

"Do you realize Duke Ramsey is here?"

"I've kept an eye out for him," Kale said as we continued to move about the dance floor.

"If he recognizes you, I don't even know what

he'd do," I said. "But I doubt trying to kill you would be far-fetched."

With our serious conversation keeping my mind occupied, I had no concern for my dancing and seemed to be gliding seamlessly across the dance floor in high heels that should have crippled me by now.

"Let him try," Kale said. "He's alone here. His people aren't close enough."

"How about the Queen's Guard? If she finds out someone's crashed her party…"

"Who's going to tell her? You?"

"No. But if the Prince—"

"Finds me dancing with you?" Kale asked mockingly. "Is he going to do something?"

"Perhaps I will."

We both spun toward the commanding voice.

Prince Byron stood before us, unmistakable even in his mask. He wore the same gray suit, white shirt, and black tie as before—only now donning a silver mask to complete the outfit.

"Your Highness," Kale said, taking his hands off me and bowing.

"Victoria," Prince Byron said. "I shouldn't be surprised you have other suitors."

"I was just being polite," I said and felt Kale's eyes glaring at me from the comment.

"May I cut in?" Prince Byron asked.

"Of course," I said.

Kale backed away a few steps. "Always a pleasure, Lady Victoria," he said and then disappeared into the sea of dancing couples.

Prince Byron picked up where Kale had left off, placing his hand on my back and leading me in a slow waltz. His grip on my hand was firm and he held me close. His smoky gray eyes were fixated on mine.

"I don't like seeing you dancing with other men," he said after a long silence.

"I don't like seeing you kissing other women, even if they're practically me," I said matter-of-factly, but the feel of Kale's touch and the intensity of his gaze lingered.

"I am committed to this process and want to make sure you are too. I'm serious about finding the girl I intend to marry."

"I am committed to this as well and open minded to whatever lies ahead for us."

"I'm glad to hear it because I don't want you to go," Prince Byron said, dipping me low to the ground. He looked like he was about to attempt another kiss, but stopped himself.

I felt guilty seeing the conflict in his eyes. When I was upright again, I said, "I know our time is short. I'm really trying."

"Which is all I can ask for," he said with one of his radiant smiles that seemed to always make me blush.

We danced for several more songs before he

excused himself, first leading me off the dance floor, then raising my hand to his lips.

"Like you said, I need to give some of the other girls a chance," Prince Byron said, leaving me in the midst of masked strangers at the edge of the ballroom.

I glanced around for familiar faces and didn't see any in close proximity. I was about to make a lap around the room to see who I could find when a familiar, chilling voice caught my attention.

"Looking for someone in particular?" Master Ramsey asked.

"Prince Byron," I said. "He's nearby."

"He just left you. Lying doesn't become you, especially with the punishments I dole out for such an infraction." Master Ramsey grabbed me by the arm and forcefully led me back onto the dance floor.

"What are you doing?" I pleaded.

"One dance is all I ask," he said.

I fought the urge to scream and allowed him one song so that afterward he'd voluntarily leave without causing a major scene.

Once we reached a clear area amidst the other—presumably happy—dancing couples, Master Ramsey turned and placed his hands on me, making my skin crawl. I tried to subdue my revulsion but was beginning to feel nauseous.

"Just because you're here, multiple wards away, and living amongst the royals, doesn't mean you're out of my reach," Master Ramsey said, speaking softly into my left ear. "Wherever you go, whoever you end up with—even this Easteria Prince—you will ultimately remain mine. I've owned you since the day you were born and will continue to own you until the day you die." His hand traveled down and gave me a swift, inconspicuous spank before returning to its rightful place on the small of my back.

I squealed, first in surprise and then in pain as the bruises roared.

"No," I said, defiantly. "I've escaped you. I'm no longer yours to punish as you deem fit."

"Yet, here we are." Master Ramsey provided a closed-mouth grin and patted my bruised cheek. "It's been concealed nicely, yet I see it still hurts. I presume the Queen doesn't know."

"It's a reminder of what I escaped."

"It's a reminder of who you belong to. Don't ever forget it."

"Excuse me, sir."

Master Ramsey was tapped on the shoulder. He turned to confront whoever was intruding on our private dance.

I was surprised to see Kale standing there. Before giving Master Ramsey a chance to say anything, Kale cocked his arm back and punched the Duke in the face.

Master Ramsey had started out off-balance from

the turn and went stumbling back into other dancers before fully collapsing to the floor.

I gasped at Kale's gall, as did other nearby couples interrupted by Master Ramsey hitting the floor. His head snapped back and bounced off the wood flooring.

Kale didn't give anyone a moment to recover and moved fast. He put both hands on my neck and planted his lips on mine. My head swam from the sudden kiss and it took me a moment to stop it—but it only took that moment to awaken something familiar inside of me. I still regarded him as the stranger I'd met outside my cellar window, but my lips—my heart suddenly knew I'd kissed him before.

Our faces were still only inches apart.

"I'm here for you," Kale said, not looking resentful, but hopeful. He glanced down at Master Ramsey who was shaking his head, pushing away people offering to help him up. "I think I've worn out my welcome here."

"Nice shot," I said. "My *hero*."

"My *Princess*." Kale brushed my good cheek with a gentle hand. Then he just as suddenly slipped in between nearby couples and disappeared into the crowd before Master Ramsey could get to his feet.

I stood there elated for a long moment while Master Ramsey aggressively collected himself. A raging fire burned in his eyes when they met mine. Blood streamed from his nose, and he wiped it with the back of his hand, leaving a crimson streak across this face. I couldn't suppress my grin from seeing him knocked to the floor and bloody. I wanted to add to his injuries—kick him while he was down or something, but he'd knock me off balance easily in these heels.

I knew I couldn't revel too long and didn't try to follow Kale. Instead, I headed in a different direction, slipping through small openings in the crowd, looking for someone I knew—anyone I could cling to while Master Ramsey calmed down—or, hopefully, left altogether. Then I saw the Queen engaged in conversation straight ahead; she would be my refuge.

CHAPTER 27

I didn't see Master Ramsey for all the rest of the ball. The remaining family members left before the ball came to a close, including the Governess, who said I was well adjusted and that her services were no longer required. I hugged them all and let them go.

During the next full week, I tried not to think of the whole clone thing, even though I saw the evidence of my so-called sisters every day. But we didn't talk about it. It felt less real that way.

I saw more of Kale as the week progressed and less of Prince Byron, though my frequent interactions with Kale were brief. He had escaped the masquerade ball unharmed and was now posing as a palace staff member. He still wouldn't tell me know he was pulling off these feats.

Kale seemed to be here to stay, but I didn't know how that would play out as the competition for Prince Byron progressed. I knew he was seeing the other girls, though he never asked about them. He seemed to have eyes for no one but me.

"So, who's the guy you've been talking to?" Bethany asked.

She was with Piper and they'd found me reading in the library—my home during the downtime, of which there'd been a lot throughout the week. When I wasn't reading, I went out to the stables and visited Misty; I wasn't ready to ride her yet, though my bruises were steadily healing every day.

"Just a guy," I said, looking up from *Northanger Abbey*.

"He seems to have taken a real liking to you," Piper said.

"Yeah," I said. "I try not to encourage him. I'm just waiting for my first one-on-one with the Prince."

"You haven't gotten yours yet?" Bethany asked. "The week's almost over."

"Danielle's out with him right now and he definitely doesn't seem that into her," Piper said.

"Have you both had one?" I asked.

Both girls nodded and took a seat on the couch across from me.

"I had mine on Monday," Bethany said.

"Wednesday," Piper said.

"Am I the last?"

"Has Constance had one yet?" Piper asked Bethany.

Bethany thought for a moment. "I think so. Umm... I'm not sure."

"That's perfect," I said. "I most likely am the last."

"He seemed to really have eyes for you on the first day," Piper said.

Probably, before I turned him down, I thought. I didn't want to say that aloud, so I deflected the focus from me. "What did you guys do?"

Piper was the first to answer. "We took a helicopter and flew over all the bordering wards, then landed atop the tallest building in Capital City, where we dined privately over the city lights and under the stars. It was amazing."

"Sounds it," I said. "What about you, Bethany?"

"He took me horseback riding on the beach. We splashed in the waves. There was no one along the entire stretch where we rode. Then he set up a picnic in the sand and watched the sun set." Bethany spoke mostly with her eyes closed as if reliving each detail as she described it. "And I'd never even ridden a horse before, never cared to *learn* before, but now... I've already requested lessons."

I couldn't help but be jealous of Bethany as she talked about her date with Prince Byron. Piper's date sounded wonderful too, but Bethany's was my dream date. I didn't know if I could have handled it earlier in the week, but I wouldn't have let my pain stop me going on a dream date like that. Riding could have been agony, but I still would have loved every second of it.

"Did he kiss you?" I asked Bethany.

"Are you keeping score?" Piper asked.

"No... I just..." I shut up.

"I'm sure you'll get your invitation tonight," Bethany said.

"Isn't there a mixer this evening?" Piper asked.

"Yes," I said. But a mixer definitely wasn't the same.

After dinner, we went to the Garden Room for the mixer. There was dessert and more champagne. Most of the girls went sparingly on the decadent puddings, but not the champagne.

Constance was absolutely glowing as she talked with Danielle and Jane. So, she'd just come back from her one-on-one date with the Prince, and here she was with the opportunity to spend more time with him. Prince Byron had taken Eleanor aside, but Constance was positioned to pounce as soon as they were done.

"You should get in there," Bethany said.

We were standing by one of the dessert tables, half a room away from the Prince.

"I'm not going to fight for his attention, especially not with all those vultures circling," I said. "If he wishes to talk to me, then he's welcome to at any time."

"There's no shame in fighting. We all need to fight for our time."

"So why don't you go over? Why are you hanging back with me?"

"I will," she said. "I'm confident in our relationship and I'll get some alone time with him tonight. I just wanted to check on you. You're my friend."

"Thanks for the encouragement, but I'm fine."

"Okay," Bethany said, put down her empty champagne flute, and strolled over to where Prince Byron was seated with Eleanor. A moment later, Eleanor was out and Bethany was in.

I snatched a chocolate pastry to make myself feel better about standing alone. The champagne was making me lightheaded and more anxious, so I set my still half-filled flute down, with the empty ones.

After Bethany, Constance finally swooped in. Bethany returned to me, scolding me more for not interrupting her and allowing Constance an entrance.

I then went to the Prince, partially to shut Bethany up and partially to piss off Constance; it worked on both counts. Constance left, but not without a scowl and a snide comment. Prince Byron didn't seem to appreciate the agitating behavior, nor did he seem particularly happy to see me.

"How's your week been?" he asked, sounding formal and distant.

"Long," I said. "Lonely. I've heard stories of a lot of amazing dates the other girls have gone on with you."

"Yes. It's been quite a week," he said, his stiff features softening.

There was a pause as we sat there facing each other, not touching like a barrier was wedged between us. He seemed to be waiting for me to speak.

"What about me?" I finally asked.

"What about you?" Prince Byron countered. "I got the feeling you didn't care. Actually, I'm not quite sure why you're still here."

"What are you talking about?" Now *I* was offended. "You said you respected that I needed to move a little slower than some of the other girls, but then you spent the rest of the week practically ignoring me."

"Maybe you don't need to go slow. Maybe it's *me*."

"I'm still not following," I said, but I was starting to get a hunch as to where this conversation was going.

"I saw you kiss him on the dance floor," he spat at me, trying to keep his voice down and his burst of rage in check.

"He kissed me. It meant nothing."

"No, no, no! Don't lie to me! It was not one-sided. You quite voluntarily kissed him."

I could feel more than a few sets of eyes on us now but had to remain focused on us.

"I don't know what you think you saw. But it was *one kiss*," I said, pleading now. "I didn't initiate it and I stopped it. I acted as swiftly as I could."

"Well, that's not all," Prince Byron said. "Not only was there the man from the party, now you're getting friendly with one of the palace staff members. I first heard about it from a few of the other girls. I didn't want to believe it after what I'd seen at the ball but then saw it with my own eyes. I could have him thrown out of here. I could have him arrested—put to a firing squad for treason!"

"You wouldn't!" I cried. I didn't want to find out what he might do if he found out the guy from the party and the one from the palace staff were actually the same person.

"If you want to run away with him or the man from the party, or both of them for all I care, go ahead. I won't stop you. But stop wasting my time." The Prince went from raging to deflated in the span of a few sentences. "This is important to me. I'm here to find the love of my life, and you're toying with me."

"No, my Prince," I said. "I'm doing nothing of the sort. I apologize for the kiss at the masquerade ball, but I won't apologize for talking with another man while I sat here all week waiting for you. It's hard seeing all these girls going on dates with you and then waiting, wondering if I'm going to be next. Then I hear about how wonderful and romantic the dates are. And it hurts, you know?"

"You haven't gone out of your way to talk to me. We've been in several group settings. There have been ample opportunities. You've had all week."

"So have you," I countered. "You seemed upset with me. I didn't know what I was supposed to do."

"I *was* upset with you—I *am* upset with you." Prince Byron let out a long breath and laid a hand on my knee. "You say you've been waiting for me. Tell me now—promise me you're not playing me for a fool," he said.

"I'm not playing you for a fool," I said, very aware of his hand on me. I made it a point not to pull away again. "I'm just waiting for you to ask me out. And I hope you still desire to."

Prince Byron removed his hand from my knee and reached into his suit coat. After some difficulty, he revealed an envelope with my name on it. "I had originally planned to give this to you Sunday evening for Monday's date, but with everything that'd happened... I held off. I hope you're still here for me and I hope you'll accept."

"Of course, I will," I said, taking the envelope. "Should I read it now?"

"If you want," he said and returned his hand to

my knee, caressing the skin under the hem of my dress.

I hastily ripped open the envelope and removed the card. "Let's ride into the sunset together," I read and then gazed up at him. "Yes. Let's do that."

CHAPTER 28

I went down to breakfast early Saturday morning. Many of the girls ordered room service, but I liked getting out of my room whenever I could, even though it was pretty spectacular.

I couldn't get much sleep thinking of the next day's one-on-one date with Prince Byron. When I'd received the invitation, I originally thought the date would be that night, but the Prince had business to attend to, so it was set for Sunday, starting the week off right.

In the dining room, I found the Queen seated with Constance and Danielle; they were all well into their meals so I was about to turn around and leave when the Queen noticed me.

"Good morning, Victoria," she said. "The best among us get our days started early. Come sit with us, my dear."

I reluctantly approached the table and chose a seat across from the other two girls. The Queen sat at the head of the table.

"May I bring you any coffee or tea?" one of the kitchen staff members asked from behind me.

"Lemon chamomile tea please," I said, making eye contact with the staff member, only to find Kale gazing down at me. *Oh God, not now.*

"Right away, m'lady," he said, disappearing into the kitchen.

"I used to read the bios of all my staff members, but my staff has grown so considerably over the years that it just became too cumbersome," the Queen said, finishing her oatmeal and moving on to a small bowl of mixed fruit. "I had to put more trust in my management team to ensure everyone employed at the Château was carefully vetted and controlled. I've only seen that boy serving us for about a week but I really like him. He's very proper and attentive. Don't you agree, ladies?"

Both Constance and Danielle concurred, maybe a little too emphatically for my taste.

"He's not hard on the eyes either," Constance said, glancing over at me.

Then they were all looking at me.

"I guess I hadn't really noticed," I said.

Kale burst back into the room with a teapot for me, along with the porcelain cup and saucer. Kale poured my first cup of steaming tea and set the cup and saucer before me.

"Your meal will be out shortly," he said. "Is there anything else I can get for you in the meantime?" When I shook my head, he turned his attention to the others at the table. "May I take your empty dishes? Was everything to your liking?"

"Everything was wonderful," the Queen said. "I haven't had the pleasure of your name."

"Jimmy, Your Highness," Kale said with a bow.

"Well, Jimmy, I will speak with the dining supervisor to commend you on what a superb job you're doing."

"Thank you, Your Highness," Kale said while stacking the empty plates on one outstretched arm and returning to the kitchen.

Constance and Danielle rose from the table and excused themselves as well. For the most part, Constance behaved herself in the Queen's presence.

The Queen was also finished with her breakfast except for her coffee, and sat back in her chair, sipping the drink noisily.

"You don't have to wait for me," I said.

"How are you handling all this?" the Queen asked.

"I was expecting to spend more time with you—get to know you since you are my real mother... well, technically the real mother to all of us."

"A lot of work goes into running a kingdom.

There isn't much downtime. I rarely have time to myself. I try to enjoy the few quiet moments I do get."

"Why is all of this happening now?" I asked. "You had eighteen years to contact us. We could have met our older sister."

"Princess Amelia," the Queen corrected.

"Yes. Princess Amelia. If we—since we were cloned from her, it would have been such an honor to meet her."

Kale returned with an omelet and oatmeal and placed the dishes before me. He then took my napkin and draped it gently across my lap.

"Anything else?" he asked.

"No, thank you. This looks delicious."

Kale bowed to each of us as he exited the dining room again.

"I didn't want to disrupt your development," the Queen said, returning to our conversation. "It was safer to separate all of you and monitor you each individually. The Kingdom can't know about this experiment; you are a beautiful and healthy young woman—a successful experiment—but still an experiment, nevertheless. There were risks, which I struggled with early on. But ultimately, I agreed with the doctors to move forward. And here you are, eighteen years later, sitting at my table. You all look like her, but *you* remind me of her the most. Your disposition. The way you hold yourself. Every time I

MICHAEL PIERCE

see you, I forget for a moment that my Amelia is really gone."

"We must seem like ghosts to you," I said.

"More like visiting angels," she said. "How are you taking to Prince Byron?"

"I have a date with him tomorrow evening. I'm very much looking forward to it."

"The time is going by fast. And all of you girls have been beyond my expectations. I'm sure his choice, in the end, will be difficult."

"What will happen to those of us not chosen?" I asked.

"Those arrangements will be discussed soon, but it needs to be with the whole group. For now, keep your focus on the Prince." The Queen took her last sip of coffee and slid back her chair. "Delicious breakfast and pleasant conversation. This has been a good start to the day, wouldn't you say?"

"It has, Your Highness."

"Duty calls," she said as she rose. "Enjoy your date tomorrow, Victoria. Make every moment count. We never know how many we have left."

No one else came in while I finished my food. I sat at the long table alone.

Kale returned a few minutes later. "May I take your plate, Lady Victoria?"

"Stop calling me that," I said, rolling my eyes.

He placed a hand on the nape of my neck and lightly rubbed it.

I jerked away from his touch, alarm always seeming to be my first reaction.

Kale took a step back. "I'm sorry."

"We need to be careful," I said. "We need to distance ourselves. The palace has eyes... everywhere," I said.

"Then let me steal you away from here. I have a place we can go, people we can stay with who will keep you safe. Neither the Queen nor the Ramseys will be able to find you. It's like we talked about before—before they stole your memories from you."

I turned in my chair to face him. "I can't," I said. "If I can win the Prince's favor and gain status here, I can save Mina, Johanna and Lady Ramsey from the monster they live with. It's a great opportunity for me. I have to see it through. It's only a few more weeks."

"And if you win, then you're gone—I've lost you."

"I don't know. I don't know how I feel about him yet. I also don't know about us. Everything you've told me about us, I have no memory of. I feel you're being sincere, but I'm not in the same place you are." I remembered the familiarity of his kiss, but it wasn't enough. I wasn't about to just run away with him—I no longer knew the girl who was.

"I know what we had," Kale said, kneeling before me. "There is no question for me."

"There's a good chance I won't win. He's seen us

together. He's watching us. That is why we need to be more careful."

"So, if you lose, then I'll be your consolation prize?"

"This opportunity is so much more than just him and you," I said, directly meeting his gaze. "It could be a new life where I could make a real difference."

Kale sighed and stood. "I'd better get back to work," he said, collecting my used dishes and silverware. "We have to be careful, right?"

He stormed back into the kitchen, leaving me alone at the table again.

How could he just expect me to leave with him? Even though we had some romantic, yet forgotten past, I currently didn't know him any better than the Prince. I didn't know who I could trust; all I could do was listen to my gut, and it was telling me not to commit to anything too early. I hoped Kale would come to understand.

After breakfast, I ventured out to the stables to visit Misty. Not knowing what the Prince had in store for me the next day, I figured I'd better get a little riding in to see how much pain it'd cause me. But once I had Misty at a full gallop across the open field, I found my injuries didn't bother me half as much as anticipated. I embraced my four-legged friend, the sweet air, and the sunshine peeking through the clouds. I spent an hour riding and another with Misty in the stable, cleaning and feeding her. The stable boy tried to take the tasks away from me, but just like back at the Ramsey estate, I didn't consider these chores.

I spent the afternoon in the library and finished *Northanger Abbey*. Bethany kept me company for a short while, and Eleanor stopped in to see what I was doing; she couldn't understand why I was spending my time in the palace reading and I didn't bother trying to explain my enjoyment of the pastime.

Kimera kept me company as I prepared for sleep. She placed my nightwear on the bed, applied some mint-scented night cream to my face, and brushed my hair. I loved having her around.

"Are you excited for your date tomorrow?" she asked as we made our way back into the bedroom.

I slipped out of my robe and into my nightgown. "I don't know if I'll get even an ounce of sleep tonight," I said.

"You're not involved with the new staff member, Jimmy, are you?"

"What? Where did you hear that? No." I felt she could see right through my feigned shock.

"I've overheard others talking," she said.

"It's just talk," I insisted. "Some of the other girls are probably trying to drum up drama where there is none to better their chances and hinder mine."

"Even if there's no merit to their accusations, it

creates doubt. And doubt will kill a budding relationship."

"I know," I said, falling back on the feathery bed. "I'll try not to give them any more ammunition."

"Just be careful," Kimera said. "That's all I'm saying. You've as good a chance as any of the other girls. Don't let them control your opportunity."

I thanked her for her advice and crawled under the covers. Kimera turned off the lights and wished me goodnight before exiting my room.

I stared into the darkness and continually glanced at the alarm clock for a long while. The last time I remembered seeing was 11:35 p.m. When I glanced over again at the sound of the phone ringing, it was already past 1:00 a.m.

Groggily, I picked up the receiver. "Hello?"

"Miss Victoria, I'm sorry to disturb you," the voice on the other end of the line said. "But there is a young girl at the front gate asking for you."

"A young girl?"

"She says her name is Mina."

CHAPTER 29

I threw my robe over my nightgown and rushed outside. At the front gate, I saw Mina being detained by two armed guards.

"Mina!" I exclaimed. "What are you doing here? She's all right. She's my little sister—step-sister."

After some brief grumbling, the guards unhanded her and opened the gate. Mina ran in and crushed me with a hug.

"What are you doing here?" I repeated.

"I had to see you," she said.

I noticed tears in her eyes. "Let's get you inside. You can stay the night in my room."

I really wished I had a lock on my door.

Mina was instantly fascinated by my room and explored every bit of it, including the closet and washroom.

"There's a lot of yellow in here," she said.

"Yeah, that's why the Queen calls it the Yellow Room. How did you get here?" I asked.

"I took the train like you did," she said, appearing in the washroom doorway. "And then paid for a ride to the palace."

"You never answered me as to why you came."

She removed her coat, turned around, and pulled the top of her dress down just past her shoulders. A crisscrossing mess of red lines peeked out from the top of her dress. I gasped and apprehensively approached, taking hold of her dress and gently pulling it down to her waist, revealing the full weight of the punishment and torture she'd endured.

"When did this happen?" I asked, unable to hold back a sob.

"Two nights ago," she whispered as if it was too dangerous to say aloud. "He visited me after we returned home from the ball. And it was bad. But then... a few nights later, he woke me in the middle of the night and dragged me into the cellar—into your old room—and... and..." She couldn't continue.

"And did this," I said.

Mina nodded. Her shoulders were shaking and I could hear her crying.

I replaced her dress to cover the wounds again, spun her around, and hugged her. I didn't know how exactly to hold her since there seemed to be welts and dried blood on every covered inch of her back.

At least her face seemed unharmed, which I'm

sure was intentional. He truly was a monster, and now with Mina gone, I feared for the rest of the family.

"I'm so sorry I didn't go with you that night," she said, tears streaming down her cheeks. "You asked me to... but Johanna talked me out of it. I was afraid. Then when they brought you back, I... I..."

I stared at her stunned, knowing what she was talking about. "Where were we supposed to go?"

"With Kale. I don't know where. You didn't tell me. I'm sorry I didn't go. And I'm sorry I didn't tell you the truth earlier. I wasn't—we weren't supposed to say anything—to even speak his name."

"Kale wasn't a secret?" I asked.

"Not until you tried to leave with him," Mina said, sniffling loudly. "I can't go home. Can I stay here with you?"

"This will be the first place he looks for you. You can stay the night, but then I'll have to find you a safe place." I thought for a moment, taking in what she'd just told me, and remembering what Kale had said earlier in the day. "I have an idea."

I called Kimera and had her come to my room. She arrived within a few minutes, fully dressed.

Does she ever sleep?

"I have to ask a favor of you, and you can't ask questions," I said.

"What is it? Is this the girl from the front gate?"

she asked with a slight stutter, noticeably nervous at my request.

"Word travels fast," I said. "Yes. This is my little sister, Mina. She's hungry and I need to order room service for her."

Kimera's shoulders relaxed. "That's nothing. Of course—"

"I'm not finished," I interjected. "And I need Jimmy to bring up the food."

"Umm… I don't believe he's on shift right now. I can't—"

"Then find a way to get him on shift. We have time. This doesn't need to be done immediately. But I do need to see him tonight before the whole palace awakes."

"I… umm… I'll see what I can do," Kimera said, her eyes shifting from me to Mina. "Why—"

"No," I cut her off. "It's better to keep you out of it as much as I can. Please just do what you can to get him here in the least suspicious manner possible. Bringing up a tray of food from an officially-placed order seems our best option."

Mina crawled onto my bed and lay on her stomach, resting her head on an outstretched arm. She wiped her visible cheek with her free hand.

"Yes, Miss Victoria," Kimera said, regaining her poise and composure. "I'll do what I can."

"And you won't mention this to anyone?" Now it was *me* getting nervous.

"I will be discreet," she said. "What would you like to eat, Miss Mina?"

Mina didn't raise her head or answer.

"Do we have any Neapolitan ice cream?" I asked.

"I'll check. If we don't, I'll have the ingredients mixed. I'll have it brought up with a glass of milk." Kimera abruptly left.

Now I was forced to wait and see if she could come through with the request.

I sat next to Mina and stroked her blonde hair, running my fingers through the pink and red accents. "It's going to be okay," I said. "I promise."

"Who's Jimmy?" she asked.

"You'll see."

While she lay across my bed, I removed her shoes and coaxed her under the covers. I kissed her on the top of the head, dimmed the lights, and went to sit on the couch. I could tell from the sound of her breathing that she was already asleep. Then I knew it was safe to let my tears for her flow freely.

I wondered if Kimera would return, but she didn't.

When Kale arrived with a dessert tray an hour later, he entered my room alone. He noticed Mina in bed and set down the tray on the coffee table.

"We should let her sleep," I said.

"The ice cream will melt," Kale said.

"There can always be more ice cream."

"Is this us being more careful?"

"This is an exception," I said. "I need help getting Mina to safety. You said you had a place, people we could stay with where the Queen and the Ramseys could never find us."

Even though I couldn't remember what we had or the plans we'd made, it seemed Mina did, which made me feel more confident in Kale's intentions. And when she awoke, her reaction in seeing him here would tell me everything.

"How is she?" Kale asked.

"He made quite a mess of her," I said, trying not to well up again just thinking about what I'd seen across the skin of her back.

Kale took a seat next to me on the couch. "It takes everything I have not to kiss you."

I smiled, but stayed firm in my seated position. He was handsome and seemed sincere, and maybe if I could remember something, I'd feel differently. But I couldn't just return to who he wanted me to be.

"Are you able to sneak her out of here and hide her with the people you mentioned?" I asked, trying to get off the subject of us.

Kale's eyes grew wide. "Are you not coming?"

"I want to make sure Mina's safe, but this doesn't change what I need to do here," I said. "I was hoping you'd be willing to help."

"I want to help *you*."

"And this would be a great help to me."

"For how long?" he asked. "What's the long-term plan?"

"I haven't devised a long-term plan. Until she's old enough to take care of herself, I suppose."

Kale's eyes dropped, seemingly upset. When I glanced down too, I noticed my robe falling open to reveal the lacey neckline of my silk nightgown, which I quickly closed.

Kale diverted his gaze away from me, his cheeks flushing, then said, "I have a guy who can sneak her out of here. He can bring her to my family where she'll be safe. Can she stay here until tomorrow night? I'll need some time to get things in order."

"*You're* not going to take her?" I asked. I'd hoped this plan would get them both out of the palace.

"Don't worry. She'll be in good hands," he said, bringing his attention back to me. "I'm not leaving. That way, I can ensure you're in good hands as well."

The way he looked at me had so much heart-broken longing—the girl he wanted was me, and she wasn't. It killed me that I couldn't be *that* girl. But she was locked away in memories to which I had no access.

"I wish there was something I could do to jog your memory," he said, as if reading my mind. Kale closed the gap between us on the couch.

When my robe began to fall open again, he took my hand before I could cover myself.

"I wish I could have done more that night—to

keep them from dragging you back." Kale shook his head like he wanted to forget what I couldn't remember.

When our eyes met again, there were tears in his.

"As much as I want you to remember me—what we had—I'm glad you have no memory of what happened that night."

I couldn't take my eyes off him. "I wish a lot of things were different," I finally said.

"I'm not crazy," Kale said and chuckled. "I know how this must look. Us. Me."

"I don't think you're crazy," I said.

And before I could say anything else, he leaned in and planted his lips on mine.

I'd planned to pull away even before consciously realizing there had been a knock at the door, which opened slowly—whoever was in the hallway not willing to wait for a response from inside the room.

Kale jumped back like a startled cat.

I frantically closed my robe and wiped my lips. My skin was burning, my face flushed. This was so *not* being careful.

imera quickly closed the door behind her. "I'm *so* sorry. I did not mean to intrude. I just wanted to check in and make sure Jimmy had come like you'd asked." Even in the dim light, her face looked as red as mine felt. Her back was against the door.

"It's not what you think," I said, springing off the couch and approaching her.

"I didn't see anything," she said, but the look on her face was not so convincing.

"What's going on?" The voice was Mina's and she was now sitting upright in bed.

"Everything's fine," I insisted. "There's ice cream for you on the table if you want."

"It's only somewhat melted," Kale added.

"Kale?" Mina asked.

"Obviously, you received what you requested, so

I'll be going," Kimera said and turned to open the door.

"No!" Kale yelled, and then realized he'd probably wake the girls in the nearby rooms. "Don't let her leave!" His voice was insistent, but much lower this time.

I threw my weight into the door to block Kimera's exit. "We can trust you, right?" I asked.

"Yes—yes, of course," she exclaimed.

"If you let her leave, there'll be guards here in seconds," Kale said, also approaching the door.

"No. I won't say anything to anyone," Kimera insisted. She was shaking uncontrollably now.

"Everyone's safety in this room relies on her keeping her mouth shut," Kale said. "The staff carry panic devices for these precarious situations. Hands out where I can see them."

"I don't think so," I said. "If she did, then she wouldn't have needed a guard in the room with me when I first arrived."

Kale walked up to Kimera and patted her down, then he reached into a pocket hidden within the folds of her dress, removing what looked like a small remote.

"I didn't press it," she said.

Kale held up the device so I could get a better look. I couldn't believe it. She'd had a panic device the whole time—whenever she was alone with me and I thought we were bonding.

"Why do you have that?" I asked.

"It's protocol," Kimera said. "It is by no means a reflection on you. I swear, I won't tell anyone what's transpired tonight."

"What are we going to do?" I asked Kale.

"This just accelerated the plan," he said. "I need to get Mina out of here tonight."

Then he turned to her and I saw them truly see each other for the first time.

"Hey there, kiddo," Kale said.

I could see the recognition on her face and knew in that moment that we really were all connected.

"Where am I going? Victoria, are you coming too?" Mina asked, dropping down from the bed.

"I wish I could, sweetie," I said, glancing to Kale, then back to Mina. "But I know you'll be safe."

"But I want to be with *you*."

Kale walked up to her and got down on one knee. "You trust me, right?"

Mina nodded. And I could see she meant it. She showed no fear or apprehension in his presence. I didn't know how I felt about him anymore. Seeing them together made me ache even more for those lost memories—to get back the feelings I'd supposedly once had for him.

"I'll keep you safe." Kale stood up and kissed the top of her head. Then he turned back to me. "Victoria, keep *her* here," he commanded, pointing to Kimera. "I'll keep this in the meantime." He slipped the panic device into his pants pocket. "I'll be back as soon as I can."

I grabbed his arm before he could leave. "Be safe," I said.

"Always," Kale said, giving me a long heartfelt look before disappearing down the hallway.

I'd thought I wasn't going to get any sleep tonight, but certainly hadn't expected things to go like this.

Kimera and Mina took seats on opposite ends of the couch. Mina left her milk untouched and began drinking her melted ice cream. Kimera leaned against the armrest and bobbed her leg nervously, while I was left to babysit them both.

"You lied to me before," Kimera said after a long silence. "You want me to trust you, but you don't trust me enough to tell me the truth."

"It wasn't what it looked like," I said. "There truly is nothing between us."

Mina gave me a disapproving glance.

"And I don't want you to get tangled up in anything that ends up happening to me," I added. "You can trust me. Can I trust *you*?"

"It doesn't matter now. She'll be gone tonight. Jimmy won't need to come back later where he could be trapped. The evidence will be gone. There will be nothing left for me to report but hearsay."

"Who's Jimmy?" Mina asked.

"It matters to me. Not just about this," I said,

trying to appeal to Kimera—to get back to the way I thought things were between us.

"I'm not going to turn you in, if that's what you're afraid of."

"Or Jimmy?"

"How did you get involved with him anyway? He's only been here since…"

"Since I got here?"

A lightbulb suddenly turned on behind her eyes. "He came with you." It wasn't a question.

"Not exactly *with me*. More like *after me*," I clarified. "And if we're truly trusting each other, his real name is Kale."

"What about the Prince? Your date tomorrow?"

"I know. I'm still really looking forward to our date tomor—tonight. This changes none of that."

"I won't say anything about Kale—Jimmy," Kimera said, looking only slightly more accepting of the situation.

Kale returned shortly before sunrise. "The shifts are just about to change," he said and handed Kimera back her panic device. "We need to leave now."

"I'll come see you as soon as I can," I told Mina and gave her a careful hug.

"He's not going to be able to find me, right?" Mina asked with big sorrowful eyes. "And you'll come as soon as you can?"

"I promise," I said, doing my best to reassure her.

"I won't let anything else happen to you. Kale won't let anything else happen to you."

"I've got you, kiddo," Kale said. "You know you and your sister mean the world to me." He glanced at me when he said it, but I wasn't sure he was talking about me.

Mina found her coat draped over my desk chair and put it on.

"Thank you," I said to Kale. I hugged him, but turned my face to keep him from attempting to kiss me.

His expression seemed conflicted. He glanced over at Kimera still seated on the couch and then back at me. He looked like he wanted to say something to me, but didn't.

"Come on, Mina. Time to go."

Kale slowly opened the door and peered into the hallway. He then grabbed Mina by the hand and they were gone.

CHAPTER 31

I saw Kale once more before leaving on my date with Prince Byron. He didn't say a word to me, which I took to mean everything with Mina went smoothly. But it didn't stop me from wondering.

"Are you feeling all right?" Prince Byron asked while we sat in the back of the limousine, on our way to whatever he had planned. "You seem preoccupied."

"No. I'm fine," I said. "I didn't sleep much last night. I was too excited. Except now I'm crashing. I drank quite a bit of tea earlier to wake up until I found out lemon chamomile doesn't have caffeine."

"It's an herbal tea. None of them has caffeine."

"Good to know."

The Prince had told me before leaving that I should dress comfortably, so I consulted with

Kimera and we'd jointly decided on dark blue jeans and a maize-colored blouse with a wide, off-the-shoulder neckline.

Prince Byron was also dressed casually, in khaki pants tucked into brown boots nearly reaching his knees and a white, button-down dress shirt. The top two buttons were open, revealing a thin patch of chest hair. I swear I wasn't staring.

"I've wanted to ride with you since the first time I met you," he said. "I wish you hadn't turned me down that day."

"I wish I could have gone riding with you that day instead of leaving you with Constance."

"Yeah… She's a lot to handle," he said. "It still gets me how similar you look, but otherwise, you couldn't be more different."

"Hard to believe we came from the same genes, isn't it?" I said and laughed.

"You asked me what I think of it, but you never told me about you. What was it like for you when you found out what you are?"

I thought my world couldn't be any more destroyed after growing up with the Ramseys, but the Queen managed to do just that. She managed to take away the little identity I had left. The little bit of myself still sacred. I couldn't tell him that.

"What I am is just another person, like you—like anyone. The Queen's great revelation didn't change that. Sure, it was surprising at first—and totally hard to believe—but it didn't change who I was. I mean, it could have, if I'd let it. If anything, it made me feel special."

I couldn't believe how naturally the words were escaping my lips. And maybe there'd even come a day when I could convince myself to believe them.

"You are special," Prince Byron said and took one of my hands in both of his, which were warm and comforting.

It took about an hour to reach our destination. The back door of the limousine was opened and Edward, the driver from my trip from the train station, lent a hand to help me out. Prince Byron followed.

I was immediately hit by a strong wind, almost masking the sound of crashing waves. We were parked on the side of the road, next to a stretch of dirt that gradually transitioned into a black sand beach. The sun was already lowering over the water.

On the beach were two of the palace trainers, each holding the reins of a horse—one of which I instantly recognized as Misty.

"How did you know?" I squealed with excitement and ran to her.

"I wanted to make today perfect," he said from behind.

The trainer gave me her reins and stepped away.

I stroked Misty's cheek and she nuzzled into the

side of my head and snorted. "I'm happy to see you too, girl."

Prince Byron took the reins of his horse and was in the saddle in one fluid movement. "I didn't think I was going to have to teach you too."

I grabbed hold of the horn, secured my foot in the stirrup, and pulled myself up. "Let's see if you can keep up," I yelled to him and signaled for Misty to take off in a full gallop, leaving the trainers, the limousine, and the Prince behind.

I was enveloped in a cloud of black sand and the wind bit at my bare skin as Misty and I raced down the beach. I glanced back under my armpit and saw Prince Byron not far behind. For all I knew, the thoroughbred the Prince was riding was a genuine racehorse. If that was the case, Misty didn't have a prayer of outrunning them.

A minute later, Prince Byron was parallel to me with a huge grin on his face, then he pulled ahead.

"You proved your point!" I shouted.

"So did you!" he shouted back.

The beach followed the coast, stretching for miles that I could see. The Prince's horse veered to the left, galloping into the shallow water. I had Misty follow him in, making sure to keep enough of a distance to remain clear of the splashing from the horse ahead of us. The kicked-up water from directly below was enough to soak me; it was icy but my exhilaration was keeping me warm, at least for now.

Prince Byron's horse slowed to a trot, then to a walk. I pulled Misty alongside him and had her match his gait. We were both still in the ocean water, but now the splashes only nearly reached my shoes.

He looked right at home on the saddle and I thought of the first time I'd seen him riding through the meadow. His hair was wonderfully disheveled again like it had been when he'd removed his helmet on that day. His five o'clock shadow was also back to match his casual attire. Even with all the beautiful scenery surrounding us, I couldn't take my eyes off him. He somehow drew me in without doing a thing.

The sun was closer to the horizon now, its magnificent rays dipping into the water. The wind blew harder, making conversation difficult, but it didn't seem awkward to ride in silence, simply enjoying each other's company.

Up ahead, I noticed the coastline turn out like a natural pier and the black sand of the beach disappeared into rocky hills. At the top of one of the hills, on a cliff overlooking the ocean, sat a dark lighthouse.

Prince Byron pointed to it. "We're headed up there."

I nodded to acknowledge I'd heard him over the wind and waves.

Once we reached the edge of the hills, I saw a

thin dirt path winding up. We took the horses up the path in tandem, with the Prince leading the slow climb.

At the entrance of the lighthouse, there was a hitching post, which we tied the horses to before entering. Prince Byron held the door and placed a hand on my back, guiding me in first. The ground floor was a small circular room with a central, spiral staircase; the Prince steered me toward it and instructed me to go ahead.

"Don't get any ideas," I warned him. At least I wasn't wearing a dress.

"I wouldn't dream of it," he said, close behind me. "When you reach the top, grab the latch and push it open."

I came to the trap door and did as he instructed. The door opened on creaky hinges and a chain kept it from crashing to the floor above. As soon as the door was open, I heard the soft melody of stringed instruments.

I climbed up into the larger room at the apex of the lighthouse. A giant spotlight took up half the space, asleep in the center. The whole outer wall of the room was floor-to-ceiling windows, and much of the ceiling was constructed from glass, where a couple of stars could already be seen against the dulled light of the setting sun.

As I rounded the room to overlook the ocean, I found a small table with chairs and place settings for two, a stretched-out blanket with pillows on the floor, and a band of four musicians to serenade us— a standup bass, a cello, and two violins. The only light from the room—besides the last of the daylight —came from candles on an end table by the blanket, and around the musicians.

My heart melted at the romantic setup; I couldn't believe someone would go to all this trouble for me.

"What do you think?" Prince Byron asked, coming up behind me.

"It's perfect," I said.

He stepped ahead of me and pulled out one of the chairs. "Please," he said.

I sat down and he took the folded napkin from the table and placed it in my lap before taking his seat. I looked out at the ocean and then back at him.

"Looks like we made it just in time," he said, turning his gaze to the sunset.

A quarter of the sun was now underwater, setting the ocean ablaze with a multitude of bright colors.

A young female server came around from the far side of the spotlight and approached the table holding a bottle of wine.

"Good evening," she said, gracefully dropping into a curtsy. "May I start you off with a glass?" She presented the bottle for the Prince to approve.

"Please," he said. "But allow me."

Prince Byron stood up and took the bottle from the server, pouring me a half glass. Then he poured some for himself before handing the bottle back to the server, who said she'd be back with appetizers momentarily.

We clinked glasses before taking first sips. The white wine was light and fruity and I knew it would be all too easy to down the whole glass in a few gulps. I needed to make sure that didn't happen, to keep my wits about me.

"You look even more beautiful as you are now, than when you're all dressed up in the formal gowns," Prince Byron said, setting down his glass.

"I was just thinking the same about you," I said. "Casual riding clothes suit you perfectly."

"Then we should move away into the country, away from all this formality where we can build a ranch and breed horses. A quiet and casual life."

"That seems quite the fantasy coming from you— from a Prince of Easteria. I wouldn't think you could just disappear into the Outlands; what about your royal and family obligations? Can they be so easily set aside to *ride off into the sunset* with me?"

"Probably not. But it's nice to pretend," he said. "If I could have what I wanted, that's how it would be."

"With me?"

"With a girl who would have me and share the same vision. I don't know, is that you?"

"It does sound like a pretty nice life," I said.

The server came back with a basket of sliced bread and a plate of bruschetta crackers.

The sun had finally set and the fiery colors painting the water were quickly receding. More stars were appearing in the night sky every few seconds, and the music filling the room enhanced the lighthouse's tranquil atmosphere.

"Are you any closer to finding your soulmate?" I asked.

"Further away, if you can believe it," he answered. "You're all so great. I don't know how I'm going to choose in a few short weeks. Each date makes my decision that much harder."

"I can't imagine being in charge of such a decision—having so many people's lives hanging in the balance. I suppose the unchosen will return to their former lives in the outer wards. It will be hard after this taste of luxury."

"But you don't care about all that, right? You'd rather be out in the country instead of being doted on by teams of servants."

"But that doesn't mean I want to go back to the 24th—back home."

"Tell me about your family—I mean, the family who raised you." The Prince took a bite of bruschetta.

"I was never really a part of their family, more like another of their servants. I didn't belong there. I may not belong here."

"I've heard the same from a few of the other girls. Some were embraced as family, but others were distanced and raised by the staff. One girl told me about the abuse she endured for years. It broke my heart. I wouldn't wish her to go back to that—but I can't finalize my decision out of pity either."

I wondered who he was talking about, but I didn't want to ask and linger on the subject because I wasn't about to tell him about my visits from Master Ramsey. Prince Byron had gone to all that trouble to set up this perfect date, and I wasn't about to destroy it with the horrors of my past.

"So, I want to help," he continued. "I want to help the remaining girls return to their old lives or start new ones. None of you deserves to go back to a place where you are not valued and respected."

"That's so kind of you, and certainly takes some of the pressure off," I said.

"Hopefully, not too much."

"I don't think that kind gesture will stop any one of us from continuing to pursue you."

"Yourself included?"

"Perhaps," I said with a sly smile.

The young female server returned with plates of fish steaks under orange sauce, potato wedges, and spiced vegetables.

"Does she have a hidden kitchen over there or something?" I asked.

Prince Byron laughed. "No. The food was

prepared earlier and kept warm, but it should still be fresh enough."

"It sure looks delicious." I peered up at him over the candlelight and found his smoldering gray eyes fixated on me, hungry for me as much as for the food before him.

We ate in relative silence, letting the classical strings take us away to a simpler world. The server checked in on us a few times, but there was nothing more either one of us wanted; everything we could ever want or need was right there.

"Should we move to the blanket?" the Prince asked after we'd finished eating.

"If that's what you had in mind," I said.

He stood up and dropped his napkin on the empty plate and came around to my side of the table, where he pulled out my chair and took me by the hand, leading me to the blanket spread on the ground. We both sat and leaned against the arranged back cushion of pillows.

The server came and cleared the table, then brought us a tiramisu to share. The Prince cut a slice with the edge of the fork, offering it to me. I let him feed me the bite, and it tasted as decadent as it looked.

With dessert finished and the table cleared, the server appeared a final time. "Is there anything else you desire?"

"Nothing more than I already have," the Prince

said, stealing a glance at me. "That will be all for this evening."

The server curtsied once again and left around the spotlight.

"Your playing has been beautiful. Thank you. However, you may leave us now," Prince Byron said and waited for the musicians to be gone—leaving us alone in the lighthouse—before saying anything more. "Thank you for coming out with me this evening. I couldn't have asked for anything more."

"No, it is I who should be thanking you for making it happen; no one's ever done anything like this for me before. I've never felt more like a princess."

"You've never looked more like one either."

My cheeks went hot at his comment and I dropped my gaze to the shrouded world outside.

Prince Byron took one of my hands in his. "Don't be nervous," he said. "You don't need to be anything other than yourself with me." He brushed my fingers with his thumb—slow, deliberate, gentle caresses. The hair all the way up my arm stood on end as his touch enlivened areas of my body I had not consciously felt before.

"I see your assistant kept you in your assigned color this evening. What shade of yellow is this?" Prince Byron asked, adjusting the pillows, and scooting closer to me.

"She called it *maize*." The neckline of my blouse was draped off the shoulder closest to him.

He slowly moved his hand up my arm, barely even touching my skin, until he reached my bare shoulder. "An excellent choice," he said. Then he leaned in to kiss me.

I stiffened from the soft touch of his lips and suppressed the urge to pull away again. I wouldn't be given another chance and… I wanted this. His attention and acceptance warmed me—stoked a growing fire deep inside that had been dormant for as long as I could consciously remember.

My lips tingled before finally going numb and my head swam from the sensations of where our bodies were joined. He smelled of ocean water and sand, and it was all as intoxicating as the wine.

The Prince pulled back and said, "I want to forget about the events of earlier in the week and move forward like I imagined from the first moment I saw you."

"You had a number of dates this week," I said. "Are you going to forget about them too?"

Prince Byron smiled from my obviously sarcastic comment but didn't respond. Instead, he pushed me back onto the pillows and kissed me under the stars like I was the only girl—not one of seven.

CHAPTER 32

*N*either of us was watching the time and it was late when we left the lighthouse. It was implied that we could have spent the night, but I didn't feel right about it, no matter how perfect the date had been.

That night, I finally got some sleep, but it was troubled as was usually the case with me.

I now felt I could better relate to what the Prince was going through with this whole clone competition. I reveled in our new physical connection and longed to see him again. His lips on me—on my bare shoulder, my neck, my lips—already felt like a dream. Too good to be true. And maybe it was. I had to remember where I really stood with him—far from the only one.

Both Bethany and Piper said I was glowing when

I saw them in the late morning, and they wanted to know everything.

"Seems like it was worth the wait," Bethany said.

"I can agree to that now," I said.

"Did you hear about the event tonight?" Piper asked.

"No," I said.

"We're having a formal dinner like on the first night with the Queen."

"I think even the Prince will be at this one," Bethany added. "Why hasn't your assistant told you?"

"I haven't seen her yet this morning," I said.

"You got dressed and everything all on your own?" Piper asked.

"Yes…? Didn't you?"

"No, I love the help. And she does my makeup so much better than I can do it myself."

"And you?" I asked Bethany.

"She always offers," she said sheepishly.

I enjoyed having Kimera around and loved her help, but certainly didn't need her for everything. I didn't want to start relying on her too much only to have her taken away at the end.

"What time's dinner?" I asked.

"6 p.m.," they both said.

"Well, then, I will have to confer with my assistant beforehand to ensure I'm presentable," I said.

I didn't have to call Kimera; I found a note when I returned to my room after lunch, informing me what time she'd arrive to help me prepare. I decided to fix myself a hot bath and soak in the water while waiting for the afternoon to pass and to have the pleasure of seeing Prince Byron again.

Kimera arrived right on time. By then, I was wrapped in my plush robe, my wet hair up in a clip, and relaxing with a book I had borrowed from the downstairs library. *Jane Eyre*.

"You're already halfway ready," she said, almost sounding disappointed.

"Doing my part to help out," I said, placing the closed book on the coffee table.

Kimera led me into the washroom to finish my hair and apply my makeup. She chose the same yellow cocktail dress I'd worn to the first dinner with the Queen. Instead of lavender, she accented this outfit with silver, including strappy wedge heels.

"I trust you remember how to get to the formal dining room?" she asked.

"I think I can manage."

"I can escort you if you'd like."

"Would you like to?"

"I don't want to be presumptuous."

I almost had to laugh. "Kimera, would you please escort me to dinner?"

"Of course, Miss Victoria."

I followed her to the dining room. She held open the towering wood door and I entered alone.

Prince Byron was seated at the closest head of the table, where I'd sat the first night. And of course, the two seats nearest to him were already taken—by Danielle on his right and Jane on his left. Piper sat beside Jane. I hadn't been the last to arrive this time; I grabbed the seat next to Piper, who gave me a friendly greeting as I sat down. Prince Byron greeted me with a smile as well, though he didn't rise and come over.

Eleanor and Bethany arrived shortly after me—Eleanor sitting beside Danielle and Bethany taking the seat on the other side of me.

Besides the Queen, the only one we seemed to be waiting on was Constance, whom I was surprised wasn't the first one there so she could be seated next to the Prince.

Queen Hart made her usual entrance with an entourage of servants and guards. Her servants stayed behind her as she glided over to the head of the table. The guards fanned out around the room's perimeter and we all rose, waiting for her to be seated, as was customary. And still, Constance had yet to arrive.

"I thought we were past all that," Piper whispered in my ear.

All the guards stood at full attention, hands

behind their backs, batons on their belts, ready for any disturbances.

"I guess we're still threats," I whispered back.

"Good evening, ladies," the Queen said. "Thank you for all being here, allowing us to enjoy another formal meal together. And this time, we have our guest of honor joining us." She raised her champagne flute and scanned the table. "*Almost* all of us, I guess." She nodded to one of her staff members who immediately rushed out of the room.

Almost as if on cue, Constance stormed into the room and made her way to the empty seat by Eleanor, close to the Queen. She made no effort to apologize for her tardiness.

"How nice of you to join us," the Queen said, glaring. Constance returned the glare full-on and raised her champagne flute to match the rest of us. "I wouldn't miss it, *Mother*."

I could tell the Queen was taken off-guard by Constance's brash tone, but dismissed it and continued with her toast. "Again, I'd like to thank you all for being here, allowing us to enjoy another formal meal together. And it is my honor to have Prince Byron joining us. To life, love, and the pursuit of happiness."

The staff members busied themselves with serving everyone at the table, starting with both heads, then working their way toward the center. Small bowls of soup were brought, which looked like little more than simple broth but the flavor from the spice combination was exquisite. Then the soup bowls were replaced by plates of salad.

The girls seated by the Prince at the end of the table were chatting the whole time. Those of us closest to the Queen were much less talkative. She seemed to be watching everyone like a hawk.

"What's going to happen to those of us remaining when Prince Byron chooses his Amelia?" Constance asked the Queen. Her tone matched her comment from when she arrived, which wasn't missed by the Queen.

"There are several options," she began, keeping her voice calm. "You will have the option to return to your home ward, to the family who raised you. We can help get you set up on your own in a ward of your choosing. You can—"

"I know, I for one never want to return to that hellhole, with what I had to endure from the family and all, but I'm sure you already know all about it."

"I assure you, I am not aware of any ill treatment. You were checked and treated regularly by my doctors—"

"More like poked and prodded like lab rats."

"I'm not appreciating your tone, Constance. If you can't control your tongue, then you can be excused."

"You'd like that, wouldn't you," Constance argued. "How about telling the table what's really

227

going to happen to the losers—what you've planned to do with us all along."

"I was already giving you the options when you so rudely interrupted—"

"And I'll continue to interrupt you until you tell us the truth—that the rest of us will be killed!"

"This is neither the time nor the place to be making such outlandish accusations," the Queen said, keeping her voice low, yet sharp like a viper.

"Is this true?" Danielle asked.

"I don't know where you got that idea, but I assure you that is not the case," the Queen said, now addressing the whole table.

"I overheard some of the staff talking about it," Constance said. "And it makes a lot of sense."

"Whatever you heard was either fully false or taken out of context," the Queen said. "I've invited all of you here tonight for a nice family dinner and that's what we are going to have. This subject is officially dropped until we have eaten, then we can talk about your options."

Constance sulked but obeyed.

The main course, which included steak, spinach, and squash, came shortly after. Two staff members carried open bottles of champagne and topped off any flutes needing more.

As the dinner plates were cleared, Piper spoke up. "When this is over, the new couple will be the face of Westeria, as well as Easteria. The return of

Princess Amelia will be huge. No one knows what she looks like now, but everyone will after this. We won't just be able to go back to our old lives, will we?"

"Looking the way you do now? No, that won't be an option," the Queen said. "But we have the technology to alter your appearances significantly. You will be able to look exactly like you want from a multitude of alterations and enhancements."

"I don't want to look different," Bethany said.

"And what will happen once we're out in the world and tell someone about your little science experiment?" Constance said. "It's going to come back and bite you in the ass. You're not going to take that chance. That's why you're not going to let us go."

"You will be leaving with many privileges still at your disposal," the Queen said. "You'll have no reason to discuss your true origins."

"You're buying our silence?" Piper asked.

"I'm taking care of you," the Queen said.

"You'll be taking care of us all right," Constance said. "Right here, under your own watch."

"I've told you I have no intention of killing any of you. I love all of you like my own daughter—which technically you all are. If you refuse to accept that, then that's your prerogative and you can leave right now. I will have you escorted out of the Château and returned to your—"

"Escorted out. Of Course!" Constance shouted. "If I walked out right now, I wouldn't make it home, would I? The only thing keeping me alive right now is remaining to play your stupid game. You wouldn't touch me—"

"I'm not going to listen to any more of this." The Queen rose from her chair.

"Are you a part of this?" Danielle asked Prince Byron. "I thought we were really building a connection, but if you—"

"No," Prince Byron said. "That is not part of this whatsoever. No one here will be harmed. The Queen and I have discussed placements of the remaining girls after this is over."

"You *would* fake offense and walk out in the middle of our discussion as a deflection for your lies," Constance shot at the Queen.

"This isn't a discussion; it's an ambush and I will not stand here and be attacked," the Queen said.

Constance rose from her chair too. Some of the soldiers were quietly approaching the table, batons being drawn.

"I haven't begun to attack you!" Constance took her champagne flute and splashed its remaining contents in the Queen's face. The bubbling liquid dripped down the front of her dress.

The Queen gasped and stumbled back a step as if she'd been slapped in the face.

One of the guards was behind Constance in a

flash and zapped her in the back with his baton. Her arms flew upward, her body arching back as the baton surged electricity into her. When the guard stopped the flow, she collapsed face-first onto the table—into a pool of spilled champagne and broken glass. Then blood began to flow from under her head.

The Queen's wet hair was falling into her face. She reached for her cloth napkin and patted her skin dry. All the servants had retreated. The table was now surrounded by soldiers, and everyone looked horror-struck, myself included. The Queen breathed heavily, scowling, her eyes on fire as she glared at the rest of us, daring the next person to challenge her.

"Please tell me it isn't true," Prince Byron said.

"The new Princess Amelia will be as public a figure as can be," the Queen said, throwing the napkin onto the table in a heap. "Those who remain will be threats to her legitimacy and I simply cannot allow that."

"This was not part of the arrangement." Prince Byron sounded wounded, in utter disbelief.

In a sudden rage, he was on his feet too. Several guards were nearby, batons blazing, but they did not approach the last few feet to subdue him.

"You never said anything about killing the remaining girls! I won't be a part of this!"

"Sit down, Byron," the Queen said. Her wet hair and running makeup made her look monstrous.

"Remember where you are. Remember *our* arrangement."

The two guards nearest him closed in, their batons only inches away.

"What? Are you going to have them electrocute me too? My family won't stand for this. My guards won't stand for this."

"Your guards are not here," the Queen said.

Prince Byron eyed the two guards flanking him, then decided to return to his seat.

Constance was groggily coming to. When she slowly raised her head from the table, there was a large pool of blood from the broken glass and several small shards remained in her face. She looked like she was still trying to figure out where she was.

"Look at her," I said to the Queen. "She needs help. You have to do something."

The Queen did not even acknowledge me. Her focus was now solely on Prince Byron. "I'm sorry it came out this way, but it's a necessity for the success of the new royal couple. I insist you be successful. I wish there were another way to guarantee the new Princess Amelia would not be challenged—that her legitimacy to the throne after me would not be challenged."

"I won't choose," Prince Byron said. His face was pure anguish. I thought about what he'd said on our date, about helping the others restart their lives. It wasn't a ruse. He truly hadn't expected this.

"Your parents want this union."

"Not like this."

"They've arranged for you to marry Amelia and that's what you'll be doing. You'll bring your Amelia home to them, they will approve, you'll be wed, and then you'll both live here as next in line to the throne under my family name. You will have children and the circle of royal life will continue."

"If they knew…"

"They will know what we tell them!" the Queen shouted. Her eyes blazed and she dug her long, talon-like nails into the table. "There will be nothing left for them to find. Any genetic test will confirm your Amelia is the real Amelia and you will live happily ever after with *my* daughter!"

"Happily ever after…" the Prince scoffed. "What about the rest of the girls at this table? The rest of *your* daughters?"

"I have but one daughter. I've always only had one daughter." Tears were welling up in the Queen's eyes and threatening to roll down her cheeks. "If you do not choose, then you kill them all."

"If I do not choose, then Amelia is truly dead," the Prince countered.

"I've accepted that for long enough," the Queen said, finishing the argument.

Prince Byron looked crestfallen. He sat amongst

the Queen's soldiers and the Queen's will and had nowhere left to go.

The Queen wiped her tears away. "This dinner took an unexpected and unpleasant turn. But here we are," she said, regaining what composure she could after everything that had happened. "There are only a few weeks left. It is true—there will be no consolation prizes or privileged placements. You are the Prince's chosen one or you are not. And if you are not, then that is the end of the line.

"Well... now you know the truth, and as usual, the truth is ugly. It's time to think long and hard —*how much do I want this?*" The Queen went to pick up her champagne flute, and when she found it empty, threw it down on the table.

Those of us closest to her shielded our faces from the shattering glass.

"I have no appetite for dessert," she said as she turned on her heel and marched out of the room. Many of the staff and guards followed, but enough remained to keep the peace.

I was speechless—frozen. Maybe this should have been expected, but I wanted to believe in the possibility something good could come from this. Now, even if I won, I'd be plagued by guilt forever. Amidst the luxury of the palace, the Queen had still managed to take everything from us.

"What are you going to do?" I heard Jane say to Prince Byron.

He glared at her with a mixture of anger and pity before storming out of the room himself. He couldn't even look at us—couldn't look at me. Everything he'd told me about helping the others would no longer come to pass. There'd be one winner. The rest of us would die.

CHAPTER 33

Most of the girls were too horror-struck by the Queen's revelation to do anything but moan, but I broke through my paralysis and rushed after Prince Byron. I didn't know what I'd say when I caught him, I just knew I had to say something—especially after the date we'd had.

I yelled to him when I reached the foyer and he was about to leave the palace, flanked by four guards —presumably his own—but he didn't respond. I wasn't about to let him leave me like this.

I ran out of the front door and down the few steps to catch him before he disappeared into his limousine.

"You're not leaving!" I screamed. "Not like this!"

He stopped at the open car door. "I can't do this," he said without turning to face me.

"You have to!" I demanded. "You don't have a choice."

"The hell I don't!" he shot back and finally turned to me. He waved his guards away and they gave us some space. "Life is nothing but choices. When you act—that's a choice. When you don't act—that's a choice too. I'm in over my head here. The Queen has taken advantage of me and my Kingdom. I cannot wage a war on her myself."

"If you leave, then we're all dead," I said, trying to plead to the guy who'd lain with me in the light-house, but who was lost within the angry façade standing before me now.

"If I choose one of you, then I'm condemning the others to death—literally killing the rest of you."

"You may not be able to save everyone… but you *can* save one. That has to be worth something."

"So, I suppose this is where the pleading starts, the begging, the bargaining, the promises of God knows what—whatever it takes—so I'll choose you." Prince Byron stepped toward me. He was coiled, tense, ready to strike. "Is that what this is?"

"I plead only for you to stay," I said, taking a step back from him. "I'm not pleading for my life, but for the life of whoever you choose. I want to make sure at least one of us has a chance. Maybe there will be an opportunity to save more—maybe there won't— but it has to at least start with one."

"So, this isn't about you?" he said. "What if I said,

today, I choose Bethany? That would be worth you running out here to stop me from leaving?"

"I would be heartbroken and don't want to die, but I would not regret anything I've said. I would be happy for her and accept the rest." Now, I was tearing up. In that moment, it truly felt like he was choosing her over me.

Prince Byron's anger and helplessness seemed to dissipate then too. "I believe you," he said after a long pause.

I heard frantic footsteps behind me and the Prince looked up. When I turned, I saw Constance, Danielle, and Bethany on the landing, gazing down at us. Constance's face was still streaked with blood.

Prince Byron closed the gap between us and kissed me on the cheek. "I have to go, but I'm not leaving," he said before getting into the back of the limousine and driving off.

I remained in the driveway shivering from my lack of a shawl in the crisp evening air. Bethany was at my side shortly after. I gave her a weak smile and glanced back at an empty front landing.

"What happened?" she asked.

"One of us still has a bright future ahead of her," I said, laying my head on her shoulder and beginning to cry.

"Then there's still time," she said, always the optimist. "Crying won't win the Prince's heart."

I started to laugh. "Don't let it go to your head, but I think you're the frontrunner now."

"How could that not go to my head? That's awesome! I'm officially sorry for you though."

"You better be!" I said and slapped her on the arm.

The tears were still flowing but we now were both laughing, which briefly lessened the sting of the evening before the reality set in of what the next few weeks would ultimately require.

Together, we went inside. We weren't about to wait for the Prince to return this evening; I just hoped he'd keep his word and come back at all.

I retreated to my room and Bethany to hers. I kicked off my shoes, collapsed face first onto my bed and cried. I had woken up on such a high—a confusing high—but a high nonetheless. Mere hours before, I'd had some semblance of control for the first time in my life and now it had been ripped away again. I screamed into my pillow and cursed the things going wrong in my life, which presently felt like *everything*.

Trying to get my sobbing under control, I reached for the phone and called Kimera, who arrived at my room promptly.

"What's wrong, Miss Victoria?" she asked, taking a seat beside me on the bed. She brushed my damp hair out of my face and wiped my cheeks with the soft fabric of her sleeve.

"Can you get Kale back here?" I asked. "Discreetly?"

She didn't answer right away, but when she did, it was a single word whisper. "Yes."

She left and Kale arrived with another tray of ice cream about an hour later.

He took one look at me, set the tray down on the nightstand and joined me on the bed. "What happened?"

"How's Mina? She did get there safe, didn't she?"

"Of course. I gave you my word. That's not why you called me here again after we swore to try and be more careful. Are you going to tell me what happened?"

I had called him there because I needed to tell him, but now he was sitting beside me with those anguished and quizzical eyes, I didn't know if I could. The only way I could manage to get the words out was by looking away. "Those of us not chosen will be killed," I finally said.

"What?" he asked. "Where did you hear that?"

"From the Queen. Six of us will be killed when this competition is over. The Prince will choose one of us, who will live happily ever after and the rest of us... will be killed... erased."

"What do you mean *erased*?"

"We shouldn't really exist—we don't really exist," I said, afraid to continue. "Haven't you noticed how similar the seven of us look? We're all the same age.

All the exact same build. Haven't you ever asked yourself why?"

"The Queen had had a difficult time conceiving Princess Amelia. That's become common knowledge. I heard she had numerous eggs implanted into surrogates—like your Duchess—so you're all twins. All pretty identical. I admit it's uncanny."

"We're all girls."

"That can be controlled, per the Queen's request."

"Wouldn't she have wanted boys? And you've seen us together. We're all completely identical. Isn't that strange?"

Kale shrugged. "I guess. But the world's a strange place."

I wiped my wet cheeks again. "What if I told you we were more than twins?"

"Meaning?"

"What if I told you the seven of us were clones?"

He stared down at me, trying to read my expression. "Are you being serious?"

"I guess there were originally eight of us, but one died," I said.

"If you're all clones, then you must be cloned from someone…"

"Princess Amelia," I said and waited for his reaction. When he didn't respond right away, I added, "That's it—now you know my big secret. I'm part of the Queen's confidential science experiment. And I have a one in seven chance of surviving past the next few weeks."

Kale's gaze was far away. He looked the way I felt when these bombs had originally been dropped on us. "I can't believe I didn't put all this together earlier."

"Put what together? How could you have known?"

"Where's Princess Amelia now? I haven't seen her since I got here. Is she really in remission?"

"She's dead," I said. "The winner of this twisted game will be announced to the Kingdom as the real Princess Amelia. It's all so messed up."

"If the Kingdom knew about this, there'd be a revolution," Kale said.

"I don't want to be the cause of a revolution."

"You wouldn't be the cause. The Queen would be the cause. You'd be the face of change. The catalyst."

"Or cursed as an abomination."

"No," Kale said. "I don't believe that."

"I'd understand if you'd want nothing to do with me now," I said, hiding my face under an outstretched arm.

"This doesn't change how I feel about you," Kale said, placing a hand on my back.

"How can it not?" I asked. He was taking this far better than I'd expected, especially since I was still trying to get *my* head wrapped around all this craziness.

He kissed the side of my head, and the gesture reminded me of how sweet and gentle he'd been with Mina. "I look at you and don't see you as anyone other than the beautiful girl I first met. Now, how about coming with me and getting away from here? I'm sure the Queen is going to be increasing her security, but if we move fast…"

I shook my head. "I don't want to do anything rash just yet. Everyone's pretty upset right now and I don't want to just abandon them. I may be able to convince a few others to come with us."

"Escape will literally get harder by the hour. And a bigger group—I don't know if it's a good idea," Kale said.

I thought of how I convinced Prince Byron to stay and couldn't simply do the same to him without feeling like a complete hypocrite, even though he wasn't the one putting his life on the line. I didn't want to make any decisions right now. "I can't leave tonight, but… what would be a good—safe time and place to meet you tomorrow?" I asked, hoping he wouldn't follow up with too many questions.

He thought for a moment and simply said, "Noon at the stables."

"That gives me time to talk with a few of the girls first," I said. "I know something has to be done… and time is short." I rolled onto my side to look at him. "I wish I could remember you from before. Maybe everything now would be different."

CHAPTER 34

"*I* saw the Prince this morning," Bethany said while we were together at breakfast. "Whatever you said to him seemed to have worked."

"Which is good news for one of us," I said.

"But we don't know who. So right now, each of us has the same probable chance."

"*You* all do." Piper had joined us halfway through breakfast.

"You have as much of a chance as any of us," Bethany said. "Well, Eleanor, not so much."

Bethany and I laughed, remembering how Eleanor had repeatedly thrown herself at the Prince without much physical reciprocation. But Piper didn't even crack a smile.

"He's not right for me," Piper finally said.

"Tall, dark, and handsome isn't right for you?" I said.

"I'm not denying his attractiveness and he seems a genuinely nice guy, but we don't have that special something... a true spark. I don't feel it. It won't work out between us."

"It sounds like you've already given up."

"Some relationships start slower. It doesn't necessarily mean there isn't or will never be a spark. You should still go for it," Bethany said. "He could still choose you."

"Don't you understand? I wouldn't want him to," Piper said. "I'd be denying him the great love story he may find with any one of you. Our relationship would be a lie. I couldn't do that to his true love. I wouldn't be able to live with myself."

"So, what are you saying?" I asked, lowering my voice and leaning in closer to her and Bethany.

"I don't know," she responded. "I don't know what I can do."

Kale strolled into the room with a dishtowel draped over his shoulder. "Can I get you lovely ladies anything else?"

"I'm stuffed," Bethany said.

"I'm fine," Piper said.

"No, thank you," I said, giving him a knowing smile.

Kale smiled back before disappearing into the kitchen. I watched him leave, thinking about what

I'd asked of him last night—along with what I planned to do next.

"What's going on between you two?" Bethany asked.

"Nothing," I said.

"I mean everyone's heard the rumors."

"And I already talked to Prince Byron about him," I said. "It's nothing." But I knew I'd have to tell them more very soon if my plan had any chance of working. "What are you guys doing around noon?"

"Nothing planned," Bethany said.

"Probably swimming or napping," Piper said.

"Okay, well; postpone those activities," I said. "Meet me out by the meadow fence near the stables at 12:15. I have something I'd like to discuss with the both of you."

"Why can't we just discuss it now?" Bethany asked just as Danielle and Jane entered the dining room.

"It's… umm… not for mixed company," I said, eyeing the girls taking seats at the far end of the table.

They eyed me back with the same intensity and contempt.

"Let's go outside now and talk about whatever it is," Bethany said.

"Yeah, don't leave us in suspense," Piper said. "I don't need any more on my mind."

"Let me get a few things in order first," I said. "I

don't mean to keep you in suspense. Can you both make it or not?"

Both girls agreed to meet me at the time I'd requested.

I WANTED to meet Kale as early as I could, so I went to the stables at a quarter before twelve. He was already there brushing Misty.

"I think she likes you," I said, leaning forward on the gate.

"The feeling's mutual," he said.

I entered the stall and patted her neck. Misty greeted me with a snort.

Kale stepped to me and met my lips with his. "How are you doing today? I hated seeing you like that last night."

"I'm feeling slightly better today and trying to stay positive, keep an open mind and give myself a purpose," I said.

"All good things. So, what's your new purpose? Is that why you wanted to meet with me?"

"Yes," I said. "One of the girls, Piper, definitely wants out."

"And you want me to smuggle her out like I did Mina."

"Yes."

"Will you be coming with us this time?"

"I'm not sure yet," I said. "I want to present the opportunity to Bethany as well."

"The more people are involved, the more dangerous it will be. As predicted, the Queen has increased security since yesterday and she's probably not done. It's getting harder." Kale was getting noticeably agitated.

"So, are you saying you can't do it?"

"No. The Queen can't lock me in."

"Good. Then will you do it?" I asked. "She's my friend and I don't want to leave her out."

Kale returned to brushing Misty's back. He walked around to her other side, but I didn't follow him. I gave him his space while he thought through what I was proposing.

"You have to agree to go too," I heard Kale say. "Or no deal."

"I'm trying to help these girls and you're giving me an ultimatum?"

"And I'm trying to help you," he said, making his way back around to face me.

"That's not fair."

"What part of this is fair?"

I ran both hands through my hair, pacing around the stall. I was making Misty nervous and had to stop myself to keep her calm.

"I'm in," I said, stopping before Kale.

"Then we're in business," he said.

I looked at my watch. "Wait here. I'll retrieve the girls."

Bethany and Piper were waiting by the wooden fence to the meadow. Piper was sitting on the top horizontal slat while Bethany paced before her.

I strolled up to them and got right down to business. "What we discuss here must stay between us," I instructed. "The only reason I'm bringing this up to you at all is because I consider you both friends in this demented competition. Do I have your word?"

"I'm not going to say anything," Bethany said.

"My lips are sealed," Piper agreed.

"Piper, you were saying earlier that you didn't know what to do since your relationship with the Prince wasn't going anywhere. What if I told you I could get you out of here—provide safe passage to wherever you want to go in the Kingdom? And Bethany, this offer is extended to you as well."

"I appreciate it. I really do," Piper said, and continued without pause. "But I can't leave."

"What? Why not?" I asked, taken aback. I certainly hadn't expected to be turned down.

"I know you had a difficult childhood, but I had a very loving and supportive family."

"Well, you can go back to them. They can help hide you if the Queen comes looking. I don't see the problem."

"You do understand our families are part of the competition as well, don't you?" Bethany asked.

"They are?" I asked.

"They are betting their statuses on us. The winning family will get a title promotion, to Archduke and Archduchess—like the Queen's extended family in the lower wards—and all the extra perks that go along with it. Families of the rest of us, provided we play the game to the Queen's satisfaction, should be left alone. But families of insubordinate contestants could potentially lose everything. I couldn't do that to my family."

"I couldn't either," Bethany said. "I don't want to dishonor them."

"Wow... Okay," I said, not sure where to go from there. "Then I guess we're all really doing this."

I leaned against the fence and looked out at the meadow. It was such beautiful land, on a beautiful day, that it seemed everything was as it should be. But I knew otherwise. This beautiful façade couldn't mask the fact our days were severely numbered.

"What are you girls talking about?"

I turned around and saw Danielle approaching from across the garden.

"Just admiring the scenery," Bethany said.

"Have you seen the Prince today?" Danielle asked. "I haven't and sure hope he hasn't run off on us."

"I saw him briefly this morning," Bethany said.

"Then there's hope." Danielle smiled, but it didn't feel sincere. She stood awfully close to Piper, who was still seated on the fence like she was ready to knock her off at any moment.

"I should go," I said and started backing away. "I'll see you girls later."

I glanced back several times as I made my way for the stables. All three girls were still where I'd left them. When I stepped inside, Kale was in the next horse stall, cleaning up.

"You're alone," he said, almost sounding unsurprised.

"I was wrong," I said. "No one seems to want out of this place."

"It's not easy to give up once you get a taste— even with your life on the line."

I walked up to the gate and he met me on the other side. It felt like I was visiting a prisoner, but the one jailed was actually me.

"It wasn't that," I said. "They talked about our families being involved with the competition too, and they didn't want them to lose everything they have over us—or something like that. They had good childhoods. I couldn't fully relate."

"So, what about you?" Kale asked, gripping the top of the gate, his arm muscles flexed.

"I don't know," I said. "What if something goes wrong? I don't want to get you in trouble either."

"We're not talking about me," Kale said. "We're talking about you. I want you to be safe. Are you still coming? Don't back out on me now just because the others aren't coming. This was never about them."

"I know." I could see the pleading in his bright blue eyes and wanted to make that look go away. I didn't want to disappoint him but didn't want to disappoint the Prince either. He had stayed. He had stayed *for us.* And I'd like to think it was mostly because of me.

"I know's not an answer."

"I know," I said again. "I mean I know it's not an answer. I want to go with you. To see Mina. But I can't lie to you—I've made a good connection with Prince Byron. I also want to know where that could go."

"There are six other girls saying the exact same thing."

"Five," I corrected. *"I know!* I don't want to make the wrong decision."

Kale ran a hand over his short hair and stepped away from the gate. He paced to the rear of the stall and back, and then placed both hands on top of the gate. Our faces were only inches apart.

"This shouldn't be a hard decision," he said softly, leaning in even closer. "This is your life."

But before I could reply, we both turned our heads to the sound of snapping twigs.

"Hey, guys," Danielle said, sheepishly. "Am I interrupting anything?"

"Not at all," Kale said. "Miss Victoria was just

telling me about her horse Misty over here." He pointed to the next stall.

"I was thinking about riding, but I've changed my mind," Danielle said, again with the fake smile. "I'll leave you to your conversation."

CHAPTER 35

"*What* do you think that was about?" I asked Kale after Danielle had left.

"Probably trying to get more gossip," Kale said.

"We are terrible at being careful," I said, shaking my head and biting my lip. "She's going to say she saw something. I know it."

"All the more reason to come with me. Whatever connection you think you have with the Prince, the competition is going to get ugly. You know that."

"I know," I said, starting to sound like a broken record.

"You seem to know everything, but you've yet to make a decision," Kale said, his stern face returning.

"I'm coming," I said after a long pause.

He almost seemed surprised but didn't say so. "Then I'll come get you tonight. I'll probably end up waking you, but be ready to go."

"I'll be ready," I said. I took a few steps and stopped at Misty's stall. "Can we take her?"

"No," he said. "We won't be traveling by horse and won't be able to transport her. I'm sorry, but she'll have to stay."

"Would you like to help me saddle her?"

"Of course, m'lady," Kale said, opening the gate with a loud creak, and strolling over to Misty's stall.

I hadn't planned on riding her now and wasn't dressed for it, but was going to do it all the same. I could have gone back to my room to change and come back, but I had the urge to go now. If I waited, I might not come back.

If I hadn't been wearing flats, I would have gone barefoot. I wedged a foot in the stirrup and kicked my other leg over, my skirt and petticoat fluttering with the movement and riding up on my thighs. I wasn't even about to ask for a helmet.

I took the reins and looked down at Kale, who had a queer expression on his face. "What?"

"Nothing," he said, a grin creeping into his expression.

Kale opened the gate and I led Misty out of the back door of the stable and into the open meadow. Once out in the sunlight and cool breeze, I kicked Misty into a gallop. It was so freeing to have the wind whipping through my hair. I took her all the way to the edge of the property, which extended for a good mile, and looped around with the same vigor with which we'd left.

By our third lap, I noticed someone standing by the fence, near the stables. From afar, I thought it was Kale watching me. But as Misty trotted closer, I realized it was Prince Byron, forearms resting on the fence, hands clasped, eyes fixed on me.

"Nice day for a ride," he said.

I had Misty walk up and stop beside him. "The best," I said.

"I recall you not riding with me on the first day we met because—what had you said—oh, that's right, that it wouldn't be proper due to what you were wearing."

"And I still stand by that," I said, smiling at his enthusiastic animation. "As you said, we had only just met."

"And now?"

"Now we are better acquainted and such formalities are less… necessary."

"I see," the Prince said. "You can finally let your hair down."

"As you can see, I am," I said, running a few fingers through my windswept hair.

Prince Byron reached past the fence and touched my calf with the tops of his fingers, moving slowly down toward my ankle. When he reached it, he opened his hand and brushed his fingers back up toward the back of my knee. His eyes moved with his hand, drinking in my bare skin. Then his expression darkened.

"What's this?" he asked and gently lifted the hem of my skirt and petticoat.

I looked down and saw he was fixated on the underside of my thigh; though the red welts had greatly faded, pink lines still crossed my skin.

"Oh, that's nothing," I said and readjusted the skirt, pulling it down as far as it would go.

"No, really."

He tried pushing my hand away, but I commanded Misty to take a few more steps away from the fence, out of his reach. Instead of taking the hint and respecting my privacy, he effortlessly hopped the fence and tried to approach.

"I said it's nothing," I repeated. "Please, just leave it be."

"Who did this to you?"

"I really should be going. I'm sorry," I said and maneuvered the reins to lead Misty away; we trotted into the stable.

Kale was still there and helped me down from my horse. He took the reins and guided Misty into her stall.

"Good ride?" he asked.

Just then, Prince Byron came running around the corner.

"I'm sorry, I didn't—" He stopped running and talking when he saw Kale.

I hadn't wanted to talk to him about this before-hand, but certainly not in front of Kale.

"Can we talk?" Prince Byron asked, glancing at Kale as he spoke.

"I really don't want to talk about this," I said. And I didn't want to move away from Kale. I knew other girls had opened up more about their past lives, and I'd talked to him about life in the 24th Ward, but not about my punishments from Master Ramsey. I couldn't talk to him about it, or anyone else.

"I'm only trying to help. I'm concerned." Prince Byron's eyes couldn't stay off Kale. "Was it him? Is that why you're afraid to leave with me right now?"

"What—no," I said. "Kale's been nothing but kind to me. You don't have to worry about me."

Kale was now looking at me, seemingly concerned, but didn't speak up. As a servant, it wasn't his place.

"I thought your name was Jimmy," Prince Byron said, now addressing Kale directly.

Now I knew where his concern was coming from. I wasn't thinking and had slipped up.

"Both, actually," Kale said, without skipping a beat. "Kale's my middle name. I told it to Miss Victoria and she seems to fancy calling me that over Jimmy. I mean no offense."

"I see…" Prince Byron said. "Can you leave us? I'd like to talk with Victoria alone."

Kale glanced at me before responding. "Of

course, Your Majesty." He exited Misty's stall and was about to leave.

"That won't be necessary," I said, placing a hand on Kale's shoulder. "You may finish your work. We'll take this outside."

Prince Byron was severely assessing the both of us, but I did my best to stay calm. All I had to do was make it until that night, and then I'd be gone.

"Very well," Prince Byron said and joined me outside. "What was that in there? He's the guy everyone's been talking about."

"Nothing was going on," I said. "I had been riding and he was working in the stable. That's all. You are cornering me to talk about private things. That is the tension you felt—and perhaps, still feel. I've tried to open up to you, but there are some things I'm not ready to talk about yet."

"I know it's hard and we've only known each other a short while," the Prince said, his tone soft. He reached for my hand. "I don't want to push you past what you're comfortable with, but we don't have much time. This isn't your typical courting process. We need to take advantage of every moment and not hold back. Myself included."

"I'm really trying," I said. "Some skeletons are hard to unbury."

"May I see?"

"Please stop asking," I said. "Because if you do, I'll end up showing you and I really don't want to."

Prince Byron sighed and looked down at my hand in his. "I trusted you enough to stay and deal with what the Queen has done. Please trust me in return."

"Please be patient with me," I said. "I know there isn't much time, but there is some. You can ask me almost anything, but this is something for which I need more time."

"I'm a patient man, but our hourglass has only so much sand left and it's draining steadily." Prince Byron brushed my cheek with his thumb, looking me directly in the eyes. "I don't want to lose you."

I tried not to let my guilt show. He already had and it was through no fault of his own—it was this terrible situation we'd all been placed into. What else was I supposed to say to him?

Maybe I should just have given him what he wanted. If it was so easy, I would have done. Showing a man I cared about—a man for whom I was developing true feelings—what another man had done to me, rendered me far too vulnerable. And I didn't yet know how to get past that feeling.

"It looks like we have company," Prince Byron said with a groan.

I thought maybe Kale had come out from the stable, but when the Prince gestured to the far side of the garden, I saw Eleanor approaching.

Perfect. She'd make for a fine distraction.

"Don't leave me alone with her," he said,

sounding worried.

I had to laugh at his plea. "Perhaps you need more time to get to know her better."

"I don't think that's the case."

"Victoria," Eleanor called to me. "Piper said you were out here. You're wanted inside."

So, this was about me. "What is it?"

"Your family's here."

"My family?"

"Yeah. I don't remember their names, but they're looking for you," Eleanor said, almost to us now.

"I'll come with you," the Prince said quietly to me.

"My Prince, is this a good time?" Eleanor asked.

"Looks like you're being summoned as well," I said with a chuckle and gave him a chaste kiss on the cheek.

I was about to leave at a time when I thought I might not see him again, giving me the clarity to know how much I didn't want to say goodbye. I felt we had that spark Piper said she was missing, and I didn't want to look at this as winning a competition but simply winning his heart. What I'd just seen in his eyes made me believe he felt the same about me.

I couldn't leave him with just a kiss on the cheek. I wanted him to know how I truly felt, even though this was ending without him knowing. Despite having Eleanor standing right there, waiting for me to leave, I kissed the Prince with the passion and possibility of never seeing him again.

CHAPTER 36

*P*rince Byron wasn't happy about me leaving him alone with Eleanor, but she wasn't about to let him get away now she'd sunk her needy claws into him.

Now, I was concerned with who I was about to find inside and could guess the reason for the unannounced visit; I could do nothing to help them.

I was greeted by one of the staff members as soon as I entered the palace; the Ramseys' arrival was announced and I was led to a formal sitting room—really a waiting room—off the foyer.

I found Master and Lady Ramsey sitting on a couch, with refreshments set on the coffee table before them. Lady Ramsey was sitting back, sipping a cup of tea, while Master Ramsey leaned forward, arms on his knees, his hands in an outward steeple.

"There she is," Master Ramsey said. His tone suggested anything other than happiness to see me.

And the feeling was mutual.

Lady Ramsey gave a weak smile, which I returned with the same wariness. Under better circumstances, I'd have been glad to see her.

"You may leave us with our daughter," Master Ramsey said to the servant.

"No. I insist you stay," I said, placing a hand on the young lady's shoulder. Her terrified eyes wavered between the two conflicting demands, but she didn't move.

"Back home, I would have you punished for your insolence," Master Ramsey threatened.

"Good thing we're not at your estate. Here, you are not permitted to lay a finger on her," I said. My hands were shaking. My healing wounds tingled but I wasn't about to back down.

"Indeed, we're not," Master Ramsey said. His eyes were ice.

"We've come to ask you about Mina," Lady Ramsey said, trying to cut through the tension.

"What about Mina?" I asked, trying my best to sound confused and honestly not know why they were here. "So, you're not here to check up on me?"

"We couldn't care less about you," Master Ramsey growled. "Mina has gone missing since shortly after the masquerade ball. We have it on good authority she came back here—to see you."

"She did," I said. There was no need to lie about it, especially since it could be verified by multiple people at the palace. "She stayed for the evening and then I sent her home."

"Did you send her with an escort? Something that can be tracked and verified?" Master Ramsey questioned.

"Why did she come here in the first place?" Lady Ramsey asked. If I mentioned why she had come, then my story of sending her home would fall apart.

"I did not send her with an escort," I said. "She made it here with no problems so I didn't see any reason why she couldn't make it home on her own. She's a responsible girl."

"A responsible girl wouldn't simply run away," Master Ramsey said. "And a responsible older sister wouldn't send a 12-year-old across the Kingdom without a chaperone. You had one if you remember, and you're five years older."

"May I go now?" the servant asked.

"Yes," Master Ramsey replied.

"No!" I insisted.

She tried to take a step back, but I clamped onto her arm to keep her beside me.

"Everyone, please calm down," Lady Ramsey said. "Victoria, this is not an interrogation. We're just worried for our little Mina."

"She didn't send her home!" Master Ramsey snapped at his wife. "She's hiding her. I'm willing to bet Mina's still here." He turned back to me. "You have no right! She is *our* daughter—*our* responsibility!"

"Then you shouldn't be driving her away!" I shot back.

"What did you say?"

I knew I was getting into dangerous water. "She's not here," I said, trying to sidestep what I'd just said.

"Then where is she?"

"I told you. I instructed her to go home."

"But she never made it home," Lady Ramsey said.

"That's all I know," I said.

The servant beside me squirmed, and I realized how tightly I was gripping her arm.

"You're lying," Master Ramsey said, his deep voice nearly a whisper now—a sinister breath of cold air.

"What seems to be the problem here?" Prince Byron entered from the foyer, his confident stride owning the room. He came to stand beside me. "Duke and Duchess Ramsey, I presume. It is a pleasure."

"Your Highness," Lady Ramsey said. She stood and curtsied.

Master Ramsey's only genuflection was a curt nod. "We're looking for our youngest daughter."

The young servant weaseled out of my grip and sped away. I didn't care now I had the Prince by my side—come to my aid.

I quickly rehashed what had already been said.

"So she's not here," Prince Byron said. "I'm sorry we could not be of more help."

"I would like to see her room," Master Ramsey said, his eyes still trained on me.

"Let's go. I'll take you," Prince Byron said. He didn't wait for the Ramseys to follow but started heading for the curved staircase.

I kept his pace with the Ramseys in tow. The Prince placed a hand on the small of my back to keep me close to him as we made our way upstairs. His touch still sent shivers through me.

"I hope this is okay," he whispered into my ear as we continued down the hallway, passing the colorful rooms of my competition, with our prize at my side.

"With you here, it is," I answered. I glanced back and discovered two guards behind the Ramseys.

Upon reaching my door, Prince Byron swung it inward and stood just outside, gesturing for the suspicious Master Ramsey to enter first. Lady Ramsey followed with a submissive *thank you.*

The Prince and I entered last and let the anxious parents explore at their discretion.

Lady Ramsey appeared to be perusing the room more than looking for something or someone. Master Ramsey, on the other hand, meticulously checked every door, drawer, and obstructed space; it was obvious he knew he wouldn't find Mina there, but he was looking for any clue to cast light on her whereabouts.

The two guards were now stationed just inside the room, blocking the doorway.

"Are you satisfied?" Prince Byron asked.

"I won't be satisfied until I've found my daughter," Master Ramsey said, walking out of the washroom.

"This is a very lovely room, Victoria," Lady Ramsey said.

"I'll tell the Queen you thought so," I said, politely.

Master Ramsey picked up my borrowed copy of *Northanger Abbey*, examined the leather-bound cover, and tossed it aside like trash.

"I understand your frustration," the Prince said. "But Victoria has told you what she knows. We have graciously complied with your request to search her room. Unless you have a social agenda for staying, I believe it's time for you both to leave."

"I demand to see the Queen," Master Ramsey said marching up to the Prince until they were nearly nose to nose.

"Your demand is noted, but no," Prince Byron said. "Demands are not how you are granted access to the Queen. You may put in a request with the Executive Assistant to the Sovereign."

"With the job we've been given by order of the Queen for the past eighteen years, this is how you're going to treat me? We raised this girl you're so fond of."

"And I thank you for your service. But protocol remains."

Master Ramsey leaned in closer and I almost couldn't hear him. "Don't think I don't know it was you," he said. "The mask didn't fool me one bit. If it wasn't for your guards to protect you…" Master Ramsey let the unfinished thought linger before snapping his fingers at Lady Ramsey. "Come, Beatrice."

Once they were gone, I let out a long breath. "Thank you for all that," I said.

"I won't ask you anymore—not until you're ready to talk about it," Prince Byron said. "I think I now understand. And I'm sorry."

I went to the door and asked the two guards to leave. They complied with my request like I had some type of power. I remained facing the closed door when I lifted the skirt and petticoat to my waist, revealing Master Ramsey's last desecration wounds on my body. The shrinking weals were still clearly visible, yet the pain was nearly gone.

I heard a gasp from behind. Footsteps approached. I couldn't turn to face him and just continued to hold up my skirt.

"Move away from the door," he demanded.

"No," I said. "You're not going after him. He's in

my past and I want to leave him there. These are reminders he'll never lay a hand on me again."

"I can have anything done to him you wish."

"I wish for him to be forgotten. I wish to move forward, not back."

I felt hesitant fingers moving across the ridges of my wounds. And again, they tingled. Then he was coaxing my hands to free my skirt and let it fall.

Prince Byron spun me around and pulled me to him. His arms wrapped around me like a warm blanket; my head rested comfortably on his chest.

"Thank you for trusting me so much," he said, his warm breath on my neck as he embraced me tighter.

CHAPTER 37

I was awakened by a forceful nudge. I opened my eyes and saw the shadowed face of Kale gazing down at me. The room was still dark, the world outside my windows still asleep.

I'd fallen asleep recalling the Prince's gentle touch running along the wounds on my thighs, and the gratitude in his eyes for my opening up to him despite me not saying a word. When he'd left, I'd felt like a part of me departed with him.

"Rise and shine, sleepyhead," Kale said. "It's time to go."

After a groggy second, I was pulled out of the grasp of slumber quickly, realizing what we were doing. My adrenaline spiked as I threw off the bed sheets and sat up. We were leaving the palace, escaping the Queen and her demented game. And we wouldn't be coming back; I'd most likely never see Prince Byron again.

Kale saw I'd slept fully dressed—in casual pants and a sweater—and seemed satisfied with my preparedness.

I reached for a hair tie on the nightstand and pulled my unruly hair into a ponytail before slipping on a pair of lace-up shoes so they wouldn't kick off when I tried to run. I'd be bringing nothing else, no baggage to slow us down. I had money left from the Ramseys that would get me started and I'd have to build a new life from there.

"I have a guy waiting out back. It's nearly the shift change, so the night shift is nearing the end. The men are tired and ready to sleep. We need to move quickly."

"Then let's go," I said, rising to meet him.

"Do you have everything you need?"

"Everything I'm bringing fits in my pockets," I said.

"Okay, now I'm totally getting déjà vu."

I shrugged, assuming he was referring to another time I couldn't remember.

Kale threw me a coat that had been draped over the desk chair. "Put this on. It won't conceal your identity that much, but at least at a glance, you won't be instantly recognizable."

I donned the black cotton coat and pulled up the hood.

"In the pocket, you'll find a small phone so we can find each other if we unexpectedly get separated."

I found the device and examined it. "It's not connected to anything." I pressed a button and a tiny screen lit up.

"There's a lot of technology out there that you haven't been privy to yet. Trust me, it works just like the phone on your nightstand." He looked me over before opening the door and peering cautiously into the hallway. "It's clear," he said and gestured for me to follow as we quietly crept to the first floor of the palace.

The first staff members we saw were arranging breakfast place settings in the dining room. They were prattling on about life in the palace hopefully returning to normal once the new Princess was announced. Kale stopped at the corner and waited for everyone's backs to be turned before leading me by the hand past the extended doorway.

We exited the palace through one of the glass doors leading to the back garden; the stables were just beyond. I saw a dark figure standing at the entrance of the stable where Misty was held, and shuddered.

"Someone's watching us," I whispered.

"Where?" Kale stopped and crouched.

I mimicked his movements. "There, by the stable." I pointed.

"Okay. We're good," he said and we continued through the winding path of the garden.

Then I heard a loud whistle sounding like it came from the direction of the stable. Kale dropped to the ground again, this time lying flat on his stomach. I did the same.

"Our lookout spotted someone—or multiple someones," Kale whispered. "Stay down and don't move."

I was on the ground for what felt like forever, waiting, listening into the night, trying to make out any sounds beyond the symphony nature provided. I flinched, hearing the crunch of boots on dead leaves and twigs; it sounded close. Kale didn't move. I thought my heart was pounding so hard it could be heard by whoever was passing nearby. Then, the footsteps disappeared.

I listened closely, trying to pick up the sound again. Then another crunch caught my attention. It seemed further away and I let out the breath I found I'd been holding onto.

We continued to hide and wait in silence.

The next distinguishing sound ringing out into the night was the clink of metal hitting metal—like a hammer to a horseshoe. There were three quick clinks.

"Okay, let's move," Kale said as he hopped to his feet.

I trailed him as we continued through the garden,

making our way toward the stable and the shadowed figure stationed by its entrance. On reaching it, I recognized the staff member from around the palace, though he wasn't someone I'd previously interacted with.

"Joshua," Kale said, shaking the bearded man's hand.

"They're saddled and ready for you both," the man said.

"Hello, ol' girl," I said as I approached Misty's open stall.

She neighed as I stroked her neck.

Joshua was then at my side, offering to help me up, but I shook my head and climbed up on Misty's back by myself. Kale was already seated on the thoroughbred in the next stall.

"Thanks for the help," Kale said to Joshua, kicking his horse into a full gallop before he exited the stable's back door.

I was right behind him in a chase through the open meadow, under the sinking moonlight. The horizon now wore its first hues of pink as we raced to what I hoped was freedom.

The perimeter wall securing the Queen's property was tall, with bird spikes atop the stone, serving more than just to prevent a perch for the birds. I wasn't aware of any exits besides the driveway gate.

But we continued to ride through the slowly dissipating darkness. As we drew closer to the wall,

Kale pulled his horse right, toward the wooden picket fence and the trees beyond. He wasn't slowing; his horse remained at full stride—and then when he reached the fence, Kale's horse leaped over it.

I'd done a lot of riding, but never attempted any type of significant jump. I tried not to over-analyze it. I was an experienced rider. There was no reason I couldn't do this as the fence was not that high. It was more of a border marker than anything else.

I braced myself for the jump, rising slightly off the saddle, one hand held tightly to the reins and the other gripping the horn for balance and support. Misty made the jump a few seconds behind Kale, and we were back on solid ground before I even knew it. I had to readjust my position on Misty's back, but I was still upright and we raced in between the trees.

After another fifteen minutes of riding, we found the perimeter wall again, with two guards idly standing by.

Is this it? Stopped at the wall?

Kale continued straight toward them, slowing only to jump off his horse in one smooth maneuver.

I brought Misty to a stop and dismounted—not quite as smoothly.

"Everything good?" Kale asked.

"You're clear to leave," one of the guards said and handed Kale what looked like a pair of train tickets.

Kale skimmed the printed information and stuffed the tickets into a back pocket. "Thank you."

One guard took the reins of Kale's horse and the other took Misty's from me.

"There's one way out and no way back in," the guard holding Misty's reins said. "Are you sure you want to continue?"

"She's sure," Kale said, taking a step closer to me.

The guard looked to Kale and then back at me.

I nodded.

The other guard kicked some of the leaves away by the wall—and I suddenly realized he was uncovering a wooden door in the ground. He pulled on the metal ring and the door opened with a tortured screech. Concrete steps descended into the abyss.

Kale pulled a miniature flashlight from his front pants pocket and shone it down the stairs, dispelling the immediate darkness ahead.

"This is it," Kale said and stepped into the tunnel that would lead us to freedom.

CHAPTER 38

*T*he door behind us boomed closed, preventing any hope of turning back. The only light left came from Kale's flashlight.

"Why do you think he asked if I was sure?" I asked.

"I was wondering the same thing," Kale said. "We've got our tickets. The train leaves in exactly one hour, so we need to move fast. As long as the car's waiting, we'll be fine."

"And if it's not?"

"Then we'll have to exchange these for a later train. The earlier the better. We want to get out of the 1st Ward as soon as possible." Kale picked up his pace, causing me to nearly jog to keep up.

We came out of a mostly obstructed drain. A trickle of water had appeared somewhere along our walk, muddying the ground. Then the enclosed space had begun to smell like mold and rotting fruit. There was something on the ground ahead of us, which from afar looked like a bolder, but as we drew closer, it revealed itself to be an animal carcass—of something large.

Kale carefully stepped over it and took my hand to help me over too. He leaned down, shining his flashlight on the mass—it was the dead body of a man, dirty and disheveled. I couldn't tell if he'd been in that condition before his demise, but there was an ugly hole in his head from what looked like a gunshot.

I gasped at the realization I was gazing upon a murdered human corpse.

"If this doesn't say *no turning back*, then I don't know what does," Kale said. "He doesn't look like he's been here that long."

"Let's get out of here," I insisted, trying to subdue the rising nausea.

We jumped down a few feet from the end of the pipe and had to scramble up a dirt hill to reach the road. Fifty yards away, a black sedan waited, parked off the edge of the road since it offered no paved shoulder.

Kale ran up and opened the back door. He ushered me inside and slid in beside me.

"Go," he said and the car sped away.

I saw the eyes of the driver glance back at us, but he didn't say a word. I removed my hood and peered out of the back window, at the spot where we'd exited the tunnel, feeling pretty good about our escape. Everything seemed to be going according to Kale's plan and I knew he'd keep me safe.

Before the road curved enough to lose sight of where we'd exited, I noticed a shadowy figure clamber up and onto the road, silhouetted in the dim light of dawn. He rose to his feet and watched us drive away. He was either one of Kale's guys checking to make sure we'd escaped, or someone had followed us.

"I saw someone back there," I said, turning to face forward in my seat.

Kale put an arm around me and pulled me into him. I rested my head on his shoulder.

"You're safe now," he said.

We drove a half hour through the early morning while most people of the 1st Ward would still be waking. The roads were mostly empty as we drove around Capital City's downtown area.

The terminal for the Inter-Ward Express seemed to be where most people out at this hour of the morning were congregating.

Kale thanked the driver when we arrived at the Capital Central train station; the man still didn't say a word. Our train was already waiting for us and we rushed toward the porter. Kale gave him both of our tickets and we were welcomed aboard.

We didn't have the same sort of luxurious accommodation given to me when I'd left the 24th Ward. Instead of our own private car, we had a bench in a shared one. I had to let go of the fantasy of royalty and reacquaint my life to that of a more common caste, but it fitted me much better anyway. I'd always been used to doing most things for myself.

"What are you thinking?" Kale asked. There was plenty of room on the bench seat, but he shuffled close to me.

I gazed out of the window at the lively terminal, the busy city we were also leaving behind. "Wondering where my life is headed now," I said.

"A place where we can be together. Where you can see Mina again. A place where you'll finally be safe," he said.

I desperately wanted to believe him, and when the train started to move, I finally let myself relax into the vision. I watched the edge of the terminal come and go as the train picked up speed. We had made it; soon, the 1st Ward would be a distant memory too.

But suddenly, with bells blaring and brakes screeching, the train began to decelerate.

"What's happening?" I asked. Passengers on other benches asked similar questions.

"I don't know," Kale answered, leaning over me to look out of the window. "I don't see anything. Maybe someone important arrived late or someone with an emergency needs to get off. Nothing to worry about." He returned to his original seated position next to me.

I wasn't so sure. After spying the guy climbing onto the road when I'd glanced from the car's back window, I was paranoid about being followed.

I kept my eyes glued to the window, looking as far back as I could, which was the edge of the terminal.

Our porter was now on the gravel outside, frantically blowing his whistle. Then I saw *him*. He jumped down from the concrete platform onto the gravel and took off running in our direction.

Prince Byron.

CHAPTER 39

*H*ad the Prince been the one I'd seen on the road?

I glanced back at Kale who was sitting comfortably, waiting for the train ride to resume. Outside, Prince Byron passed by our window and stopped to question the porter. Six of his guards were trailing him. I was about to mention what was happening when Prince Byron ran up the stairs and burst into our car.

"Amelia!" the Prince exclaimed.

There were gasps from other passengers in the train car who recognized him, a wave of murmurs spreading the word like wildfire. Kale shot up from his seat and backed up into the aisle.

"Have mercy on her," Kale pleaded, his hands up in surrender.

I sat frozen in my seat, staring at the Prince's

melancholy gray eyes, speechless. It took a moment for the name he'd used to register. *I* was Amelia.

"Don't go," Prince Byron said, making no effort to address Kale. He was breathing heavily from his race to get to us and now took slow, apprehensive steps toward me. "You came after me. You convinced me to stay. I trusted you that we could make the most of the unsettling situation we've all been thrown into. Now trust me. I beg of you, don't go."

Glancing back outside, all his guards seemed to have stopped. No one was joining him on the train to drag either of us away.

"Does she actually have a choice?" Kale asked.

"She does. You're not really one of the Queen's staff, are you?"

"No use in lying about it now."

"I can't go back there," I said. "I can't go back knowing what time I have left."

"You can't know that," Prince Byron said. "Because *I* don't know that. When I discovered you'd gone, I didn't want to continue this journey without you. I know it's selfish, but I need you in this—I need *you*."

"What happens if I refuse?"

"Then I'll walk off this train and let you go with your chosen protector. I will not follow and I will not reveal anything to the Queen. She will most likely pursue you, but she'll get no assistance from me. I'm not here to force you to do anything. I'm here to beseech you to stay—to stay *with me*."

I couldn't believe what I was hearing. I wanted to be able to decide and know I was headed in the right direction. I was standing before two closed doors with no idea what was behind either one. I'd come to trust Kale's intentions were true, but I didn't know if I'd be safe with him, especially with Master Ramsey in search of Mina. And I didn't know if the Prince would choose me.

Unexpectedly, Prince Byron dropped to one knee. "In this moment, I am not your Prince. I'm simply a man asking for a chance from a princess —*my* princess."

"Is that her?" I heard someone say.

"Is that the Princess?"

"It can't be..."

"Princess Amelia?"

"It's actually her?"

"What's she doing here?"

"Why's she dressed like that?"

"She looks so beautiful."

"It's a miracle!"

My head was spinning from all the comments and questions flooding the train car. How could he hide this? The word was out now and would spread from this train car to the far reaches of the Kingdom. With the competition ending in a few short weeks, maybe it wouldn't matter. But the Queen would still know something had happened—something beyond her control—and who knew how she would react?

I couldn't tear myself away from the mixture of anguish and hopefulness in his eyes. I believed for a moment that I was the only one—but then had to remember there were so many other girls waiting back at the palace, vying for this man's affection. But still, I wanted to believe there was something we had —something we shared that the others couldn't match.

"You opened up to me yesterday with something I know was incredibly difficult. And it wasn't the fact you opened up, but how hard it was for you to do so, yet you did it anyway; you let me in. Well, I'm in. *All* in. I know these are not normal circumstances and these are irregular times, but I ask you to put your faith in me."

"Are you saying I'm the one?" I finally managed to ask.

"I've never knelt for anyone other than my own parents. I am your servant. I'm saying I can't go on without you and I'll do whatever possible to find a way to save the others. I know you want to help them as well. We will not let the Queen have the final say."

Kale reached out to me. "Vi—Amelia, you can't be seriously considering this."

"I can't stay here," I said, gazing up into his

pleading eyes. Murmurs from the other passengers continued echoing throughout the car. "My cover is blown."

"That's not a reason to go back," Kale said. "We can make other arrangements and slip back to anonymity."

I sadly shook my head. Both men wanted me to do things for them, but in the end, I had to follow my heart and make the decision that was best for me —which didn't necessarily mean the *right* decision. "I'm sorry, but I think I have to do this," I said.

"Are you doing this for *him* or *them*?"

"Why can't it be both? Why can't it simply be for me?"

Prince Byron returned to his feet. "I will not let any harm befall her."

"You'd better not," Kale warned. "I'm not just going to disappear."

"I wouldn't expect anything less," the Prince said. "In fact, I'd be disappointed if you did."

"Please keep Mina safe until this is over," I said. "Then I'll come for her."

Kale nodded. "I wish there was something else I could say or do."

"Please don't make this any harder than it already is," I said and dashed out into the aisle. I hugged Kale and it took him a moment to return the embrace. "Thank you, for everything."

"Keep your eyes open," he whispered into my ear.

"I'll be careful," I said and let him go. My eyes were stinging and my composure threatening to crack. I had to turn away, but then facing the Prince didn't help with holding myself together.

His hand was outstretched, beckoning me forth. I fretfully went to him, becoming more unsure of my decision with each step. I wanted him, but not everything that choosing him would come with.

"I won't let anyone else hurt you," the Prince said and drew me into him.

He tried to kiss me, but I didn't feel comfortable with being physically affectionate in front of all those people—especially Kale. I felt I was hurting him enough by leaving.

"I'm sorry," Prince Byron said to Kale. "But please be assured, she's in good hands."

"I lost Victoria the moment she boarded the train to the 1st Ward," Kale said.

I couldn't bear to glance back as Prince Byron ushered me off the train.

CHAPTER 40

The Queen greeted us upon our return to the palace. She was in the front sitting room, off the foyer, waiting like a concerned parent.

"I heard there was a commotion this morning," she said as we entered the room. "Would you care to elaborate?"

"I don't know about any commotion," the Prince said. "We went out to watch the sunrise over the mountains, then stopped for an early morning breakfast."

"Dressed like that?" The Queen was certainly directing the comment at me.

"Not everything has to be so formal. I asked her to dress comfortably and that's what she chose," Prince Byron said. "She's beautiful in whatever she's wearing."

"It was chilly this morning," I added.

"I'm sure your assistant could have found you something more appropriate, more befitting of a princess."

"But I'm not a princess yet, am I?" I countered.

"You should be dressing for the part you're striving to get."

"She's fine and there's no problem," the Prince said in his formal, diplomatic tone, coming between the Queen and me.

The Queen excused us and we went up to my room. I unzipped my coat, shrugged it off and threw in on the back of the desk chair.

"I must admit, I'm pleasantly surprised I convinced you to come back," Prince Byron said, pacing the room.

"I wasn't expecting to be back," I said. "But I want to be with you, as well as save the other girls from the Queen's slaughter."

"I want you too. And I want to announce it to the world, but we can't yet. I need to continue playing the Queen's game until I can secure the safety of the other girls."

I collapsed onto my bed with a sigh of exhaustion, anticipation, and overwhelm. "Just as long as you don't go falling in love with one of them."

"Not possible," Prince Byron said, redirecting his pacing over to the bed.

I had curled up on my side. He crawled behind

me and lay with his warm body pressed against mine.

"Anything's possible," I said.

The Prince draped an arm over me and found one of my hands. I craved his touch and couldn't wait for the day he'd be exclusively mine. I wanted it to happen straight away but knew we needed a plan before making an announcement to the Queen. Otherwise, the rest of the girls would die and it would be all my fault.

Then I saw a card propped on the desk. I didn't remember seeing it before, so I wiggled out of his arms to go take a closer look.

"What is it?" the Prince asked.

I didn't answer him and proceeded to open the card and read what had been written inside. "Oh, it's just a note from Kimera," I said and turned back to him. "She wanted to let me know she'd dropped by this morning."

"That was nice of her. Are you going to come back and lie down?"

I was up now and still reeling from the deluge of emotions that made up the past few hours. I needed time to myself. "I think I'm going to take a bath and fix myself up," I said. "The Queen was right. I'm a mess."

"You're gorgeous," he said.

"I'm sure you say that to all the girls."

"Only the ones who look like you." He flashed a mischievous grin.

"That's a whole lot."

"I'm kidding, Victoria—if I may still call you that."

"I'd prefer it, actually. I don't think I'll ever make a good Amelia."

"You'll always be Victoria to me." The Prince shuffled to the edge of the bed and pulled me to him. He turned my head to nibble on my ear, then trailed kisses down the side of my neck until he reached my collarbone. "Would you like any help getting cleaned up?" he whispered.

Every place his lips touched burned for more… and it scared me. "It wouldn't be proper." My voice was breathless.

"Indeed, it wouldn't," he said. "But the offer still stands."

I stepped back to reduce the temptation of everything he was implying. "I've already taken more than a big step today—for you."

"Yes, you have," he said, getting to his feet. "I do not mean to overstep or offend. I will give you your privacy." He cupped my face in his strong, yet smooth hands and delivered a kiss that took away any lingering thought of dying.

When he was gone, all I could do was drop to the floor and cry; all my emotions had reached their brim and could do nothing but overflow.

What was I doing? Was I making a huge mistake? Was he still just playing a game? Was I still a meager one of several? I didn't know the answer to any of it. I wanted to believe everything he'd told me that morning—on the train, in my bed. But how could I be sure? How could I be certain his actions weren't a performance to spare his own ego? I couldn't know it until he announced his decision—*us*—to the Queen.

Ultimately, I knew I had to own my decision to come back and not mourn the path I'd denied myself. If the Prince went back on his word at the final moment, then I'd have to accept it was the risk I'd been willing to take.

For the first time in my life, I had to find some way to take control of my destiny and not be the pawn in everyone else's games; I needed to find insurance of my own.

I'd let the tears run their course, then stand up and find a way to secure my life myself.

CHAPTER 41

*P*iper introduced me to the indoor pool down the hallway from the Garden Room. It was nicknamed the Roman Bathhouse, which referred to a civilization in the old world. The Romans took up about a page in the history books I'd been allowed to read and were famous for their grandiose entertainment and notorious excesses, which eventually led to their demise. I guessed the nude statues around the sublime indoor room resembled those of the lost civilization.

The water was hot, steaming up the room, creating an almost foggy atmosphere. Skylights brought in natural light, and at night, lights from beneath the water illuminated the room with a flickering, aquamarine hue.

It turned out most of the girls loved coming here

and I'd been the last to be introduced to the palace's hidden gem.

Piper loved to swim and did endless laps for exercise. The humid atmosphere wasn't ideal for reading, so I tried relaxing in one of the lounge chairs lining two sides of the pool. Jane and Eleanor were lounging on the other side, already with a plethora of empty drink glasses.

Piper climbed out of the pool and grabbed her towel from the chair next to me, beginning to dry herself off.

"One of these days, I'll get you to take off your wrap and come in."

"It looks nice and all, but I'm not much of a swimmer," I said.

"You can't relax without a book, can you?"

"A good book keeps my mind focused," I said. "Daydreams don't agree with me. My idle mind likes to return to things I don't want to think about."

"I know what you mean. Exercise keeps me focused." She laid her towel down on the lounge chair and lay back.

A platinum blond male waiter who looked younger than us stopped between our chairs. "Can I get you ladies any cocktails? Appetizers? Lotion?"

"A water for me," Piper said.

"Same," I agreed.

He typed our order into a small computer tablet

like it was too much for him to remember, before moving on to the girls on the far side of the room.

"That reminds me," Piper said. "Thanks again for the offer yesterday. I was kinda surprised to see you today. I thought you might have left."

"Nope," I said. "You guys made me think and I want to see where this could go."

"I'm glad you're still here, and at the same time, I'm not. You know? But regardless, since you're here, I wanted to repay the favor. I have something for you that I think you'll enjoy in the meantime. Remind me to show you later."

"Later—you're seriously going to keep me in suspense?" I frowned. "I would never do that to you."

Piper laughed. "Okay, okay. Since I owe you and all." She stood and wrapped the damp towel she'd been lying on around herself.

"I was kidding. Whenever you want to show me is fine."

"Get your ass up, Vici. We're going now." Piper led me out of the Roman Bathhouse and through a multitude of rooms and hallways.

We reached a wing of the first floor that I'd never ventured into before.

"Every time you think you've seen it all, there always seems to be one more room," Piper said as she stopped in the middle of a long, lounge-like room that rounded a corner. There were windows at least ten feet tall with tied-back curtains on one side and ornate chairs, statues, and oil paintings on the opposite side. It seemed to extend much further than it was supposed to.

Then she stopped and turned to the wall. When she started to push, I noticed a seam. A door in the wall swiveled, allowing us enough of an opening to enter a hidden chamber.

"How did you find this?" I asked as we crossed into the new layer of the Château.

"I seem to have plenty of time on my hands. I like to explore," Piper said.

The room we'd entered was all in darkness, but Piper flipped a light switch on the wall. We were in a library twice the size of the one I'd been using, with bookcases so tall they spanned two levels. A spiral staircase on either side of the room led to a perimeter platform above. Brown leather chairs and accompanying end tables were arranged throughout.

"You love to read and seem to like your space," Piper said. "I thought this place would be a nice sanctuary for you."

"It's wonderful," I said, in awe of the Queen's collection of books.

"I don't think any of the other girls know about it. I found it a few days ago and have kept it to myself. And each time I've spent time in here, no one's come in. So, I don't know how many people in the palace know about it either."

"Our own private getaway," I said.

"Do you like it?"

"I love it."

"I thought you might." Piper walked up to me and gave me a hug. "Enjoy your fictional worlds. I'm gonna get back to the pool."

"Okay," I said. "I'm going to look around and see what this library has to offer. I'm in need of a new book anyway. I'll join you in a little bit."

I watched Piper go—mainly to make sure I knew how to get back to the main part of the palace.

There were no windows or other doorways. Large golden chandeliers hung from overhead, providing plenty of reading light.

I wondered why this room was even there and why the Queen needed two libraries. She didn't seem to read much. But—as with all the artwork—there seemed to be status in the collections.

I approached the nearest bookcase and slowly circled the room, reading spines at random to determine whether the books were arranged in any type of order. If they were, I wasn't seeing it.

I reached a corner of the room with a large globe attached to its own wooden stand. I spun it and realized it wasn't like one I had ever seen. It depicted countries and territories of the old world, many of which were long gone. I found where Westeria should have been, and found the country of California in the time before The Cleansing. I'd been told there were still a lot of artifacts from that decadent time in The Outlands, but Westeria had been cleared of much of it. Most of what seemed to be left were their different creative media—like the titles filling this room.

I turned the corner and kept perusing the bookshelves. I chose a great hardback cover of a book called *Breaking Dawn* and took it back to one of the chairs. I flipped through the pages and read the first few chapters. It was told from the perspective of a girl my age, beginning with preparations for her wedding and then the telling of a cautionary tale of baby vampires. The way Bella talked about Edward made it certain he was her true love. I yearned for that kind of certainty with Prince Byron, and for that kind of storybook ending—yet this was just the beginning.

I flipped to the start of the book, to the copyright page, so I could see when it was written. 2008; such a long time ago. How much the world had changed in the last few hundred years. While looking at those introductory pages, I discovered this was the fourth book in a series—that it all began with a volume called *Twilight*.

I closed the book and slid it back into its rightful place in the bookcase, scanning the nearby titles for *Twilight*. Still not finding it, I climbed one of the iron spiral staircases to the second level and continued my search.

Halfway down the wall, I found it and pulled it

out from the shelf. I figured this would make for a good read and fill my downtime for the next few days.

I was just about to return to the lower level when another title caught my eye.

Pride & Prejudice.

I was instantly reminded of the previous copy I'd had at the Ramseys' estate—and of how Master Ramsey had given it to me as a gift then taken it away—torn it into little pieces.

I was a long way from there now and didn't want that association to become permanently allied to my favorite story.

I went to pull the book out as well, but it was caught on something—maybe the lining hardcovers were stuck together after years of compressed storage? I pulled harder and the top of the book pivoted downward, but the bottom seemed hinged in place, somehow. The immediate section of the bookcase moved, something clicked, and the section of the bookcase directly before me slowly swung inward.

I pushed it open wider to get a better look at what lay beyond, but the light from the library only extended so far. I was standing before a narrow hallway stretching into darkness, but as my eyes adjusted, I began to see a dim sliver of light; this palace was like an onion.

"Hello?" I called into the newly-discovered hallway.

I thought I could hear soft music coming from deep within and looked back at the doorway in the library wall. It was still closed. I was still alone.

After a moment's deliberation, I decided to venture into the secret passage and see where it led.

I closed the bookcase again and it clicked into place. For a moment, I panicked that I wouldn't be able to get back into the library and might be stuck in there forever. My corner of the passageway was shrouded in blackness; I felt around the back of the bookcase and the adjacent walls, looking for a trigger to reopen the door.

I breathed a sigh of relief when my exploring hands found a small lever, which worked to reveal the exit again. My nerves slightly calmed, I proceeded down the small hallway, the dim light growing brighter as my eyes adjusted more to the darkness. There seemed to be no lights at all. If it wasn't for the diminutive light ahead of me, I'd have no guide.

I didn't call out again, just creeping quietly until I came to another spiral staircase. Now, the light was coming from below—accompanied by ethereal music.

I descended the staircase and cringed with each creak that sounded out like a beacon of my arrival. The staircase extended far below the upper platform of bookshelves, all the way to the ground floor. By the time I reached the bottom, I knew I was in a cellar. It was cool and damp and the light coming from ahead, where there was a single door about 100 paces away. It was closed, yellow light pouring out from all four edges like a rectangular eclipse.

I padded softly toward the light and stopped before reaching the door. A thumbscrew deadbolt was affixed this side of the door and a typical door-knob sat beneath that. I unlocked the deadbolt and apprehensively reached for the doorknob, by the second getting more and more frightened of what I'd find on the other side. A voice in my head was telling me to *turn back, turn back*. But the soft music seemed to be beckoning me forth.

As the door swung inward, I found I was entering a bedroom in the cellar, to which I could definitely relate. The room was sparsely, but nicely furnished. First, my eyes were drawn to the medical machinery, much like the units used when the doctors had come to the Ramseys' for my check-ups. Then my eyes rested on the movement in the room's far corner where the music was coming from; it suddenly silenced.

A girl in a wheelchair was taking great care, and with what seemed like great effort and difficulty, to change the record on an old-fashioned phonograph. She was slumped to one side and her hands shook terribly.

"Hello?" I said, keeping my voice low in an effort not to startle her.

The girl didn't turn, but the wheelchair turned from the use of a joystick on the armrest. Even in her condition, it was plain to see she was another genetic identical—she was one of us! And then I thought about where we were and who would be locked away in this secret chamber...

"Princess Amelia?"

CHAPTER 42

The girl gave me a half smile, and when she tried to speak, one side of her face didn't even move.

"Where's my mother?" she asked.

I stepped into the room, leaving the door open. "Is your mother the Queen?"

It looked like she was trying to nod, but it was hard to distinguish a deliberate movement from a tremor. Her head was cocked to one side. She seemed to have very limited control over her movements.

"Yes," she then when I didn't respond to show I understood.

"Then you're Princess Amelia, right?"

"Yes. What's happened to my mother?"

"Nothing's happened to her," I said. "She's around here somewhere."

"She sent you? She hasn't sent anyone to visit me —besides doctors—in so long." Princess Amelia rolled closer to me. She was dressed in a long, thick nightgown with yellow flowers, and wore slippers. Her hair was cut short. There was saliva collecting on the corner of her mouth that wasn't moving. "You're so beautiful," she whispered.

"Thank you. So are you." I didn't see a mirror in the room and wondered when was the last time she'd seen herself? "The Queen did not send me. I accidentally found you."

"What is your name?"

"Victoria," I said. "How long have you been down here?"

"Al—almost ten years." She turned her chair to face the way she'd come. "Can you help me with my music?"

"Of course," I said, following her to the phonograph in the corner of the room.

One record was on the floor, the other on the turntable but off-center, refusing to fall into place.

I adjusted the record and gently placed the needle onto it; more soothing instrumental music began to pour from the shell-like speaker. I picked the fallen record off the floor and found a sleeve for it on a shelf to one side of the phonograph.

"There," I said. "You like music?"

She rolled away again. She went to her nightstand where there was a large plastic cup of water with a lid and long straw, so she could drink without picking it up.

After a sip, she turned back to me. "I don't like the silence," she said. "What book do you have?"

She rolled over to the dresser by the door, where I had put down my book from the library without thinking.

"*Twilight*," I said. "Have you read it?"

"Yes. Several years ago. I've read all four of them. But my favorite is still *Pride & Prejudice*, which I've read many times. I have a hard time turning the pages. I read on here. See?"

She went to a desk with a slanted top, formed of one large piece of glass. She was able to roll right up to it, her legs fitting underneath, even from her elevated position in the wheelchair. She instructed the tabletop to "wake up" and it came alive—it was in fact entirely a screen. From there, what looked like open pages of a book appeared. She then said, "Next page," and the page on the screen simulated flipping the page of a real book.

"It's really something," I said, taking a closer look. The Ramseys had a computer, but all the actions were performed through a keyboard. Before coming here, the doctors visiting me throughout the years were the only ones I'd seen to carry little tablets with touchscreens resembling this one. "My favorite is *Pride & Prejudice* too. What are the odds? Do you read a lot?"

"It's the only time I can explore beyond these four walls anymore," Princess Amelia said.

"I understand," I said. "I've read for years as the escape from my home too."

"Where is your home?"

"Here," I said, still working through what I was going to tell her. "I'm your younger sister."

"I have a sister? Why have I never heard about you before?"

"The Queen—Mother has kept us apart. I didn't always live here. But I've recently been allowed to return home."

"I have a sister... This is so..." Her facial expression did not change, but tears formed in her eyes and began to spill down her cheeks. "...amazing."

I was almost about to cry too. "I'm sorry I haven't visited until now."

"But you'll visit me again?" She tried to wipe away her tears, but her hand couldn't seem to find her cheek.

I noticed a box of tissues on her nightstand and took one to wipe her tears away, as well as the spittle collecting at the drooping corner of her mouth.

"Every chance I get," I said. "Can you do me a favor?"

"Yes."

"Can you not tell the Qu—Mother I was here? I don't know if she'll be upset that I came to visit you—you know, since she's kept us apart for so long. I don't want her to take this time away from us."

"No. I don't want that either," Princess Amelia said.

"Then you won't mention I was here?"

"No."

This poor girl before me was the one from whom I'd been created—the one from whom all the girls upstairs had been fashioned. After the Queen's announcement the first night, I took her words at face value and figured I'd never get to meet Princess Amelia, yet here she was, as much a prisoner as the rest of us. She certainly didn't seem in some miraculous state of recovery, but she was far from dead.

"Have you heard of Prince Byron?" I asked.

She mouthed a few words before any sound came out. "Mother has talked about him before. She's shown me a picture. She says he's from Easteria and I will marry him someday. I don't know why he would want me, but she tells me he's a very understanding man. He's supposed to come here soon."

She sounded skeptical, yet hopeful, and it broke my heart. "Yes, he is supposed to be coming soon," I said, sad to be substantiating the Queen's lies.

"Why do you ask?"

"No reason," I said. "There's so much going on in the world outside. I don't know what information actually reaches you down here."

"Just what Mother tells me," she said. "And now you can tell me things too."

"Yes, as long as what I tell you stays between us. We don't want Mother to become suspicious."

She certainly seemed to understand, especially with her thirst for knowledge of the ever-changing world outside of her cell. I wished I could take her out of here, steal her away like I did Mina. But this was a task well beyond me—and Kale was gone, and I doubted even he would have been able to pull this off.

I gave Princess Amelia a hug before leaving and locking her room. It was so hard turning that deadbolt, but I knew it had to be done. It wasn't like she could climb the spiral staircase on her own, but I couldn't leave any evidence of being there. That's when I remembered the book I'd been carrying when I ventured down. I went and retrieved it before returning to the hidden library.

Luckily, the library was still empty. I gazed up at the book that had led me to the Princess—perhaps it had always been leading me to her—and couldn't believe what great design had been at work to fit the pieces together so perfectly.

Just then, the door in the wall opened and Piper returned, still in a mere towel wrapped over her bikini.

"I should have known you wouldn't be coming back," she called up to me.

"I'm sorry. This place is amazing," I exclaimed, descending the spiral staircase.

"I knew you'd like it and just couldn't keep it a secret."

"But let's not invite too many people," I said.

"How about Bethany?"

"I'm good with Bethany."

"Okay," Piper said. "She's the cut-off."

I helped her close the wall once we were in the empty hallway, securing our new sanctuary and the secrets held within.

CHAPTER 43

I kept Piper company for a little while longer, lying by the pool. Jane and Eleanor were still on the far side collecting glasses of cocktails and getting louder with each one they emptied. When Bethany made an appearance, I excused myself to head back to my room.

While changing into a casual yellow sundress—I didn't have Kimera around to inform me of the shade—I noticed another card tented on the desk. Assuming it was another note from Kimera, I opened the card and read what had been written inside.

Let's disappear together. I'll meet you in the foyer at 8 p.m. in formal attire. Wear whichever color you desire. Your humble servant.

I fell back on the bed, clutching the card to my

chest, thrilled to be getting a second date so soon. My heart sang with the thought of spending another evening with Prince Byron and my thoughts raced with what he meant by *let's disappear together*. Of course, I wanted to leave with him and disappear into the countryside, starting new lives for ourselves; I was sure that wasn't what he meant in his note, but a girl could dream, couldn't she?

I typically liked doing things for myself, but I wanted Kimera's help for this occasion. I gave her a call and informed her of the good news, and she agreed to show up an hour before my meeting time with the Prince. She sounded as excited as I felt.

She showed up right on time. I was finishing tying my robe after a long bath when she entered the room. I picked at the little bit of food left on my room service tray, and then we went straight into hair and makeup.

"What color dress do you want?" she asked.

"Anything but yellow," I said.

"And you said something about disappearing together?"

"Yes. The card said *let's disappear together*. Whatever that means."

Kimera thought for a moment and examined the makeup at her disposal before saying, "I think I have just the thing."

She curled my hair, braided my bangs and looped

them to the back. The smoldering eyes she created were dark and severe. The dress she chose was a long black gown with a plunging neckline, three-quarter-length, loose, lace sleeves and black crystal pickups in the skirt. Once I was in front of the full-length mirror, I hardly recognized myself. I couldn't believe how sultry I could look with a little professional help.

"This dress will keep his eyes on *you* all night long," Kimera said, stepping back to admire her work more fully. "I think it needs one more thing."

Kimera ventured into the back corner of the closet where there was a cluster of coats, coming back with a black velvet item draped over one arm. She opened the material and placed the thick velvet cape over my shoulders. On the inside, the color was deep violet. She turned me to face her and tied a bow at my front. A loose hood hung at my back; Kimera lifted it and tucked my hair carefully inside as she placed it on my head.

"What do you think?" she asked.

"I look—dangerous," I said.

"Yes. I like that. You're a true siren of the night." Kimera squared my shoulders and adjusted the cape. "You're carrying too much stress in your shoulders. Try to relax them a little. Well, would you look at the time—not a minute to spare."

I thanked Kimera for all her help and glided into the hallway at the stroke of eight.

Constance exited her room as I passed by her doorway and scowled as she looked me over.

"You really played up the innocent girl-next-door when you got here, but the true whore's coming out now," she said.

"You're one to talk," I snapped and kept right on walking, doing my damnedest to keep her out of my head.

When I reached the top of the curved staircase, all thoughts of Constance vanished as I saw Prince Byron standing in the foyer with a single red rose, gazing up at me. His serious expression dissolved as I cautiously descended the staircase.

"And here I thought we'd be able to disappear," he said as I approached. "You'll stand out wherever we go. At least I don't have to worry about being recognized because no one's eyes will be on me."

"Mine will be," I said, trying not to blush.

The Prince was wearing a black tuxedo with a long coat, white ruffled shirt, with more ruffles peeking out through the coat sleeves. He didn't wear a tie, but kept his collar open. His muscular upper body filled out the suit coat, accentuating his broad shoulders. I had an urge to run a hand down the ruffles of his shirt and ended up evening out the cape on my shoulders to keep from doing anything embarrassing.

Prince Byron offered me the rose. "My Princess."

"My Prince," I said and did my best curtsy as I

took the floral gift. The Governess would have been proud of my grace.

He offered me his arm and I slipped mine through.

Two staff members opened the main double-door entrance.

"Let us do our best to disappear. Shall we?"

"We shall," I said, letting him lead me out toward the circular drive, where a black sports car awaited us.

The Prince opened the passenger door, and—as I sank into the car—he crouched next to me and pulled the seatbelt across my body, securing me in like his most prized possession. Then he took up his position in the driver's seat; he was fully taking the lead this evening.

The beautiful little car roared to life. We crept down the drive and Prince Byron waved to the guards at the gate before zooming away. I was thrown back in my seat from the acceleration far superior to that of any horse, which brought a smile of exhilaration to my face.

"Where are we in such a rush to get to?" I asked.

"The rush is merely to get away," he said, reaching a hand across the center console and resting it on my thigh. "The drive won't be long. We're going to one of the estates nearby, to a party being thrown by one of the biggest business tycoons in the Kingdom, Sir Leonard Duncan."

"I haven't heard of him."

"That's fine. He's not a hugely public figure. But he does business past the border and all the way to Easteria. My parents have entertained him before— that's the main reason I know who he is. But his wife, Delores, loves to throw these lavish parties."

"I see," I said, spinning the rose between my fingertips.

And he was right. We'd barely left the neighborhood when he turned into another long driveway, entering a parade of other fancy cars slowly inching up to an elegantly lit estate. It wasn't quite the Queen's palace but was still quite impressive.

Prince Byron reached into the snug back seat and set a small paper bag in my lap. Inside were two masks, and if I didn't know better, they were the ones we had worn to the Queen's masquerade ball.

"Let's disappear," he said as he took hold of his mask. I placed mine over my face and tied it behind my head, vividly remembering the night of the Queen's masquerade ball, when all this craziness of my new life was just beginning.

Prince Byron was now donning his mask. He looked as handsome as I'd ever seen him, which was maybe only due to my growing feelings for him. It was hard to be objective, but I didn't care.

Both doors were opened simultaneously by the parking staff. I set the red rose on top of the dashboard and took hold of a man's offered hand to help me from the sports car.

"Good evening and welcome, m'lady," the man said. Like us, he also wore a mask, but his covered his entire face—as was the case with the rest of the parking attendants.

"Thank you," I replied and found the Prince at my side in an instant.

We walked up to the main entrance arm in arm. The evening air was brisk, and I pulled at my cape to keep it over my shoulders. Each couple before us stopped at the two exquisitely dressed female staff members in black lace skeleton masks. When it was our turn, the Prince pulled an invitation from an inner coat pocket and handed it to the lady now holding a stack of them.

Once inside, the Prince was asked if he'd like to check in his coat. A small room off the foyer was being used to store everyone's outerwear, and Prince Byron handed over his long coat. He then untied my cape, pulled down my hood, and relieved me of the layer of material allowing my body to hide at all.

As Kimera had said, he couldn't take his eyes off me. Then there were the gazes of other men as they passed by, the attention sounding better than it currently felt. The Prince seemed to notice as well.

"I don't want to share you with the whole party," he said.

"Now you know how I feel," I said.

"At least it's better than the whole Kingdom looking at you, which it soon will be." Prince Byron took my hand and led me deeper into the mansion.

I certainly wasn't ready to have the whole Kingdom's eyes on me.

CHAPTER 44

I didn't know life could be like this. We talked, we danced, we laughed. We hardly talked to another soul at the party and no one seemed to recognize either of us—if anyone did, it was never expressed. We'd succeeded in disappearing into the sea of anonymity.

Prince Byron never left my side, nor took his eyes off me. He held me close as we moved across the dance floor and made me feel I was truly his.

Each time I touched him, I waited for him to disappear—for all of this to disappear and for me to awaken in my room again, in the cellar of the Ramseys' estate. I felt the dream coming to an end as I fought hard not to let it go, not to let it dissolve into real life where fairytales didn't come true for servant girls like me, or for someone even less than that—an unnatural human and the Queen's secret science experiment.

But the music played on, the Prince continuing to spin me in circles until I felt almost drunk. He kissed me in front of everyone around, with no concern for who was watching. Midnight came and went without the magic that had transformed me into a princess wearing off.

"Would you like to find a place to sit for a while?" the Prince asked.

"Yes, please," I said. My legs and feet were sore from all the dancing, but I hadn't wanted to stop.

Many rooms were serving as lounges, but all seemed taken by the multitude of guests throughout the estate, all partaking in sophisticated conversations, sipping from elegant glasses, engaging in intimate moments in full view of the rest of us.

Prince Byron led me to a balcony off one of the lounges. It had fewer people than were gathered inside. The night air was cool, but portable heaters were spaced at regular intervals.

We claimed an empty couch by one of them. I slipped my feet out of my heels to let my toes breathe. My feet had become toughened from a life of being barefoot and receiving regular switchings, but wearing all these different heel styles and heights since coming to the palace seemed the biggest punishment yet given to them.

Prince Byron peered down at my bare feet, then

without saying a word, stretched one of my legs across his lap. With both hands, he began to rub my foot. The attention hurt at first, but as soon as the aching muscles slowly relaxed, it began to melt all the tension in my body. Through my foot, he seemed to be reaching areas all over. I sank into the cushions of the couch and closed my eyes.

"How's this?" he asked as he dug his thumbs deeper into the sensitive flesh on the bottom of my foot. I felt some of the lingering bruises that were no longer visible, but they didn't diminish the ecstasy brought forth by the Prince's expert fingers. "I usually don't like people touching my feet," I said.

"I can stop," he said.

"Don't you dare."

"Yes, m'lady." Prince Byron leaned in to kiss me while continuing to massage my foot.

"Prince Byron, I thought that was you," a woman said, standing over us.

I'd been so enraptured in the Prince's handiwork I hadn't noticed her approach.

"Good evening, Lady Duncan," Prince Byron said. "You continue to stand out from the crowd and look as lovely as ever."

"Always the charmer," she said.

Lady Duncan wore a long burgundy A-line gown that shimmered in the lights from the estate. Her masquerade mask matched her gown and was accented with plumes and sequins. From her voice and the lines on her face, I guessed she was in her sixties, but her toned arms and shoulders didn't reflect the body of an older woman.

"And this must be the elusive Princess Amelia," Lady Duncan added, offering me a hand. "Don't worry, child. Your secret's safe with me. No one else suspects a thing."

"How do you—" the Prince started, but Lady Duncan interjected.

"I hear everything," she said with a brilliant smile. "I make it my business to know. Word has spread from your little stunt on the train. It was so sweet though. You two make an adorable couple."

"Thank you," the Prince said.

"It's nice to meet you," I said.

"You look well," she said. "More than well. You look absolutely radiant. Has the Queen actually been hiding you all these years, or have you spent time in other kingdoms for treatment and healing—Easteria for instance?"

I didn't know how to answer, but luckily, Prince Byron spoke for me.

"The Queen has been protective of her and remains protective of her, especially since she hasn't issued her official statement of reintroduction."

"Like I said, my lips are sealed," she said and performed the gesture. "I'm just glad I had the chance to see you with my own eyes. I saw a few of the pictures from the train and heard the talk, but didn't fully believe it. Until now. You really are back. The whole Kingdom will rejoice once it's official."

"It's a lot of pressure," I said. "I hope I can live up to the Kingdom's expectations."

"I'm sure this young man can help you with that," Lady Duncan said, patting the Prince on the shoulder. "You'll do fine. Now I'm sure you didn't want to get stuck talking with an old woman on this romantic evening. I'll let you get back to your anonymity."

Once Lady Duncan was gone, I turned to Prince Byron and said, "There are pictures of us on the train?"

"Yes," he said. "They've been circulating like wildfire. I haven't seen any really good ones though, so... they can't be particularly damaging. The Queen is aware and she's not commenting on the reports—she's waiting for the end of this process, which is quickly approaching."

"And I have nothing to worry about?"

He placed my first foot gently back on the floor and lifted my second, taking it in his hands. "There can always be something to worry about, but I don't want you to worry about me—about us."

"What are we going to do about the other girls?"

"I don't know yet," he said, looking off into the distance. "I need to get my guards into the room when the announcement is made to protect the other girls from whatever next step the Queen has in store. The biggest problem will be that whatever guards I can get in will be grossly outnumbered by the Queen's own. She'll be thoroughly protected and I don't want there to be any bloodshed."

"That makes two of us," I said. "I want to keep everyone safe—even the few I despise, who will remain nameless."

The Prince laughed. "They're certainly not nameless. But yes, I want to keep everyone safe as well. I'll work something out. I don't want you to worry about this either. This is my problem to solve."

"They are *my* sisters," I said.

"But they're *my* responsibility," he countered. His hands left my foot and moved over to my waist as he leaned in to kiss me. "A responsibility that can wait until tomorrow. I want to enjoy my time with you now. This is our night. No Queen. No competition. Just us."

I climbed onto his lap, my lips inches from his. "That's all I want too."

"Then we both have everything we want and need right here." The Prince kept his hands on my waist, repositioning himself under me. "This choice wasn't supposed to be so easy—but it is. It's simply you."

I smiled from his conviction and sincerity and kissed him with a fervor that matched my dress. It was no longer the nearby heaters keeping me warm, but him. I pressed every possible inch of my body to his because I just couldn't bear to be apart any longer.

As we devoured each other's bodies, I never felt so alive. In some ways, I was already Princess Amelia. And with that thought, an idea came to me of how to save the other girls... and myself, if needed. But I had to keep this idea to myself.

CHAPTER 45

The last time I'd come back on a high from a date with the Prince, the Queen had dropped a bomb on all of us. I was afraid of some new, terrible revelation punching me in the gut again. When Kimera told me of my afternoon appointment with Dr. Crane, I figured this was it.

Kimera wanted to know everything about the night before, and I told her, save for my new idea. But with my sense bad news was on the way, it was hard to get fully into the story. Kimera didn't seem to mind; she was simply excited for me.

She led me to an empty bedroom on the third floor, in which the doctor had set up his usual machinery. But when I entered, I was surprised to find Dr. Sosin as well. He'd checked me out a lot when I was younger but had delegated most of the check-ups of the last few years to Dr. Crane.

Dr. Sosin looked like he'd aged more than a decade since I last saw him. His hair had gone from peppery to completely white and he seemed to be steadily gaining weight. But his smile was still the same and looked genuine when he saw me.

"Victoria, my dear. You are looking well," Dr. Sosin said.

"I hear you're making quite an impression on the Prince," Dr. Crane said, finishing setting up the machines. "It seems your accident hasn't hindered you at all."

"Thank you," I said. "I feel great."

"Are any of your memories returning?" Dr. Crane asked. "How are your energy levels? Mental clarity?"

"All fine, I think. And no—no memories have returned."

"That's okay. Nothing to be alarmed about."

"I think you know the routine by now," Dr. Sosin said.

I nodded and took a seat that they'd placed by the machinery so I could be hooked up and their string of tests could begin. While the machines did their work, Dr. Crane examined the results on his miniature tablet computer.

"Everything is looking good," he said. "Though your Vitamin D is slightly below average. A little extra sunlight may do you some good. You love to ride, don't you?"

"You know I do," I said. "I'll try to get out more."

"The benefits would be twofold," Dr. Sosin said.

Dr. Crane handed me the cup for a urine sample, and I filled it in the en suite washroom and brought it back to him.

"Dr. Crane," I said. "You told me I was the Queen's daughter, but not what I truly was. I wasn't being checked so often, like now, because I was the Queen's daughter. And now to learn about the rest of us…"

"It was a sensitive subject," Dr. Crane said.

"Would you have believed it if you were told earlier—told without seeing?" Dr. Sosin asked.

"I don't know," I said. "It hard to put myself back there at this point. A door's been opened for me that I can't seem to close."

"And I wouldn't want you to close it," Dr. Sosin said. "I want you to be proud of what you are. You're a marvel, as are all your sisters."

"I don't think everyone will see us as such," I said.

"Not everyone in the world will be ready for and accepting of your kind, but such is the reaction to progress. You are a huge leap forward in human evolution. You are the future."

"If we're the future, then why are you letting the Queen kill us off?"

Both doctors' expressions became morose. I could tell right away this was something they hoped would not come up.

"We are still trying to reason with her," Dr. Crane

said. "Killing any of you is not the answer. There are available alternatives. But she is afraid."

"Afraid of what?" I asked.

"Looking weak," Dr. Sosin said.

"We're still her daughters," I said. "Even though she didn't birth us."

"You're as much our daughters as hers."

"Then you should be doing more to protect us," I snapped.

"The Queen is not so easily persuaded. But I assure you, we're doing whatever we can without risking everything," Dr. Sosin said.

"You should be risking everything. *We are.*" Here I was with people saying they were trying to help us, but not actually doing anything. I couldn't count on them and couldn't count on the Prince to find a way either. I wondered if any of them knew about Princess Amelia, but didn't want to mention her since she was the central component to my idea. Now I just needed to turn my idea into a plan that would save all our lives.

Our meeting did not end on a happy note, but I hadn't been floored with a terrible revelation as I'd been anticipating. Instead, I found myself frustrated with every word they uttered.

There was a time gap before their next appointment, so both doctors left the room shortly after me. I went back to the second floor and they continued down another level.

Once they were out of sight, I sneaked back upstairs into the bedroom-turned-exam-room and looked around. Set atop one of the portable machines, I found the small tablet computer Dr. Crane had been using. I grabbed it, clutching it to my chest with both hands, and rushed back down to my room.

I sat on my bed, folded back the cover of the tablet, and stabbed a finger at the screen. A keypad showed up, along with a message asking for a password.

That puts a hindrance on my plan. What was I supposed to do?

I started by typing all our names, including Princess Amelia. But none of them was the correct password. I tried more seemingly relevant words, but they all came up with error messages.

As I continued to fiddle with the tablet, my typing was interrupted by a buzzing. I followed the sound to the desk, and more specifically to my coat draped over the back of the desk chair.

From the pocket, I removed the phone Kale had given me and flipped it open.

"Hello?" I said.

"Hey, Victoria."

I instantly recognized the voice as Kale's, which brought a smile to my face. Even after my wonderful evening with the Prince, it was good to hear him.

"Hey," I said.

"How are you? You've been on my mind."

"I'm good… except this stupid computer tablet I stole from the doctors has a password on it. I can't get in."

"I seem to be rubbing off on you," Kale said with a chuckle. "Why are you stealing tablets?"

"I'm sure they have information on me and the other girls that they're not sharing and I want to know what it is."

"Are they going to know it was you who took it from them?"

I hadn't really thought about it when I went back to the room. I'd been the last one in there, but the door wasn't locked and it could have been anyone. I'd have to keep it hidden well in case anyone came snooping around my room.

"It could have been anyone," I said, hoping my thought would sound as plausible when spoken aloud.

"You need to make sure you cover your tracks. Be careful, okay?"

"I will."

"If I was there, I could hack into it for you," Kale said. "There's always some type of back door."

I flipped over the device. "I don't see anything," I said.

"You wouldn't see something so obvious. When I come back to check up on you, I'll look at it."

"You're not coming back—you can't. They'll never let you back in here."

"I wasn't planning to ask the Queen's permission."

"How about mine?" I asked.

"Do I have your permission?"

"No. I don't want you to risk your safety by coming back. I don't want to think about what would happen to you if you were caught."

"So, I don't have your permission because you're concerned about my safety or because you don't want to see me?"

"I *do* want to see you. But I don't want to jeopardize what I'm building with Prince Byron. And I *am* concerned for you. You're looking after Mina, right? You can't go getting yourself into trouble. Like I said, when this is over, I'll come for her."

"By that time, it may be too late," Kale said.

"No. The Prince gave me his word."

"And you trust him?"

"I do," I said, even if that wasn't the entire truth. "I'm going to be okay."

"Forgive me if I don't share the same level of confidence in this prince of yours."

I could hear the bitterness in his voice. I had chosen Prince Byron over him and the wound was still fresh. But the choice had not just been between the two of them. I wished he'd be able to understand that someday.

"I know you don't agree with my choice and I'm sorry," I said.

"It was hard watching you walk off that train," Kale said.

I walked back to my bed and lay down across it. "I know."

"There are pictures of you everywhere now."

"Pictures of Princess Amelia."

"Who is *you*."

I heard footsteps coming down the hallway and took the phone away from my ear to listen more closely. When a knock sounded at my door, I brought the phone back to my ear. "I've gotta go," I whispered.

I didn't even give Kale the time to respond before closing the phone and stuffing it and the tablet under my pillows.

"Victoria, are you in there?" Dr. Crane asked.

Oh, crap!

CHAPTER 46

"You can come in," I called from my bed.

Dr. Crane entered but stayed close to the door. "Did you happen to see anyone going up to the third floor after our appointment?"

"No," I said, sitting up on the bed. "Why? Is something wrong?"

"Nothing to concern yourself with. I was just curious. You saw no one when you were going back to your room?"

"No. The hallway was empty."

"Did you forget anything in the exam room?"

"No. I didn't bring anything."

Dr. Crane glanced around the room. He was trying to look casual—not to appear like he was searching for something. I watched him attempt to mask his actions during a long moment of silence.

"Well, I should be getting to my next appointment," he finally said and turned back toward the door.

"Okay," I said and waited until he'd closed my door and his footsteps had disappeared down the hallway before pulling out the tablet.

I made more attempts to get past the password protection, but they continued to come up short. I thought about calling Kale back but didn't want to get into an argument. I already had enough problems with the tablet that wouldn't open; if it was going to be useful and aid me with my plan, then I'd somehow have to break into it.

With my failed efforts compounded, I grew tired.

I dreamt of my sultry night of wonderfully physical connections with the Prince and wanted him to hold me right now. I longed for his hands on my feet, his breath on my skin, his lips on my neck and his sensual whispers in my ear. If he was here with me now, I didn't know if I'd have the resolve to turn him away again.

I couldn't recall when my daydreams turned into real ones, and when I awoke, it was dark outside.

My stomach was growling and I thought of calling for room service but decided to get out of my room. So I planned to go down to the dining room and see who was around and what food I could scrape together.

As I descended the curved staircase, my heart

leaped at the sight of Prince Byron standing in the foyer with a single red rose—just like he'd held the night before for our date. He wasn't in a tuxedo this time, but a well-fitted gray suit.

He smiled when he saw me, but it was restrained.

"I was just dreaming about you and here you are," I said as I reached the ground floor.

He moved his hands to reach behind his back, hiding the rose. "It's good to see you," he said.

I walked up to him and leaned in for a kiss. He turned his head and offered a cheek, which I took, but it was hard hiding my disappointment.

Then I heard the rustling of fabric and clinking of jewelry. I turned and saw Bethany descending the staircase in a long, flowing lavender dress. She looked gorgeous and my excitement to see the Prince drained at the sight of her. We were supposed to be happy for each other. I knew that, but it was hard now, seeing the two of them together.

Prince Byron offered her the rose and bowed like the gentleman he was. She was beaming; her cheeks flushed.

"Hi, Victoria," Bethany said, glancing over at me, unsure of how to take my presence.

"Hi, Bethany," I said.

She forgot about me almost immediately as she lifted the rose to her nose and took in its sweet scent.

"We should be going if we want to make our reservation," Prince Byron said. "Shall we?"

"Yes," Bethany said as she took his arm.

"Goodnight, Victoria," the Prince said as he led his beautiful date out the front door.

"Goodnight," I said weakly, watching them disappear into the night air.

I shuffled up to the door to see how they were leaving and saw the open back door of a limousine. I watched them climb in and the car circle the drive and make its way to the gate.

The staff member at the front door asked if I'd like the door to remain open. I shook my head and left for the dining room.

Throughout the walk to the dining room, I couldn't get the image of the Prince leaving with Bethany out of my mind. I was the one for him, his choice, and here he was, still going on romantic dates with the others. I knew he had to keep up appearances, but it still felt like a punch to the gut. And the fact it was Bethany almost made it worse because she was my friend, a great girl, and she'd make a fine Princess Amelia—probably a better one than I would.

The dining room was dark when I arrived; surprisingly, the table was already set up for breakfast. I continued into the kitchen and rummaged through the refrigerator for leftovers and anything else edible that I wouldn't have to cook. I arranged a plate of random food items no one with any taste would combine, but I didn't care. It silenced my stomach, which was all that mattered. Now—if only I could silence my mind.

After eating, I wandered through the downstairs. A few staff members were around, all cleaning various rooms, but overall the palace was quiet. In one of the hallways, I passed Danielle and Jane. They both said "hi," but I heard laughter shortly after, which made me think it was something to do with me. At least my frustration with them took my mind off Bethany and the Prince for now.

I ambled to the hidden library and up to the *Pride & Prejudice* that couldn't be read. It was kind of a cruel joke. I followed the secret passage to Princess Amelia's room.

"Hello, Sister," she said. "I was wondering when you'd come back to visit me. But you can't stay long. It's approaching my bedtime. At nine, one of the doctors will be down to put me to bed. Maybe even Mother. She hasn't come down for a couple of nights."

"I'm sorry," I said. "I didn't realize."

"But maybe it's okay. Maybe it will be okay if the doctors know you come down here."

"Maybe, but I don't want to take that chance just yet. We're just getting to know each other."

Princess Amelia rolled from her illuminated glass table, trundling closer to me by the bed. Her hand shook as she maneuvered herself with the joystick. Her head was still cocked to one side, which looked painful, but she couldn't seem to reposition herself.

"Can you tell me about your day?" she asked. "I want to hear all about it. Everything."

"Everything... wow. Where to begin..."

"At the beginning."

I sat down on the bed and looked her in the eyes with a smile. "I don't think we have enough time, but I'll get through as much as I can," I said and fabricated a story of what I envisioned a normal day in the palace to be like, away from all things clones and competitions.

CHAPTER 47

*I*t felt so good to talk with Princess Amelia that I didn't want to leave. I ended up staying too long and hid in the closet when Dr. Crane came and helped her into bed, then gave her a shot of her latest treatment. He didn't seem to suspect an intruder, even though I couldn't lock the exterior deadbolt. I crept out when he went into the en suite to wash his hands.

I wanted to kiss Princess Amelia on the forehead. She had just been tucked in, yet she was already asleep; she looked so peaceful but I knew I couldn't linger and slipped out of the door before Dr. Crane could emerge and discover me.

The next morning before breakfast, I took out the computer tablet again and took another stab at guessing the password. But this time when I touched the screen, it didn't ask for one; the *Home* screen appeared completely unencumbered.

There were only a few icons and I clicked on each of them. Nowhere did I see anything with our names on. No information. No medical records. No pictures. There seemed to be nothing specific on it whatsoever.

I called Kale and he didn't sound surprised.

"It was probably reset to factory defaults remotely, wiped clean of all sensitive material," he said. "I'm sorry you didn't find what you were looking for."

"Not entirely," I said. "The camera still works." That was what I really needed for the plan I was devising. "If I take pictures, how can I get them to you?"

"What kind of pictures?" Kale asked.

"Incriminating pictures," I said.

"I'm listening."

"I don't want to jinx myself. Will I be able to get pictures to you or not?"

The line went silent for a moment, then he went into a speech about the old internet, downloading applications, cloud storage, and granted user access. I didn't fully understand, but I tried following his directions.

"Why have I never heard of any of this before?" I asked.

"There's a lot the general public in Westeria

doesn't know still exists. We've built over the old world, but there is plenty of its infrastructure still in place behind the scenes. Those who control the information retain the power."

"What if the doctors reset it again?" I asked.

"Why would they unless they suspect something? Besides, if I've already downloaded what you've uploaded, it won't matter." There was another pause. "Are you going to tell me what you're up to?"

"Princess Amelia is alive," I said. "And I'm going to send you proof. She doesn't know it, but she's going to save the lives of all the girls here."

"Where is she? I didn't hear about this when I was there," Kale said, sounding disappointed.

"What can I say, I've got my connections too." When he didn't find my comment amusing, I continued. "She's locked in a secret wing of the cellar. The Queen's apparently had her down there for years. She's definitely not well. That part wasn't a lie. But she's such a nice and hopeful girl. She doesn't deserve how she's been treated."

"You're going to be careful, aren't you?" Kale asked.

"Of course," I said. "You don't have to worry about me."

"I always worry about you."

"Well, stop. It's not your place to always worry about me."

"If I could help it, I would," Kale said. "But I can't.

I care about you too much. And I'm still worried what's going to happen at the end of this."

"I know." I was worried too but didn't want to keep thinking about it. If I did, it would consume me and drive me mad. I had to put some trust in the Prince that he'd keep his word, choose me and find a way to save the other girls. And if all that failed, then Princess Amelia would have to come through and save us all.

After breakfast, I ventured toward the hidden library again. I was wearing shorts under my dress, with the tablet inconspicuously tucked into the waistband. As I reached the secret door area that led to the library, the wall opened up and the Queen stepped out into the hallway.

I turned to race back in the direction from which I came, but she saw me before I could make an escape.

"Victoria, is that you?" she asked.

I froze, then slowly turned back to her. "Yes, Your Highness."

"Where are you going?"

"I was just… umm… just wandering the halls," I said, stumbling over every word.

"In that case, come, walk with me." She linked arms with me and dragged me along. "I've recently received a call from Queen DuFour—Prince Byron's mother."

"Oh?"

"There has been a lot of speculation as of late about Princess Amelia—speculation all stemming from your stunt on the Inter-Ward Express."

"It was all a misunderstanding," I said. "Everything is going really well with the Prince. We're developing a very strong relationship."

"More so than the other girls in the house?"

"I can't speak for the relationships he's building with the other girls, but I feel good about ours."

"I'm glad to hear the process is working, despite the added pressure." The Queen was looking out of the passing windows as we walked, then decided to continue our stroll into the gardens. "You seem in good spirits," she said once we were in the sunlight.

"I am," I said, which couldn't be further from the truth. "I feel like everything's going to work out. I'll marry Prince Byron, meet his parents and visit Easteria. And I will learn from you how to rule a kingdom."

"I'm sure it will all work out," was all she said. Her words carried very little emotion. She stopped and turned to me, her eyes suddenly staring intensely into mine. "But if you try to run away again, I'll have you disemboweled, stuffed as a scarecrow, and posted out here as another permanent palace fixture. Do we understand each other?"

"Yes, Your Highness." I gulped. A chill ran through me despite the warm, sunny air.

The Queen left me in the garden to digest her

threat. She knew. Of course, she knew. She'd made it clear she was playing nice for the competition, for Prince Byron—but her leniency would only go so far.

The Queen's actions made me want to return to Princess Amelia even more. Since she'd just visited with her daughter, I figured it would be safe for a while.

"Two days in a row," the Princess said. "Is it my birthday and I've lost track of the days again?"

"No," I said. "Nothing special. I just wanted to see you. Is that okay?"

"I love having you here with me. I only wish it could be every day."

"And maybe someday it can," I said and reached under my dress to pull out the tablet.

"That looks like one of the computers the doctors have."

"Similar," I said. "I bought it in the city." I didn't want her to know I'd taken it from the doctors. "I noticed you don't seem to have a mirror in here and the one in the washroom is rather high. When was the last time you were able to really see yourself?"

"It's been a long time. I don't remember."

I held the tablet up and clicked a picture of her. Then I brought it up on the screen and showed it to her.

"I've grown so much older," Princess Amelia said.

"I wonder—if I wasn't sick—if I'd look more like you?"

"You look beautiful," I said.

"Take another picture," she answered.

I snapped a few more and showed them to her. With the little control she had over her facial muscles, I noticed her attempting a smile.

"I wish I had long hair like you," she said.

I had the tablet up, and instead of taking more pictures, it was recording video.

"Long hair looks nice and all, but it's a lot of work," I said.

"Yeah, but all I have is time. The doctors or Mother would be taking care of it for me. Then they could let me see it sometimes."

"I could do that for you. Help wash it and brush it every day. I'm sure it would be very similar to mine. Do you know what day it is?"

"Wednesday, isn't it?"

"Yes. February 18th, 579."

"I know what year it is," Princess Amelia said. I sensed a bit of sarcasm in her comment.

"I wasn't implying you didn't—it was just a habit when saying the date. How long did you say you've been down here?"

"Almost ten years. Since July 2nd, 569. That was back before I had the motorized wheelchair and I could still push myself. I wish I still had the strength."

"But the doctors are working on getting you better, right?"

"I don't know. I feel like everyone's given up. I've been on the same treatment for years now—a daily shot—and nothing seems to be changing... I mean, for the better anyway."

"I'm sorry," I said.

I turned off the video. "I'll do what I can to help you get the treatment you need. What these doctors are doing doesn't seem to be working, so there has to be someone else who can help. New technologies. New breakthroughs. Something."

"Can I see the pictures again?"

I brought the tablet to her and scrolled through the pictures I'd taken, not stopping to replay the video.

"This is the best day I've had in a long time," Princess Amelia said.

I stroked her short hair and gave her a kiss on the temple. "Me too," I said.

CHAPTER 48

I tried calling Kale, but he didn't answer. On his phone, there was an automated message reciting the number. I promptly hung up without recording a word. Another number was listed in the call directory; I had no idea whose it was but didn't think it would hurt to give it a try.

It rang four times before a young girl answered.

"Hello?"

I wasn't sure, but I thought the voice sounded familiar enough to ask. "Mina?"

"Yes? Who's this?"

Tears came to my eyes almost immediately. "Hey there, sweetie. It's Victoria."

"Victoria!" she squealed into the receiver. "I can't believe it's really you!"

"Are you safe? Happy? Comfortable? Where are you? Have you seen Kale?"

"He's been here. I haven't seen him recently though," Mina said. "It's nice here. Everyone's been nice to me. Kale's mother is a good cook. I love what she makes."

I fell back onto my bed as I continued talking to Mina.

"What number is this?" I asked.

"The house phone," she said.

"Where did he bring you? Where are you?"

"I don't know exactly, but we're out past the fence."

"In the Outlands?"

"Yeah."

The Ramseys definitely wouldn't find her out there. They'd never venture past the Kingdom border and out into the land of outlaws, even though that's where Master Ramsey belonged.

"I can't tell you how good it is to hear your voice. I'm so glad you're safe. I knew Kale would come through, but… it's just hard. You know?"

"There's a lot of good people here," Mina said. "Now we can talk to each other every day." That little girl excitement was infectious.

"Yes, we can," I said. "See, it's like we're still together."

We talked for almost an hour and when I hung up, the tears returned. I just wanted this to be over. I didn't know how much longer I could take the looming uncertainty.

I met up with Bethany and Piper for lunch and then we all headed down to the pool. We had the whole place to ourselves to choose whichever lounge chairs we wanted.

Bethany was eager to share all about her date with Prince Bryon, while I was eager for her to finish the story. I wanted to be happy for her and share in her excitement—as we'd said we'd do for each other—but it was too hard to think about the Prince with other girls at this point. I already saw him as mine and had no intention of sharing.

"Did you hear about Eleanor?" Piper asked after Bethany had finished regaling us with the specifics of her romantic evening—or so she thought.

"No. What about her?" I asked.

Bethany perked up as well.

"She was electrocuted in her bathtub last night," Piper said. "She's not dead, or so I was told. Her hairdryer was in the tub, connected by an extension cord. I guess it blew a fuse before she was pumped with too much juice. She's with Dr. Sosin now."

"Oh, wow—that's awful!" Bethany cried. "Was it a suicide attempt?"

"Or attempted murder?" I asked.

Piper shrugged. "I was hoping one of you knew something. I just heard it had happened and she was no longer in her room."

"I can't believe she'd do it to herself," I said.

"We're all under an impossible amount of pressure," Piper said. "It's one way to control your own destiny."

"That's so sad," Bethany said. "I wouldn't wish it on anyone."

"Maybe we should all start sharing a room," I said. "Watch out for each other—just in case. I don't trust those other girls."

"Do you really think they're capable of something like that—trying to kill one of us?" Bethany asked.

"What if it was the Queen?" Bethany asked. "Maybe she's trying to turn us against each other and make us all paranoid."

"One more reason why we should start bunking up," I said. "We don't have much time left."

"What do you think is going to happen in the end?" Piper asked, directed at both of us.

"I don't know if Prince Byron's said anything to either of you, but he's told me he's developing a plan to save the girls he doesn't pick. He won't leave us to the Queen to dispose of."

"He mentioned that to me last night," Bethany said.

"I hope that's true," Piper said. She stood up and dropped her towel. "I need to do some laps and clear my head. I don't want to end up like Eleanor."

"You both good with moving into my room today?" I asked.

Bethany and Piper agreed. They each moved a suitcase of personal items into my room before dinner. I had more than enough clothes in the closet for all three of us and it wasn't like my clothes wouldn't fit the other two girls.

Piper set up sheets and a pillow on the couch. The bed was so large, I said there was ample space for all three of us, but she insisted on the couch and I wasn't going to argue with her.

We all went to dinner together and had almost finished eating when the Queen joined us. I lost what appetite I had left by just being in her presence after our conversation from the morning.

"Don't you want dessert?" the Queen asked as I rose from the table.

"I ate too much already," I said. "I couldn't possibly eat more." I looked to Bethany and Piper to see if either of them would leave with me, but both remained seated, waiting for dessert to be served. So I left alone.

The girls returned to the room about a half hour later. I was looking forward to having some company for the night—for the remainder of my nights here.

Piper arrived carrying what looked like a dress box, topped with a ribbon. "This came for you," she said.

"Oh?" I took the box, untied the bow, and removed the lid.

"He said it was important we give it to you."

Inside were green tissue paper and a note. The

girls were gathered around me so I picked up the note and read it aloud.

"You deserve this. Put on the dress and meet me outside. Always yours," I read.

"Let's see it," Piper said.

I parted the tissue paper to reveal an emerald dress inside.

"It can't be," I said, staring at the dress.

"It can't be what?" Bethany asked.

I removed the emerald ballgown from its box; it had beautifully beaded lace appliqués and a plunging V-back; it looked just like the one I'd received from the tailor before coming to the palace—the dress fabricated for Princess Amelia, that was given to me and destroyed by *him*.

I didn't even want to think of his name but seeing the dress, I knew I'd have to. This was a bold move, even for him.

"Who gave this to you?" I asked Piper.

"A staff member in the foyer. Why?"

"Did you recognize him?"

"No, but there are so many."

"I can't believe you're getting another date so soon," Bethany said.

"It's a gorgeous dress," Piper said.

"It was originally made for Princess Amelia," I said, thinking of trying on the original at Lady Adriana's boutique.

"That's fitting," Bethany said.

"Well, what are you waiting for?" Piper asked. "Go get dressed."

"I can't deny it's a beautiful dress, but I'm not up for wearing it tonight. I'd like to keep it casual, which I'm sure the Prince will understand." I walked over to the phone on the nightstand and picked up the receiver.

"Hi, Kimera," I said, picturing the man who awaited me outside—probably in the back of an idling limo. "Please come to my room as soon as you can. I need your help."

CHAPTER 49

I told the girls I'd see them soon.

"Hopefully not too soon," Bethany said. From what I could tell, Bethany was genuinely wishing me well on my date, making me feel even more guilty of my jealousy the night before. I couldn't really compete with her.

Kimera looked nervous due to the help I'd privately asked her for, but in the company of my sisters, she remained quiet.

I made my way to the foyer. It was empty except for the staff member stationed at the front door. He opened it as I approached and wished me a pleasant evening.

In the circular drive, a black limousine idled just as I'd pictured, with the driver holding the back door open. I stared him straight in the eyes to see if he'd let slip that something was amiss—to provide a non-verbal warning of some kind. But he didn't.

"Good evening, Miss Victoria," the driver said.

I shook my head in disgust, not masking my expression whatsoever as I climbed into the back of the limousine.

The driver slammed the door shut and I gazed upon *him*—and my throat went bone dry at the realization he wasn't alone.

Maybe this was too risky after all. It took me a moment to take in a breath, which was labored from the stench of whiskey and cigar smoke hanging in the air.

"It's so good to see you again, Victoria," Master Ramsey said, sitting between three other strange and burly men.

I went for the handle; I could pull it, but it wouldn't open the door. I was committed to this now.

"She's a cutie," the man to Master Ramsey's right said.

"I told you she would not disappoint," Master Ramsey said.

The back of the car was dimly lit. Flashbacks of my last encounter with him flooded back to me. Last time there'd been one observer. This time he was intending three—if they were actually meant to be merely voyeurs.

Then I felt the car start to move.

The rising fear was immediate, but I couldn't let it cripple me. "I suggest you stop the car," I said in an almost confident voice.

"Didn't I tell you you'd never be beyond my reach?" Master Ramsey said. "You are mine. You will always be mine. And I will do with you as I please. Tonight, I've invited some friends—"

I dug into the folds of my skirt and held up a small electronic device. "Maybe you didn't hear me," I said louder, cutting through the chuckles and chatter. "I suggest you stop the car right now because you won't be getting past the gate anyway. Do you know what this is?"

"Nothing of consequence," one of the guys said, scooting closer to me.

"Wrong," I snapped. "And back the hell off!"

When he listened to me, it momentarily caused me to lose my train of thought.

"This is a panic device. All the staff in the palace carry one. If I press it, there will be guards from all over the palace descending on this car."

That got their attention.

"And I've been assured this car isn't getting past the gate without my consent," I continued. "So I suggest you have the driver stop so we can have a little chat."

Master Ramsey's eyes gleamed with murder. He rapped on the partition and the limo slowly came to a stop. "Okay, *Princess*. Let's play your little game."

"I am *not* yours to do with as you please. I needed to tell you in person and make it so you understood, rather than sending Prince Byron or the Queen after you. But as for me; all ties between us are cut."

"Is this a joke?" one of the other guys asked, the sentence sounding like one elongated word.

"No," Master Ramsey said. "I obviously haven't done a good job of teaching you your place in life."

"Oh, you have. But I don't accept it. You do not get to touch me ever again."

"Is that a challenge, *Princess?*" Master Ramsey growled. "Because I always accept a challenge."

I held the panic device high like a bomb—a reminder of what was about to blow up in their faces. "If any of you advances toward me, you're all as good as dead. I assure you."

Master Ramsey made a move to lunge at me, but just before I pressed the button, one of his men pulled him back.

"Get your hands off me, Mackenzie!"

"Don't be stupid, Ramsey," he said. "You know what will come through the door if she presses that button. And if she's beaten and bloody... well, it will be all our heads, not just yours. And I'm not losing my head tonight."

Master Ramsey settled down, shrugging off Mackenzie's hands.

"As you can see, I have the means to get in the

gates whenever I please," Master Ramsey said. "I will not—"

"If only you had the means to leave at such will," I said, a smugness growing in my voice and probably spreading across my face.

My plan might not have worked if it had only been Master Ramsey, but his friends were forcing him to acknowledge the consequences of his actions and keep his eager hands off me.

"Where is my daughter?" Master Ramsey growled.

"She's safe," I admitted. "You won't be touching her again either."

Master Ramsey screamed in frustration. "I knew it! I knew it! You lying little bitch!"

Mackenzie's hands—and those of the other man seated adjacent—were on him again, keeping the unraveling master from diving for me.

"Let go of me! She needs to learn! She needs to be punished!" Master Ramsey strained against the grips of those he'd invited but was unable to break free.

"I think it's time you left," Mackenzie said to me.

"Good," I said. "Because I've said everything I've come here to say. *We are done.*"

"We are so far from *done!*" Master Ramsey screamed. I'd never heard his voice reach such an octave.

Mackenzie rapped on the partition and it slowly descended. "Open the back door." Then he turned his attention back to me. "Will you let us through the gate?"

"I guess you'll have to drive up to it and find out," I said just as the door beside me opened. "I hope this has been as fun for you as it has for me." I stared Master Ramsey straight into his murderous eyes and climbed out of the back of the limo.

"This is your lucky day," I told the driver and walked toward the palace's main entrance.

Once I reached the front landing, I turned back and watched the limousine as it approached the gate, stopped before the stationed guards, and was waved through to disappear into the night.

CHAPTER 50

*K*imera was still in the room when I returned. She'd expected me back shortly, but the others hadn't even though I'd told them before leaving that I wouldn't be long.

"What kind of a date was that?" Bethany asked.

"It wasn't," I said and dropped down on the bed with a sigh. I was exhausted. Every part of me felt entirely drained, even though I'd escaped the limo—and Master Ramsey's clutches—unscathed.

"What happened?"

I retrieved Kimera's panic device and tossed it to her.

"Are you okay?" she asked.

"I've never been better," I said, stretching out across the bed.

"I don't understand," Piper said. "What's going on?"

"It wasn't Prince Byron who called on me for a date, but my sadistic stepfather." I hadn't told them what I'd endured back home, but I could tell tonight's story without mentioning it. And we'd come so far in such a short period of time that they had truly become sisters to me. "I was punished a lot growing up in the 24th Ward—in the Ramsey household. When I was younger, I was made to believe it was justified and noble, but I've come to realize it was for sport and pleasure. Duke Ramsey didn't want to let me go and he's gone to great lengths to demonstrate that."

"I know you said you didn't have a happy childhood, but I didn't realize it was so bad," Piper said.

Bethany came over to the bed and gave me a hug.

"Yeah, well, I guess it's made me into who I am today, which I don't want to complain about. I feel I'm stronger because of it. And tonight, I proved that to myself."

"I wish you'd said something before you left," Bethany said.

"Then I wouldn't have been able to face him on my own. Someone else would have gotten involved," I said. "I needed to do this. And look at the bright side—I prevailed."

"I'm relieved you're all right, Miss Victoria," Kimera said. "Is there anything else you require from me?"

"You don't have to go," I said. "You can stay with us a while if you like."

"Yes; stay," the other two girls repeated.

Kimera started to flush. "Thank you for the offer, but I should go unless there's something specific any of you need."

I shook my head. "We'll see you tomorrow then."

"Good night," Kimera said as she made her way for the door.

"What if you hadn't known right away?" Piper asked, kneeling to face backward over the couch. "What if you'd walked right into the trap?"

I shrugged. "I'd rather not think of that."

"I'd feel so guilty," she said. "I gave you the box. I didn't know. We didn't actually see the Prince; I was given the box by a staff member who instructed me to give it to you. I didn't ask any questions."

"Someone would have had to let him in the gate," Bethany said.

"And staff members saw you get into the car," Piper added. "He got help from someone within the palace."

"Maybe," I said. "Do you really think someone was trying to sabotage me—that this reached beyond his own motives?"

"First, Eleanor," Piper said.

"Eleanor wasn't even a threat."

"But she *was* an easy target."

"I thought I had the upper hand. Now you're both making me paranoid."

I rolled on my side to face Bethany. "Where's the dress I was given?" I asked.

"Kimera hung it up in the closet," she said. "It really is beautiful and so exciting it was made specifically for Princess Amelia. Piper tried it on."

"Bethany!" Piper cried. "You said you wouldn't tell."

I laughed. "It's cool. I just don't want to lose it again."

"What do you mean?" Bethany asked.

"It doesn't matter," I said with a sigh and closed my eyes. "I'm so tired."

"It's hard work being the hero."

I'd hoped for a peaceful night's sleep, but all the ways the evening could have gone wrong ravaged my dreams.

I awoke sweaty and shaking. Bethany was no longer beside me and the yellow curtains were glowing from the sunlight behind them.

My breathing had just about returned to normal when I heard a voice from across the room.

"Good. You're up."

I pushed up on an elbow and found Constance sitting at the desk.

"I heard about what happened to you last night," she said and approached the bed. She had something in her hand—something small and shiny.

"Is that so? What did you hear?" I asked.

"I can't imagine what that would have been like. Oh wait, I can."

"What are you talking about?"

She tossed the object onto the bed. It was a broken-off blade of a razor.

"If it had been me who'd gone through those violations last night, I wouldn't be able to live with myself. It'd be too much to bear; I'd need to find an escape." She gestured to the razor next to me on the comforter.

"You go first," I snapped.

Constance didn't bat an eye. "I did," she said and extended both forearms to me.

When I looked closely, I could see the hint of a silver vertical line on each arm, stretching from inner elbows to wrists.

"They brought me back," she said bitterly. "*He* brought me back. I wasn't allowed to leave."

I couldn't look away from her scars. She seemed to become self-conscious and crossed her arms so I could no longer see them. I gazed up at her face. The cuts from the broken glass were still healing, but they too would scar.

"I'm sorry about all that's happened to you," I said. "I know how hard it is."

"Even when the wounds heal, the pain never goes away," she said.

"That's not necessarily a bad thing."

Constance didn't look the same as she had a few minutes ago; something within her had changed. Her anger seemed replaced by a profound sadness and I waited for the next snide comment, but she remained quiet.

When I stood, she still didn't seem to notice I wasn't hurt; she'd sunk too far into her own horrific memories.

"I know what you're going through—" I started to say, but the door suddenly opened and broke my train of thought.

Bethany and Piper entered the room. Bethany was carrying a breakfast tray.

"What's going on here?" Piper asked, glaring at Constance.

"I was just leaving," Constance said. She discreetly snatched the razor from the bed and concealed it within a loose fist.

"No, seriously, why are you in here?"

Constance didn't answer as she marched for the door, pushing past both girls and disappearing into the hallway.

"What the hell?" Piper moaned.

"What was that about?" Bethany asked, bringing the tray over to the bed.

"Are people talking about what almost happened to me last night?" I asked.

"Not that I've heard," Bethany said.

"I haven't told anyone," Piper said.

"Then how did Constance know about it?" I asked.

Both girls looked blankly at me and then each other.

"What was the name of the family that raised her?" I asked.

"I don't remember," Bethany said. "Forget her. Let's eat before breakfast gets cold."

"Thorton? Does that sound right?" Piper asked. "I could be wrong."

"I don't know," said. "The name sounds familiar. It's probably right. I guess it doesn't matter."

CHAPTER 51

The next morning, a knock at the door came while Bethany was finishing getting dressed so we could leave for breakfast together. Piper answered; Prince Byron was standing in the hallway with a breakfast tray.

"Is that for all of us?" Piper asked, allowing the Prince into the room.

He immediately looked embarrassed. "I—I didn't realize I'd be entertaining a group. How many are here?"

"Bethany's in the bath," I said.

"I'm ready," Bethany said, emerging from the washroom. "Oh, good morning, Your Highness." She curtsied.

"Sorry, I did not mean to intrude on girl time," the Prince said.

"Don't be silly," I said, walking up to give him a

hug. "We can all share."

"We were just heading out," Piper said, grabbing Bethany by the arm.

"I don't mind sharing," Bethany said.

"Don't make me eat alone," Piper said, pulling Bethany toward the door. "We'll be back later."

Bethany gave an awkward wave as she was ushered out. Once the door had closed, Prince Byron gave me a look of sheer confusion.

"It gets lonely in these huge suites," I said. "It's good to see you. To what do I owe the pleasure?"

"I heard something happened to you last night, but not what," Prince Byron said, walking into the room bearing a tray of pancakes, scrambled eggs, and fruit salad. "I brought breakfast. Are you okay? What happened?"

"I'm fine," I said. Did everyone now know about my previous night's endeavor?

Prince Byron set the tray on the desk. "Are you sure?"

"Okay, you have to promise to remain calm," I said, trying to prepare him for what I was about to say. "There was an... incident two nights ago. The Duke paid me a visit and... and arranged his own idea of a romantic date with me."

The Prince's eyes widened in horror. He knew what Master Ramsey was capable of and what he liked to do to me.

"But like I said, I am fine. Nothing happened. I handled him."

"Let me see you." He stepped closer and was about to touch me, but didn't know where would be safe. "I will have him killed," he said, venomously.

"He did not so much as lay a finger on me," I said. "Like I said, I handled him. I met him head on and sent him on his way—unfulfilled."

Now he took me in his arms. "Thank God you're all right. I don't know what I would have done if I'd lost you," he said and hugged me tighter. "You went to him alone?"

"Yes. But with precautions in place. I wasn't reckless." If I gave him too many details, I was afraid he wouldn't agree on that point.

"Even so, the fact he was here and coming after you is grossly offensive. I'll have him hunted down like the animal he is and delivered back here in chains."

"I don't need you hunting him down," I said. "I handled the situation. He's gone. And he won't be back. Please let this go. Can we eat now?" I looked deep into his eyes and could see his vow of revenge wouldn't be doused so easily. I pressed my lips to his to bring his mind back to me. "Are you with me?"

"I'm with you," he said. "I'll always be with you."

I hoped that was true, but knew better than to count on absolute declarations; I could hope for the best but needed to plan for the worst—which was exactly what I was doing by not telling the Prince about Princess Amelia. I needed to protect her to protect myself.

We ate in silence for a few minutes, and then he simply said, "I love you, Victoria. I don't want the first time I say it to be in front of everyone."

It was the first time I'd heard those words in a very long time. The only other person to ever say it to me was Lady Ramsey, and not since I was much younger.

The sincerity in his voice made me forget about the upcoming Choosing Ceremony that would happen in a few short days. He kissed my forehead; I truly felt loved, maybe for the first time in my life. There was no doubt of the way I felt.

"I love you too," I said. "And I'm not just saying that because of the competition."

"And I shouldn't be saying it *because* of the competition," Prince Byron said. "But I can't help it. I love you."

When Bethany and Piper came back a few hours later, we were lying comfortably entwined on the bed. They went to excuse themselves again, but Prince Byron insisted they stay as he rose from the bed.

"I've already monopolized too much of Victoria's time." The Prince brushed a hand over my hair but did not give me a parting kiss before leaving.

Bethany came and dropped down on the bed beside me. "None of us really has a chance, do we?"

"I don't know," I said. "You seem to have a pretty great relationship with him. Who knows what's really going through his head?" I hoped I actually *did* know the answer.

"I see the way he looks at you."

"So do I," Piper added, heading straight for the washroom.

I tried to suppress a smile at the outside validation of our relationship. It lit a fire in my belly that warmed me all over—much like when he told me he loved me.

We lounged around the room for most of the afternoon, talking, watching television, ordering snacks through room service. Johanna, Mina, and I had never hung out together like this. This was what having sisters should be like, but it was disheartening to think this joyous time had a three-day expiration date. What happened to any or all of us after that remained as shrouded as the landscape on a foggy morning.

While Bethany and Piper ate dinner in the room, I drew myself a warm bath. I snuck my phone into the washroom and closed the door. With the water running, I called Kale. It rang a bunch of times before going to an automated message. I tried the other phone number and Mina picked up again.

"Is Kale around? I asked. "I tried calling him, but he didn't answer."

"He's been gone a few days," she said. "He seems to do that a lot—leave for several days at a time. I don't know where he goes."

"Well, when he comes back, can you have him call me?"

"Of course."

I needed him to be available if my plan was going to work. It made me nervous not being able to get in touch with him, making me feel something was wrong and there was nothing I could do about it.

I stepped into the tub, inching down into the warm water and trying to expel all my negative thoughts.

Soon, the Prince would make his announcement to the Queen and my new life as a Princess of Westeria would begin. Kale would be ready and waiting on the other end of the line, and I'd force the Queen to spare the lives of the other girls. Then I'd be able to free the real Princess Amelia from her dungeon. All I had to do was expel my negative thoughts.

CHAPTER 52

*P*rince Byron brought breakfast again the next morning, and this time had a plate for each of us. We gathered around the coffee table and all ate the eggs Benedict sandwiches he'd retrieved from the kitchen.

"We'll let you have some private time," Bethany said as we all finished up our food.

Prince Byron glanced at me, and then said, "I insist you stay. This is nice with the four of us. Casual. Sweet. And the hours grow short. I'd like to spend them with each of you."

Then everyone glanced at me.

"Why are you all turning to me?" I asked. "I couldn't ask for better company." And it was true. Even though I did want to steal him away, I loved every second of our collective time together.

So we made the same breakfast date for the following morning.

I followed him into the hall as he was leaving, and he kissed me goodbye and told me he loved me. It was always hard watching him go, but it was easier with my waiting sisters just inside the room.

"Let's get out of here for a bit," I said, sauntering back into the room.

"To get our lovely Prince out of your head?" Bethany said. "What are you up for?"

"Amongst other things. Piper, have you shown her the library?"

Piper shook her head.

"I've been to the library a bunch of times," Bethany said.

"There's a secret one that Piper found," I said.

Bethany's eyes lit up. "A secret room? How exciting! Let's go!"

Bethany was giddy the whole way and we had to shush her squealing when Piper pushed on the hidden door leading to the concealed two-story library.

"How did you find this?" Bethany asked as she meandered around the room.

"I'm kind of a snooper," Piper said. "I'm good at finding things."

I laughed at her comment, thinking of the hidden corridor waiting just beyond the upstairs bookcase.

"Who else knows about this?" Bethany asked.

"Of the seven girls—" Piper started.

"Clones," I clarified.

"Sisters," Piper said, sardonically, rolling her eyes. "Of the seven *girls*, just the three of us."

We perused the endless shelves of books. One at a time, each of us claimed a leather chair and began reading. I could read straight into the afternoon, but Bethany and Piper became restless after about an hour.

"I need a break from reading," Piper said. "Want to visit the pool?"

"I'd rather not," I said, laying my open copy of *The Graveyard Book* across my lap. I'd needed a new story. The first book in the previous series I'd been reading had been enough. "I'll stay."

"I'll stay with you," Bethany said, but I could tell she'd only offered out of a sense of obligation.

"You don't have to," I said. "I'm okay by myself."

"You sure?"

"Totally. Go."

"You know where to find us if you need anything," Bethany said, coming over to give me a hug. Piper waved, and both of them disappeared through the pivoting wall.

I waited about five minutes before slowly climbing the spiral staircase and pulling on the copy of *Pride & Prejudice*, opening the *real* secret door.

Princess Amelia was listening to her records like the first time I'd come down. Her facial expression was mostly frozen in place, but I could see an extra sparkle in her eyes when she saw me.

"Hi, Sister," she said.

The song she'd been listening to ended and I picked up another record and placed it on the phonograph, setting the needle down gently to reduce the crackling.

"Did you bring the tablet today?" Princess Amelia asked.

"No, I didn't. Sorry, but I forgot."

"That's okay. You can bring it next time and show me more pictures."

"Next time…" I said, truly hoping there'd be one. If I could have carried her out of there, I would have done so, but there was no way I could get her up that spiral staircase. I didn't know how anyone could do that—unless there was another exit?

I talked to her all about Misty and horseback riding. We listened to several records and I read to her from the book on her desk screen. After I finished a few chapters, I stopped and noticed tear tracks running down her face.

"What's wrong?" I asked.

"I'm just so happy—happy to have someone—you to spend time with me. These have been the happiest days of my life." She lifted one shaking arm to wipe her cheeks, though she could only really reach one.

I jumped up and grabbed a tissue from across the room and finished wiping her face. It was also a chance to turn and take a moment to retain my own composure.

By the time I said goodbye, returned to the corridor and locked her door, I'd completely lost it. I surrendered to uncontrollable, air-sucking sobs.

None of us could replace Princess Amelia. She was the real deal. She was a beautiful, amazing human being, the rest of us pale and unworthy copies.

I had to wait quite a while before re-emerging into the known living quarters of the palace without letting everyone see the emotional wreck I'd become. I didn't know how red my eyes were, so I averted my gaze at the passing of each staff member.

When I reached my room, I heard a phone ringing and quickly realized it wasn't coming from the nightstand. I ran over and flipped open the phone I'd stashed in the bottom desk drawer, seeing Kale's number on the screen.

"Sorry, I didn't get back to you sooner," he said.

"You had me worried," I said, relief rushing over me.

"What? You, worried about me?"

"Don't start with me," I warned. "You know I do. So is everything okay?"

"Yeah. Nothing to worry about."

"I just wanted to make sure you were good with what we talked about. The Choosing Ceremony's in two days. It's supposed to start at 8 p.m."

"Wow. I can't believe it's already here," Kale said.

"I need to make sure you'll be ready?"

"I'll be eagerly awaiting your call." He didn't try to downplay his sarcasm, but then his tone turned solemn. "I hate the fact I'll be standing by and not actively doing something to help. It kills me I won't be there."

"You know you can't be here and you *will* be actively helping. You're the one getting me and the other girls out alive."

The line was silent.

"You're going to make it through this," Kale said, proclaiming it as fact.

"We all will," I answered.

CHAPTER 53

*I*t felt like the next day was stolen from me. I was in such an anxious state that time seemed to keep accelerating until the morning of the Choosing Ceremony arrived.

Prince Byron continued our breakfast routine but the morning was not like the others, the air hanging heavy with an overwhelming tension. It was obvious he felt it too, that it wasn't just us girls.

Bethany and Piper left after breakfast, allowing us some private time together; this time, he didn't protest.

"I know it's nearly impossible not to worry about this evening, but I don't want you to," the Prince said, once we were alone.

"You seem just as worried," I said.

"It's an easy decision as I've already told you. I love you and I wouldn't choose anyone else. But I will still be breaking the hearts of six other girls and trying to secure their safety."

"And you have a plan for doing that?"

"Yes. I have a plan in place. And I hope to God it works," Prince Byron said, not sounding entirely confident in his answer. I had a feeling the lives of the other girls were still going to come down to me —and I had plenty of concerns of my own.

"But worrying now isn't going to solve anything," he said, sitting down on the edge of the bed. "It will just make us crazy. Everything's in motion that needs to be and we'll attack whatever happens together."

"I like that *together* part," I said, taking a seat next to him.

The Prince smiled, deepening the dimples in his cheeks. He kissed me and his stubble scratched my face, but I wasn't about to complain. I wanted his reassurance that this night was the beginning, not the end. And right now, his lips were giving me the guarantee I needed.

Prince Byron had a lot on his plate already. Bethany and Piper went back to their respective rooms to prepare for our last formal event as a group. I welcomed Kimera's company and her help to transform me into a girl looking fit to be a princess—because that's who I would be by the end of the night.

"I'll need to find you the perfect dress," Kimera

said once I was out of the bath and wrapped in a plush robe.

After a long search through the cavernous closet, she found me a radiant, golden gown with three-quarter-length sleeves and a skirt that dusted the floor when I wore no shoes.

Without asking, I donned a pair of shorts under my robe, and when Kimera helped me into the dress, she either didn't notice or simply didn't comment on it.

Instead, Kimera continued picking out a pair of shiny black heels, which luckily weren't too high. My hair was styled in what she called a *French roll* updo, my look completed with dangling onyx earrings encircled with diamonds and a thin diamond tiara.

"Simple and elegant," Kimera said. "The true effortless-looking style of a princess."

"There seems to be a *lot* of effort into looking effortless," I said.

"What do you think?"

"I never want to wear yellow again after tonight," I said, viewing myself in the closet trifold mirror. "But I hope you'll continue to be my assistant."

"You'll have to put in a good word for me," she said.

"You know I will."

Kimera walked me to the formal dining room like she had done on our first dinner with the

Queen, but instead of coming in, she left me at the door. I was the last to arrive except for Eleanor and the Queen, but there was miraculously an open seat next to Prince Byron.

He turned back and gave me a warm smile as I crossed the expansive room to reach the daunting table.

Everyone was back to their room colors: Bethany was attired in orange, Piper in blue, Jane in champagne, Danielle in purple, and Constance in red. After what had happened, I didn't know if Eleanor was in any kind of condition to join the group this evening.

But as soon as I sat down, the door I'd entered opened again and Eleanor shuffled into the room in a silver dress. She used a wooden cane and hung onto the arm of her assistant for help as she headed for the final open seat.

Prince Byron jumped to his feet and pulled out Eleanor's chair to help her get seated. When he returned to his spot, I found his hand under the table. I squeezed it and he squeezed back.

Whispers were shared between Constance and her friends, probably commenting on Eleanor who looked like a zombie at the far end of the table. Piper turned to Eleanor and tried talking to her, which wasn't greatly reciprocated.

Everyone grew quiet when the opposite door opened and soldiers and servers entered the dining room, followed by the Queen. Prince Byron rose and urged us to do the same, which we all reluctantly did. The Queen glided across the hardwood floor in a long emerald gown with an extended train that looked like a hitchhiking demon. Two servers were tasked with helping the Queen to sit, adjusting her gown and fixing her train.

"The evening is finally here. My, how time flies," she said and raised her champagne flute. "Here's to love and the future of our fine Kingdom." She took a sip, signaling for us to follow. Then she continued. "I look at each of you and see my Amelia. She would be so proud and honored to know one of you will be stepping into her shoes, continuing her legacy and leading the Kingdom into a new generation. I'm very excited for Amelia's public reemergence and the announcement of the new royal couple at the Kingdom's birthday celebration.

"Prince Byron, are these girls all that you expected?"

"They all have greatly exceeded my expectations," he said. "It's been a pleasure getting to know each and every one of you over the past four weeks."

"Can't we just hear his choice now and get this over with?" Constance asked angrily.

"I insist we have one more meal together before this is over," the Queen said, glaring.

"You mean before you…" Constance glanced over

at the Prince. "Never mind. Let's eat. I'm freakin' starving."

The dinner was painfully long, with course after course served separately. It seemed she was dragging this out intentionally.

Each of Bethany's plates was removed from her place setting untouched. She'd pick up her fork, dab at her food, and then place the cutlery back on the table without taking so much as a bite.

"I'm scared," she said during the fourth course which was pepper-crusted duck breasts. "I don't think I'd be able to keep anything down."

"It's going to be okay," I whispered. "Have some champagne to calm down."

She shook her head and picked up her fork again. She cut a small slice and looked at it like she was being asked to eat rat poison.

"I can't," she said, placing it back on her plate.

Prince Byron leaned closer. "You're going to get through this." He smiled to reassure her.

His attention seemed to calm her slightly, but she still didn't eat any of her food.

I glanced across the table at Constance, who seemed to be mostly drinking her dinner. She noticed me looking and simply raised her glass with a smirk.

"If it's free and flowing," she said.

"Keep your wits about you," Prince Byron whispered to her.

"We had a good connection. Didn't we?"

"You're a strong, self-reliant, amazing woman. We've had a strong and genuine connection from day one."

"I thought so too," she said, her words beginning to slur.

For dessert, we were served chocolate cake with a middle layer of strawberries. Each plate was garnished with a strawberry rose, a dollop of whipped cream, and a few mint leaves.

"Each course served tonight was among Princess Amelia's favorites," the Queen said.

Each time she mentioned Princess Amelia I wanted to scream at her, curse her for what she was doing to her own daughter. The Princess deserved to be at this table with the rest of us—to see the lives of all these girls she'd made possible by her unique genetics.

With the Princess in the forefront of my mind, I leaned in close to Bethany and asked her to nudge Piper. "You both know *Pride & Prejudice* is my favorite book. Well, there's a very special copy of it in the secret library, on the second level. If either of you gets the chance, you should check it out."

"I guess," Piper said. "You would be thinking of books at a time like this."

"Sure thing, Victoria," Bethany said.

It was obvious they were both confused by my bringing it up, but I hoped it would lead one of them to Princess Amelia if it wasn't me who was chosen tonight.

The Queen only took a few bites of dessert before rising from her chair. Several servers rushed to her side to keep her gown in perfect condition.

"Thank you for this pleasant dinner," she said. "I couldn't have asked for more. Now it's the time you've been eagerly awaiting. Follow me."

The Queen led the way out of the dining room, followed directly by her servers and several soldiers. We were allowed to join the procession afterward, with Prince Byron taking the lead. Then the remainder of the soldiers brought up the rear to keep us in line.

Bethany took my hand as we marched into the Event Room. I hadn't been in there since the masquerade ball. As we descended the steps, I saw the entire room was filled with palace staff members and soldiers. Doctors Sosin and Crane, along with a few other doctors I knew by sight but not by name, were among the crowd. I glanced up and noticed more soldiers positioned on the balconies.

A dais was set up on the far side of the room with two thrones, one larger than the other, centered atop. The Queen ascended the few dais steps and claimed the larger throne.

On the right side of the room were risers, which we were directed to by several staff members. Piper, Bethany, and I took the second row, along with

Danielle. Constance, Jane, and Eleanor were positioned on the bottom.

"Prince Byron," the Queen said from her throne. "Who will be our Princess Amelia?"

The Prince paced before us, seemingly gathering his thoughts. When he stopped and faced us, his eyes found mine. "I want to thank you all for opening up to me, for letting me into your hearts and your lives. I feel so grateful for the opportunity to get to know and build connections with each of you. I wish I didn't have to make this decision. It's much harder than I ever thought possible. But in the end, there can only be one Princess Amelia and one woman for me." He took a slow breath and glanced over at the Queen.

My heart was pounding, thinking of everything he'd told me over the past few weeks, the wonderful moments we'd shared and the promises he'd made. Now I wished I hadn't eaten so much.

I noticed a few soldiers inching their way closer to the risers we were standing on, but I tried to keep my focus on the Prince and the name he was about to call.

When his attention came back to us he finished his short speech. "I choose Victoria. That is, if she'll have me."

My smile matched his at hearing my name. My shoulders relaxed. In that instant, I forgot about everyone else in the room. All I could see was Prince

Byron standing before me. I truly would be a princess!

"Of course, I'll have you," I exclaimed.

"I love you, Victoria. You are my everything." The Prince held out his hand, beckoning me forth.

"I love you too," I said and maneuvered past Constance and Eleanor to reach the floor and go to my Prince. But I was stopped by a single word slicing through the room.

"No." The Queen was on her feet, looking all the more larger-than-life and intimidating from her dais.

CHAPTER 54

"What?" I gasped and heard Prince Byron simultaneously utter the same question.

"I have always reserved the right to veto your decision if I feel it's detrimental to the Kingdom," the Queen said. "I do not feel Victoria Sandalwood is a suitable choice and have voiced my veto."

The risers were surrounded by soldiers now. I stood halfway between the Prince and the girls, unsure of what to do next. My eyes met Prince Byron's, pleading with him to say something—do something.

"Queen Dorothea, I beg you to reconsider," the Prince said. "I feel Victoria will provide great service to you and the Kingdom. She has a tremendous heart and will take on her new role with grace and fortitude. I have found my true love and can no longer imagine my life without her."

"You said to all of us that this was a harder decision than you ever thought possible and you had genuine connections with each and every one of the girls standing on those risers. You may prefer Victoria, but there are other girls here with whom you can have a fulfilling future. A girl more suitable as a partner for you and as a leader to this great Kingdom."

"Why then?" Prince Bryon asked defiantly. "Why do you object?"

"She's attempted to run away once since she's been here," the Queen began. "She's been hiding an affair with a boy posing as one of my staff members, whom she knew from her home in the 24th Ward—"

"I was not having an affair!" I shouted.

"This was your second time planning to run away with this boy, was it not? He infiltrated my palace because of you—" she snapped.

"Which shows the gaps in your own security—" I said.

"Do not interrupt me!" the Queen demanded. "This girl was reset due to numerous instances of insubordination back home, which was also withheld from me to keep her and her guardians in good standing. All of these things are unacceptable, making her an unacceptable candidate for Princess Amelia's replacement.

"Now, Prince Byron, we need to move on from this. My decision is final. You must choose another if our two kingdoms are to continue building and strengthening our alliance. You don't want to be the one responsible for destroying all the work your parents have put forth over the years to bridge our Kingdoms, do you?"

Prince Byron dropped his head. "No, Your Highness."

"A prince, and one day a king must be able to make difficult choices—many of which are not popular—for the good of the many, for the good of the Kingdom as a whole. This is a difficult choice. I understand. But one you *must* make."

I couldn't believe what I was seeing. The Prince looked crestfallen—and worse, he looked like he was going to comply with the Queen's orders.

I ran over to him. "You can't do this!" I pleaded. I grabbed his hands and gazed up into his sorrowful eyes. "You have a choice. You do. Please…"

After what felt like forever, he returned my gaze. His hands were clammy in mine. "I know. A choice I have to make and I *will* make it right—I promise. But for right now, I'm sorry."

"No…" I cried. "Don't say that. You can't…"

"Victoria, please—please go back and stand with the other girls," Prince Byron said, letting go of my hands and lifting his gaze. His expression was wiped clean of any lingering emotion.

"You can't be serious."

"Please," he said. "Let's not make this harder than it needs to be."

I felt so stupid for trusting him, for allowing myself to believe I deserved love. My heart was shattered and the pieces scattered about the floor like tiny shards of glass. There would be no way to piece them all back together.

I returned to the group of girls, tears streaming, unable to meet anyone's curious and shocked eyes. What should have been the best moment of my life had instantly been turned into the worst.

"Prince Byron, please continue," urged the Queen. She was once again seated on her gaudy throne.

"I'm sorry—I'm sorry for all of this," the Prince said. "I'm sorry to all of you, but most importantly, I'm sorry to Victoria."

I couldn't look at him.

"I've also developed an amazing connection over the past few weeks with this thoughtful and giving young woman." Prince Byron paused. "I will choose Bethany for Princess Amelia."

Bethany turned to me, tears also in her eyes. "I'm sorry," she said and gave me a hug. "He said he'd help us." She wiped her cheeks and raised her chin before stepping down from the riser and joining the Prince in the center of the room. She wrapped her arms around his neck and kissed him on the cheek.

I had to look away, unable to bear seeing her with him. A smile finally crept onto her face as her dreams came true, her heart blooming over the scattered shards of my own.

"A very fine choice," the Queen said. "Welcome back my dear daughter, Princess Amelia."

The room roared with applause, all welcoming the new Princess. It hurt so much more knowing how close I'd come to being in her position.

The Queen rose from her throne and descended the dais. Her staff members rushed to her side to help with the train of her gown as she approached the Prince and new Princess. On reaching them, the Queen embraced them both. She took Bethany by the hand and led her up the dais to the secondary throne. By the time the Queen and new Princess sat down, the applause finally subsided.

Then Prince Byron spoke up. "You have to give me the others," he said. "I can provide them safe and discreet passage to Easteria where they will be no threat to the legitimacy of Princess Amelia."

"And you placed your soldiers around the girls to stop any advance I might take toward them, I presume," the Queen said in an amused tone.

"I want to appeal to your mercy and compassion. I've developed feelings for all of them and cannot bear to see any ill fate befall them. Please, as a gesture of goodwill toward the alliance of our kingdoms."

"One day, my young Prince, you will come to understand why this was necessary. This will be painless, I assure you," the Queen said and turned her attention to the doctors huddled by the dais. "Hit the kill switch."

The Prince gasped. "What? No!"

"Wait!" I screamed and jumped down from the riser, frantically waving my hands in the air to get the Queen's attention. I was stopped by the ring of soldiers encircling us, now ready to shoot anyone who approached.

Dr. Crane had a computer tablet out and was systematically jabbing his finger at the screen. When he stopped and finally looked up, I heard a chain of crashes behind me. Then the room went silent apart from a few nearby gasps.

I spun around and found Danielle, Jane, and Eleanor on the floor, out cold. They didn't seem to be breathing and their bodies were contorted in grotesque positions from the way they had fallen off the risers. Piper and Constance, on the other hand, were quite awake and looked like they'd each had a bucket of ice water thrown in their faces. They both were in shock from what had happened and from wondering why three girls were seemingly dead and the three of us were still standing.

CHAPTER 55

"**W**hat happened?" the Queen demanded.

"They didn't all take," Dr. Crane said, glancing at the other doctors in his vicinity.

"Why?"

"I—I don't know."

"What did you do?!" Prince Byron shouted. He moved toward his men to form a united front against a multitude of soldiers in the balconies, all aiming down at us.

Sitting beside the Queen, Bethany was horrorstruck.

"Prince Byron, come here," the Queen said. "Instruct your men to stand down. There is no need for any of them to die today."

I swallowed hard, reached under my dress, and

pulled out the tablet and phone. "Let me pass," I told the soldiers tasked with protecting us.

"Victoria, don't," Prince Byron said. "Stay back. I will handle this."

"Queen Hart!" I screamed from behind my human wall. "Bethany can't be Princess Amelia because Princess Amelia is not dead! I've seen her and I can prove it!" I pushed the soldiers before me and this time they made room and let me pass.

Prince Byron took a step toward me. "What are you doing?"

"What you couldn't," I snapped. "Getting the rest of us out of here." I walked purposefully toward the Queen. "You've lied to the Kingdom. You've lied to us. You've lied to your own daughter for her entire life."

With a few clicks to the screen, I lifted the tablet so the Queen could see as the video of her daughter played.

"How did you…" The Queen actually looked surprised. "You've visited my Amelia? What have you told her?"

I glanced at Dr. Crane and he looked furious. As I drew closer to the dais, Dr. Crane rushed over and snatched the tablet from my hand. He ran up to the Queen.

"It's okay," I said. "I don't need it anymore."

"And there are pictures," the Queen said somberly. "Erase all of this."

"Those aren't the only copies," I said. "There are copies of all of them outside the palace right now, out of your possession. Out of your reach."

"Are you blackmailing me, you little whelp?" The Queen was on her feet again, approaching the edge of the dais. She remained at the top of the stairs, glaring down at me.

"You will let Piper, Constance, and me leave or I'll have your entire plot exposed to the Kingdom." I thought my voice would crack, but it didn't. My hands shook from the rush of adrenaline, but I stood my ground.

"How do I know there's any surviving evidence?"

I waved my phone to get her attention. "I will make a call to someone outside the 1st Ward who has copies of the pictures and videos, as proof that what I'm saying is true. Then, if I don't meet him by a certain time, all the information will be released. The only way you can stop that from happening is for me to meet him at that appointed time, for which I also need to feel safe—like you're not having me followed. And as a final caveat, I'm not leaving without my sisters."

"Prove it," she challenged. "Make the call."

She didn't seem particularly fazed, which scared me more than I wanted to show. I flipped open the phone and pressed Kale's number. I clicked the speaker button and held my breath, anxiously waiting for him to answer.

When the phone rang, I heard it echo. At first, I thought I was hearing things, but when the Queen held up another phone continuing to echo the ring, I knew what—or whom—she had in her possession. All hope of escape drained with each ring.

"Is this *you* calling?" the Queen asked haughtily.

Just then, I saw Kale being led from the crowd in shackles, two soldiers leading him by the arms. There was dried blood on his face and he staggered like he could barely walk.

"I'm sorry, Victoria. I had to try," he said warily.

The Queen had bested me and there was nothing left for me to do, but await her reprimand and execution.

The ringing of her phone stopped and I waited for the automated message. But my phone continued its ring; I glanced down at the screen and saw a new number displayed, then the ringing stopped and there was crackling on the line.

"Hello, Victoria," said an unfamiliar male voice. "Is Queen Dorothea there?"

"Yes," the Queen answered. "With whom am I speaking?"

"That's not your concern," the man said. "What *is* your concern is that I have all the files Victoria has sent regarding Princess Amelia. I have been instructed to release those files if Victoria does not meet me at the predetermined place and time. She must be provided safe passage and must meet me alone.

"Victoria, be at the devil's tree at 8 p.m. tomorrow night. If all is good, then you'll get the files back. If not, they will promptly be released. You will not be able to call this number again. As soon as I hang up, it will be disconnected and these events will be set in motion. Is everything I've just stated clear?"

"Yes," I said.

"Wait a moment…" the Queen said.

"Thank you," I said. "The clock starts now." I clicked the end button and closed the phone.

"What have you done?" the Queen demanded.

"I wouldn't sacrifice your plan. But I'd sacrifice myself for you," Kale said, and for his comment, he was jabbed with an electronic baton, immediately sending him to the floor in fierce spasms.

"Don't hurt him!" I yelled at the soldiers and quickly turned my attention back to the Queen. "I did what was necessary—made a hard choice if you will. Like you. You're letting me walk out of here and I am taking the girls—and now Kale as well. If that information gets released, it will bring about a revolution. Your reign will come to a quick and violent end and your family name will be demonized."

"Maybe—maybe not," she said. "There are always options, ways to spin the story. I can release information about my Amelia first."

"But do you want to risk those options? The risk of those versus the risk of letting us go to continue with your original plan seems clear. It's much less risk for you to let us go and guarantee this information doesn't get released."

The Queen was silent for a long moment. "But you can't guarantee that information doesn't get released, can you? It's not strictly your decision anymore. That information is now in the hands of someone else. How do you plan to guarantee *me* the information is destroyed and never sees the light of day?"

"It was *my* plan and *my* information," I said. "I am in control of it."

The Queen laughed. "No, you're not. You're not in control at all."

"And neither are you!" I shot back.

"It seems we are at an impasse," the Queen said. "If I don't let you leave, then potentially damaging information will be released. I can take preemptive action to minimize the impact, but the outcome of such action would be unknown and potentially just as damaging.

"If I let you leave to make your rendezvous, then per your word, the information will not be released. But that is also dependent upon you keeping your word and retaining full control over the information, which you currently do not have. Have I missed anything?"

"Difficult choices," I said.

"Difficult choices, indeed." She scanned the room of transfixed faces, then returned to her throne by Bethany's side. "I do not regret my decision to veto you, but I did underestimate what you're capable of.

"Here is my offer—and I want to make it abundantly clear you are not holding all the cards. I will allow you to walk out of here unguarded. I retain a link to you. With the phone I've confiscated, I have your number. You will leave alone and I will hold the others until you return with some type of definitive proof the information currently out of your possession has been destroyed. Do that and the rest of your sisters and your boyfriend here will go free. If you do not return, they are in my possession indefinitely. If the information is released, then they will be executed."

"That's not good enough," I countered. "I'm not leaving alone."

"Then you're not leaving. Either you can all die together right now and I'll deal with the aftermath— or you can bring me what I want and try to play the hero. That is *your* choice."

I could tell by the look in her fiery eyes that she wasn't going to back down. I'd made my stand, but didn't entirely have the upper hand and I knew it. I couldn't help anyone if I was dead. Walking out of here alone at least bought me some time to figure out my next move. I could sense the gears turning in the Queen's head, already hard at work calculating her next steps. I needed to act fast.

"If you hurt any more of them, the deal's off," I warned.

"As long as you uphold your end of the bargain, I'll uphold mine."

"Then you're letting me walk out of here right now?"

"You're free to leave," the Queen said. "I'll expect to see you again soon."

I nodded, taking a few backward steps, nervous of turning my back on the predator hungrily eyeing me from the dais.

I met Kale's eyes. "I'll be back for you."

"I know," he said.

As I continued to back out of the ballroom, I looked to Piper and Constance still behind a ring of the Prince's soldiers. "It'll be okay. I promise," I said.

Piper's mascara was streaked down her cheeks, but she was no longer crying. She was the sole girl still standing on the riser, tall and strong. Constance was on the floor, cradling Danielle's head in her lap, her expression morose and murderous.

Then my eyes met Prince Byron's.

"Victoria…" he said, a painful timbre to his voice.

"Don't," I said. I didn't want to speak to him. He didn't fight for me and I couldn't trust him. As magical as our short time together had been, the sun had set on us and the night ahead of me was dark.

I ran up the stairs to exit the ballroom, finally letting it sink in that I was leaving the Château alive. I had no idea who I'd be meeting at the devil's tree, but it didn't do any good worrying about it.

I kicked off my heels and made a mad dash for the stables in bare feet. I freed Misty from her stall, and when I climbed onto the saddle and hiked up the skirt of my gown, I was thankful I'd had another reason to wear shorts under the dress. I kicked Misty into a gallop and we headed for the main gate.

As the cool evening air whipped through Kimera's masterful French roll updo, I ripped off the diamond tiara and flung it onto the ground. It no longer suited me. I was no princess.

EPILOGUE

*B*ethany awoke in a cold sweat. It took her more than a moment to remember where she was—back in her orange room with Piper and Constance. Piper was still sound asleep beside her, and Bethany could hear Constance's heavy breathing coming from the couch.

Bethany would become the new Princess Amelia, which would be announced at the Kingdom's upcoming Foundation Day celebration—but for now, she was confined to her room like a captive. All three of them were captives.

She sat up, taking deep breaths, trying to calm her pounding heart. It had felt like she was there; the dream was so vivid. She gazed down at her stomach where she'd been struck, with blood pouring down her dress from the ragged hole—but there was no wound. She was not dying after all. The memory of the pain slowly lost its grip. It had only been a dream.

Bethany took another long breath and sighed.

"Are you okay?" Piper asked.

Bethany turned and found Piper gazing up at her in the dim, early morning light. Her face was etched with concern.

"I am now," Bethany said. "Just a bad dream."

"What was it about?"

"Oh, you know how dreams are," Bethany said, shaking her head. "They rarely make sense. And so many of them are dispelled from memory on waking until only a faint feeling remains."

"What *do* you remember?" Piper propped herself up on an elbow.

The problem was, Bethany did remember, and in all too vivid detail. She couldn't wait for this dream to fade like the rest, so only a sickly feeling would remain. But it didn't feel like any other dream she'd ever experienced. It felt like... she was there... or would be there. But that wasn't possible. Was it?

Bethany swallowed hard and said, "Blood, death, and the Kingdom collapsing."

Piper laughed, causing Constance to stir. "Good thing it was only a dream," Piper said, dropping her head back down to the pillow.

"Yeah," Bethany said, her eyes fixed on the far

wall, yet not seeing anything in front of her. "Good thing."

# # #

ABOUT THE AUTHOR

Michael writes YA speculative fiction. He currently lives in Southern California with his wife, kids, and two blood-thirsty chiweenies.

When he's not at the computer, he enjoys spending quality time with family, practicing yoga, playing guitar behind closed doors, and listening to as many audiobooks as possible.

Connect with me online:

michaelpierceauthor.com
michael@michaelpierceauthor.com

Made in the USA
Coppell, TX
17 February 2020

15886808R00240